DEEP DEVOTION

M.C. NORRIS

For Annie, my life mate,

and for our beloved brood,

J.J. and Jill

"How does it feel to be holding an impossible dream in your hands? Dream big. Be bigger"

- Dad

Chapter One

Whatever became of their ocean moon would remain a mystery, because none but two survived. They knew things, these frozen travelers, who slept for eons, dreaming together of the crystalline depths that they would never know, where elaborate courtship dances were performed that could last more than a thousand years. They were an exceedingly long-lived species. Blessed with a vast awareness that extended beyond their eggshells, beyond the rock walls of their hurtling prison, they reached out to the seas of the new place they would soon call home. It was a world of light and shadow that spun beneath an infernal sun. It was a world of tyrants and terrible extremes, where flesh-eating abominations roared in the shadow of the cataclysm, as the pair of new immigrants descended. Like seeds of life enveloped in a husk of fire, the tiny destroyers plummeted toward the new world, ushering in the promise for a new and gentler creature endowed with the capacity for love for its family, and devotion to its gods.

Sara lowered her chopsticks into the ramekin. With a gentle swirling motion, she muddled a dollop of wasabi in the soy sauce. A perfect balance was key. To this end, she went partly by viscosity, and partly by color, which was kind of hard to describe, but she knew the right hue when it appeared. It was the color of forest moss. Once the solution was blended to her satisfaction, she pinched hold of an albacore cutlet, dipped it twice into the greenish pool, and then raised it to her lips. Just as she was about to enjoy her first bite, her eyes happened to flick up to meet with a revolted stare, from across the table.

"What?" Sara said.

Collin just grunted and shook his head.

"Yours came from the same cutting board, you know. Same ocean."

Collin looked down at his lobster tail. "Yeah, but mine is cooked, see?"

"That's more than I can say for your steak." Sara popped the albacore into her mouth, and then pointed her chopsticks at the pool of watery blood beneath Collin's sirloin. Such hypocrisy, forever extended from so many eaters of raw beef, toward lovers of sushi. Fish was always going to be the cleaner, healthier, and the more sustainable choice.

"You can't go wrong with a medium-rare steak," Collin replied, picking up his knife and fork, and slicing a pinkish sliver from his sirloin, "but sushi? Blech. That's just wrong to begin with."

"Mmm." Sara closed her eyes and smiled while she chewed. "How can anything possibly be wrong, when it tastes so right?"

Ryuu Grill and Galley was a pleasant stimulation of all the senses. Clouds of savory steam billowed up from a dozen teppanyaki tables, where chefs clattered their steel instruments and flipped acrobatic shrimp through the air, right into the open mouths of diners—sometimes. Strange and lurid fish swam an endless promenade through a huge saltwater aquarium that was mounted just beyond the sushi bar, where glistening cutlets rode a conveyer over mounds of shaved and sparkling ice.

Trademarked by a massive dragon pendant cut from brushed steel, Ryuu was the latest addition to downtown Kansas City's relatively new and booming Power and Light District. For four decades, a person could safely and easily roll a bowling ball down the middle of Main Street at the stroke of midnight, all the way from Liberty Memorial to the banks of the Missouri River, without a chance of striking any living thing, beyond a stray cat. It had remained a woefully dead part of town, but the culture of downtown KC had recently undergone some major revitalization.

Thanks to the addition of the downtown arena, a dome of mirrored glass situated at the confluence of two major highways, the nightlife of downtown Kansas City was resurrected from the darkness and desolation of an oversized cow town to a dazzling labyrinth of bars, trendy restaurants and thumping nightclubs. For the first time since the roaring twenties, Kansas City had become cool.

"I guess when you boil me down, strip away the car, and the loft, I'm still just a simple Kansas boy, at heart," Collin said, "scared of anything that ain't beef."

Sara smiled and winked at her boyfriend of six months. "Lobsters ain't beef, baby."

"Oversized crawdads, that's all." Collin shrugged. "Crawdads and cows? Shoot, they never hurt anybody. But all of that crazy stuff on your plate ... well, let's just say I don't eat anything that I can't pronounce."

"Repeat after me." Sara leaned over the table, narrowing her eyes seductively. "Shiro."

"Shiro," Collin said, leaning in to meet Sara, nose to nose, over their food.

"Maguro," Sara said, airily.

"Maguro."

"Guess what?"

"What?"

"You just said albacore in Japanese." With her chopsticks, Sara selected a small but choice cut of the pale meat. She dipped it once in the wasabi-soy sauce, and lifted it near Collin's mouth. "Will you?"

A mischievous smile spread across Collin's face. "Only if you will."

"If I will what, exactly?" Sara wrinkled her nose and cocked her head.

Collin rose from his chair. He reached for the inside pocket of his jacket. His hand reappeared with a black jewelry box, as he dropped to one knee, beside their dinner table. He flipped it open in one smooth motion, to display a sparkling ring. "Sara?"

"Yes?"

"Will you marry me?"

Mitch Poole transferred the wriggling minnow from his dip net into a Mason jar filled with water. Then, he threaded on the lid. He turned from the aquarium of feeder minnows to the group of teens, who would be his last tour group for the day. In the manner of a street magician about to perform some amazing trick, he raised the Mason jar to eye level, passing it steadily back and forth before the row of bemused faces. Inside, the minnow darted to and fro. It bumped its snout against the convex walls of its glass prison, gulping, and fanning its little gills.

"Human beings, we like to think of aquatic life as being brainless," Mitch said, while turning on a heel, "unless of course, it can be trained to jump through a hoop. Then, all of a sudden, it seems more intelligent to us. But, what exactly is intelligence? Can it be measured? Is there more than one kind? These are the questions we have to ask ourselves when we're suddenly confronted by a creature so unlike us, so alien to our world, and to our limited human experience, that a true comparison of our brand of intelligence against theirs seems difficult, if not impossible."

Mitch hitched an eyebrow, smiled, and then turned. Minnow jar in hand; he began walking slowly along the ranks of aquariums that lined the back wall of the Henderson Beach State Park visitor's center. The teens eyed each other uneasily, before shuffling after him. The last kid in line, peering out from the portal in his green hoodie, blew a bubble and snapped it with his tongue.

The rear of the visitor's center was a living laboratory, with rows of percolating lift tubes and humming fluorescent lights. Weird and wimpling creatures fawned up at Mitch, as the marine biologist strode through their neighborhood of glass houses. Some glowered cantankerously from holes in the coral, while others wriggled excitedly back and forth against the glass like gilled puppies, eager to play. Mitch stopped before a large and foreboding aquarium that emanated the ethereal glow of black lights, mounted beneath a latched hood of solid steel. It appeared to be empty, except for a jungle of dark rocks that were heaped at its center. Champagne bubbles rushed through lift tubes that jutted up through the layer of black gravel. Bits of wavering and translucent waste lay scattered about the aquarium floor.

"Let me introduce you to a very good friend of mine," Mitch said. His voice was barely audible over the mesmerizing hum of aquarium pumps, and the hiss of billions of bubbles, bursting constantly on so many surfaces. Mitch set the jar containing the frantic minnow atop the aquarium hood. He was careful to place the vessel softly, and soundlessly, before withdrawing his hand. But the sacrificial offering did not go undetected. As if stirred from its slumber, a grotesque entity emerged from within the stacked rocks like a living bulge of intestines. It gathered its complicated and writhing mass atop the rock pile. Puffing and pulsating in a show of changing hues, it engaged its crowd of onlookers through slitted goat's eyes. "Kids, meet Ursula."

Mitch lowered his bare arm into the water. A few of the teens gasped as the bulbous monster threw a heap of purplish coils around his arm, and dragged itself upon him. The tentacles tightened and released, changing grips, leaving little red circles on his skin, wherever the rows of suckers had seized hold. "Right now, Ursula is just greeting me in her weird octopus way. Each of her eight arms is equipped with its own brain, and each is loaded with tons of sensory receptors that not only can touch, but also can taste and smell. She's just taking it all in, making sure that it's really me, her old buddy."

As if satisfied with the data she'd sampled, Ursula slithered back down off his arm and studied the faces of each of the kids. It seemed to linger longest on the face of the kid in the green hoodie. "I think she finds you pretty interesting," Mitch said, glancing over his shoulder, at the boy.

"Why me?" the kid croaked.

"I don't know. It's hard to say what might be going through her head, right now. They don't think the same way that we do. What we do know is that an octopus is a highly intelligent, emotional, and even opinionated animal."

"How can an animal be opinionated?" the kid in the hoodie asked, popping his gum.

"Well, there used to be a biologist who worked here, named Kelly. And, for whatever reason, Ursula decided that she hated her. Any time Kelly got too close to this tank, Ursula would rush to the top and spurt a jet a water right at her. She's a pretty good shot. Kelly eventually left Florida for another opportunity, but a couple of summers later, she came back through Destin, and she decided to stop in here, to pay a visit. No sooner had she stepped into this room, Ursula rose to the top of her tank, and soaked her." Mitch turned to the teens, and grinned. "And get this, Kelly had even colored and straightened her hair."

Mitch took the jar containing the minnow, and he lowered it down into the tank. He positioned it upright in the black gravel, and then he withdrew his hand. In an instant, Ursula was upon it. Flashing black and red, the seething mass of tentacles explored the jar from every angle, tumbling it over and over, testing surfaces, changing grips. Glimpses of the terrified minnow could occasionally be seen through the monster's constricting coils.

"What's perhaps most impressive about Ursula, and all octopi, for that matter, is their ability to solve problems. We've tried all sorts of ways to keep her from getting to that fish, but she always manages to crack the code." The great mollusk then flexed its whole body, turned a weird shade of purple. The jar came open with an audible pop, and a rising bubble of expelled air. From the center of Ursula's restless mass came a chuff of minnow scales that settled to the gravel like a blizzard of silvery snow. The octopus then released its grip, and writhed back into its dreary tumulus with its eyes directed backwards, as if the creature trusted nobody. It left behind nothing but an empty mason jar, and a litter of minnow scales upon the gravel.

From the front of the room came the jangle of bells, as someone else entered the visitor's center. A heavyset man wearing the same khaki uniform as Mitch rounded the corner with a flushed and breathless expression. He took a moment to catch his breath, eyes bulging, before addressing Mitch in an urgent tone. "We need you down at the beach, right away."

"What's the problem, Skip?"

The panting man just shook his head and put his hands on his hips. "Dude, I'm afraid you're going to have to see this one to believe it."

Sara's jaw dropped open. Her chopsticks fell from her hand, clattering on the plate. She gaped down at the man with the dazzling ring. This was Collin, after all. He was impulsive, emotional. Not much of a planner. From the moment he first hit on her, from the opposite side of their gas pump, to his first phone call five minutes later, to their first lunch date, an hour after that ... the guy always seemed to be rushing the next play. On one hand, she found it flattering. However, on the other, his doggedness could sometimes make her a little anxious. She wasn't sure why.

It was as if sometimes it seemed as though he unconsciously knew something that she didn't. As if, he somehow intuited a shortage of time, and to compensate, everything needed to happen right this minute, right now-now-now. Maybe she was overthinking things, giving him more credit in the intuition department than he was due. But seriously, what guy thought the way Collin did--at least, beyond those first physical milestones in a relationship? And heck, what if it was intuition, and what if his intuition was right? What if this man kneeling before her in the middle of downtown Kansas City's Ryuu Grill and Galley, bearing her ring, with that heart-melting look of hope in his eyes, actually possessed a deeper sort of awareness?

Or, maybe this was just Collin being Collin.

"I will," Sara replied, falling into Collin's arms, just as a teppanyaki chef summoned a great plume of fire, prompting a perfectly timed cheer throughout the restaurant. He kissed her, and he told her that her breath smelled like sushi, but that he loved her anyway. And he did. Sara knew that much to be true. He showed it every day in both big and little ways. No one had ever loved Sara as well as Collin did. Plus, he was the first guy she'd ever dated who she knew she could trust completely. Collin hid nothing from anybody, because he never had anything to hide. He was an open book, and it was a good book. "I love you too. So, so much."

They'd not even finished their tableside embrace before a host with the keenest eye and the most impeccable sense of timing swept up to their table with a chilled bottle of champagne and a couple of glasses. He singlehandedly popped the cork right into the palm of his hand, as though he'd practiced this maneuver a thousand times. Before the bottle had a chance to foam, he'd filled both their flutes overflowing with froth, and then he turned to make an announcement of their engagement. His toast to their love, and to their future together, brought about an uproarious applause that made the both of them blush. Laughing, they obliged their onlookers with a delicate clink of their flutes, and a sip of the cloying fizz. Their host congratulated them again, before slipping respectfully away.

Collin removed the engagement ring from the velvet box and slipped it onto Sara's finger. "Is it the right hand?" he asked, hesitating, with the ring halfway down her finger.

"No, that's my left hand," Sara replied, with a smile, "and the left one is the correct one."

"It's supposed to be a little big," Collin said, allowing a nervous chuckle, "because you have to take it back into the store and they, you know, resize it exactly to fit your finger. I guess they cut a chunk out of the band, or something, and then weld it back together."

Sara tried her best not to laugh at his endearing innocence. "You're doing fine, babe."

"Thanks." Collin sighed, and leaned back in his seat, smiling. He picked up his napkin and blotted his forehead. "I've never done this before, you know."

"Are you scared yet?"

"Scared? No way." Collin leaned forward, kissed her again, and then smiled. His face was flushed. "This is exactly right. I've never been happier, never more excited."

Sara beamed across the table at her fiancé. Not her boyfriend. Her fiancé! This was the man with whom she was going to spend the rest of her life, raise a family, and grow old. The guy from the other side of the gas pump. The whole thing just seemed so surreal. So fast. It was almost—dare she say, flippant? No. If it hadn't felt right, she wouldn't have accepted his proposal. There was no such thing as flippant, when a match is just right. "So, who should we call first?"

"What do you mean?"

Sara furrowed her brow at him. "What do you mean, what do I mean, silly? Who are we going to call first to announce our engagement? My mom or yours?"

Collin picked up his napkin again. He smeared his face in the white linen folds. When he reappeared, seconds later, it looked to Sara as though he had aged five years. "I don't know," he replied. He reached for the champagne flute, then apparently changed his mind, and went instead for the glass of ice water. He took a few drinks and leaned back in his chair, staring intently down into the cluster of ice cubes. The color of his face waned from the flush of excitement to a rather sickly pallor.

"Are you okay?" Sara asked.

"I'm just, not really feeling so good all of a sudden." Collin's glassy gaze swept around the restaurant. His knee began to jiggle.

"Aw, babe ..." Sara placed her hand lovingly atop his, but he abruptly pulled his hand away from her. "You probably just got yourself all worked up over everything."

"Maybe." Desperation clouded Collin's face.

Sara glanced down at Collin's half-eaten steak and lobster tail. "You don't have a shellfish allergy, do you?"

"No, I've eaten lobster plenty of times."

"Well, I've heard that it can just come on, all of a sudden, even if you've eaten it before. My cousin had eaten oysters lots of times, but when she and her husband went down to the French Quarter, they ordered this huge platter of raw—"

"Would you please?"

"Sorry ... maybe it's the prospect of a lifetime with me that isn't settling so well."

Collin squirmed, pulling at his collar. "I think I just need to get to a restroom."

"You want to go home?"

"I don't think I can wait that long."

Sara rose in her seat and looked around the room. "It looks like they're over there, beside the bar."

Collin rose from chair. He dropped his napkin on the table, and clenched his fists. "Could you—could you get the check if they come around?"

"Yeah-yeah," Sara replied. "Are you going to be okay?"

"I'm going to be sick." Collin extracted his wallet and keys and placed them on the table. "Get the check. Meet me out in the car." Pushing in his chair, Collin then turned in the direction of the sushi bar. He took three ungainly steps, and then collapsed onto the restaurant floor.

Chapter Two

Mitch stood frozen on the boardwalk. His arms dangled limply at his sides. Beyond the feathered dunes of hissing sea grass, shocks of wild rosemary, sprawled Henderson Beach, a pristine hem between the strip of sugary sand, and the lapping emerald waves, all backlit by the natural brilliance of a Florida sunset. This was the place where Mitch had spent nearly all of his childhood, and the better part of his adult life. He'd achieved his bachelors degree in marine biology in order to drop anchor here, to secure a spot on Henderson Beach, from which he would launch his career, and pledge a lifelong commitment to his one and only true love. For all intents and purposes, Mitch was married to Mother Nature. And the sight thrown now before his eyes felt like looking at his wife's malignant tumors on an MRI. "How many are there?"

"Close to fifty. And different species."

"Different species?"

"Mostly pilots, but you've got a couple of humpbacks, right over there. A few false killers, a northern right, and down there, there's the big guy."

"A sperm." Mitch surveyed the awful collection of dying whales that lined the beach for as far as the eye could see in either direction. In another day and age, such an event might have been a joyous occasion. It might've meant a feast, or a glut of profitable oil gifted from the sea. But in the twenty-first century, a mass stranding in North America was nothing but a massive environmental disaster.

"Different species. Different species." He ran his fingers through his hair, and then, he just stood there, hands atop his head, as though he were preparing to be placed under arrest. "This has never happened before, Skip. Different species. Anywhere, I don't think. I don't know. I've never heard of this. Why would this happen, Skip? Have you called up to State? This rules out geomagnetism and navigational errors. It's something else. It's something new." Mitch lowered his hands and began to march rapidly down the boardwalk, murmuring to himself like the quintessential mad scientist. His colleague struggled to stay on his heels. At last, he stopped spinning his cogs, and turned to face his trainee. He grabbed him by the shoulders. "This is going to be a long night, Skip."

"What's first?" Skip asked. "What do we do?"

It was Skip's first season out of college, and his first experience with a beaching. Much less, one of this scale. One whale out of water was a stark enormity of a problem, and in this case, there were so many of them, all dying at the same rate. Even for Mitch, with his nine years of experience with the State of Florida, it was a paralyzing dilemma. The logistics of a strategy were positively mindboggling.

"Call down to Grayton," Mitch said, getting nose to nose with Skip, "and have them scramble the barge with the corset, cables and rings. I'll get the cat and canvas stretchers. Muster all biological staff, both here and Grayton. Muster everyone … grounds keeping, maintenance … pull the volunteer roster. Send your emails and tweets to the Friends of the Park network. Call up our local construction vendors, anyone we've used in the past. Check the Grayton parking project file. There's a bunch in there. We need bulldozers, cats, every free hand we can get. Are you getting all this? Skip! Give me sign, Skip!"

"Corset, cables, rings, barge, dozers, volunteers, vendors … yeah-yeah-yeah." Skip turned, with a look of desperation on his face that suggested that his brain might literally explode. He began running back up the boardwalk toward the visitor's center.

Mitch continued seaward, still murmuring. Different species. There were plenty of reasons for a whale to beach itself, all with the same monumental result. And in every case, it was always a challenge to pinpoint the cause. Pilot whales were notorious for stranding themselves. False killers, as well. Most often, the phenomenon was attributed to anomalies in the geomagnetic field that these species depended on for navigation. However, when a rare northern right whale was involved, humpbacks, and a mighty sperm whale, well, that certainly complicated an already difficult search for a rational explanation. For better or for worse, military sonar, or experimental submarine maneuvers, had traditionally been blamed for recent anomalies in whale behavior, when no natural explanation could be embraced. It was a lazy train of thought that couldn't be proven or disproven, and for that reason, Mitch had always been somewhat reluctant to buy into those conspiracy theories. But in this bizarre situation, he found himself struggling to arrive at a more likely explanation. It had to have been some sort of a major disruption. That much was certain. Something had happened, way down below, something sizeable enough to have caused every species of whale in the vicinity to make a suicidal run for the shallows. But, what was it?

Mitch turned to the Gulf of Mexico. He dealt a long and questioning stare out across those waves into the torrid whorls of the sunset. He felt as though he were actually expecting, or just hoping, for the answer to the mystery of the beached whales to rise up from the depths and show itself. But of course, nothing did.

When he was a child, Mitch used to like to imagine all of the water in the ocean just disappearing--without consequences, of course. He would sit right here in this same stretch of sand, and just imagine that mysterious green curtain being drawn suddenly back, exposing everything, allowing access to all of the deepest trenches, the submerged mountain ranges, and everything hidden down there, shipwrecks, sunken treasure, and of course, every monster of the depths. Animals had always been his greatest fascination. Now, as an adult, not all that much had changed. As he gazed out over the Gulf, he still found himself yearning to pull back that curtain, to get a glimpse of what the heck might be down there, terrorizing the world's largest creatures. So long as the curtain remained closed, the sea would always hold great mysteries. It was a fact that mankind knew far more about the surface of the moon than they did of the sea floor.

Mitch quit scanning the sea. He jogged down the beach toward the black mountain of flesh that was a sperm whale. All he'd ever seen of this beast were its bones in museums, photographs, and fantastic renditions of its image, breaching the waters of old paintings. Amongst whales, this species had perhaps earned the most unfair reputation of being a monster, a rammer of wooden ships, and a smasher of whaleboats. The closer he drew, the more awestruck he felt in the looming presence of the thing, the living battering ram that achieved most all of its infamy in a single instance, when one sperm whale purportedly sunk the whale ship Essex. So far as Mitch knew, that was the only documented incident suggestive of a sperm whale's latent aggression. That very incident inspired a young Herman Melville to write his masterpiece, *Moby Dick.*

Nearly the size and shape of a railcar, the creature lay prone on its side, waggling a skyward fin as if it were hailing Mitch, with a friendly wave. But the situation was hardly a lighthearted one. Here, one of nature's greatest living wonders lay hopelessly grounded, asphyxiating beneath the weight of its own bulk. The waving fin was probably an outward sign of the agony that it was suffering, as its upturned eye slowly wrinkled and dried in the hot air. Its saw-toothed lower jaw opened and closed, as if the creature was struggling to find the right words to communicate what was hurting it the most. Then, Mitch saw all of the blood.

At first difficult to discern in the blushing sunset, and then, it was frightfully obvious, rafting up around the great whale in crimson surges. Mitch placed his hand on the whale's rippled hide as he waded out into the surf. He could feel its titanic heartbeat. His gaze swept over the mottled acreage, searching for the injury that he knew must be there, somewhere, hidden amongst the scads of barnacles. He found it midway up the tail from the flukes, where blood oozed from a grinning crevice behind its dorsal hump, slashed from its severed spine, all the way down to its vent. With its every labored breath, the injury opened and closed. A sliver of sunlight shone through the gap. This whale had been sliced neatly in half.

"I really think we should've taken you to the ER, babe," Sara said, shaking her head as she studied Collin's every lethargic step from the parking lot, up the path, to the entrance to his apartment complex. Strange. It was suddenly easy enough to imagine the two of them growing old together, and it no longer seemed so romantic. All he needed to complete the portrayal of his future self was a shabby cardigan, suspenders, and some thin slacks hitched up to his chest.

Bats looped and spiraled through the twilit sycamore trees. It had been an unseasonably cool summer. More than a few genres of music could be heard playing simultaneously through open windows. The River Market was a pleasantly trendy place to live for an eclectic melting pot of young professionals, Bohemians and hipsters. The area suited Sara, who, like many of the River Market residents, grew up in the surrounding suburbs and satellite communities. It was a natural transition after graduating from MU to move into the beating heart of her city. Especially now that downtown had been revitalized, it was the cool thing to do to pounce on a loft apartment, and embrace the urban lifestyle.

Not so much for Collin, who affably admitted following a few of his fraternity brothers toward the River Market after graduating from KSU with a basic degree in business. He was a small town boy who had never fully adapted to life in the city. He didn't particularly like to drive on the highways, or leave his safety zone in the River Market. It was kind of a scary place for him--though Sara knew he would never admit it--filled with all strange shapes and colors of people who were totally alien to his rural experience. Sara guessed that she found this quality endearing. For some reason, his quavering innocence turned her on. It made her feel stronger, as a person, to see her man peering shyly out at her strange city from behind his thin shield of Midwestern American machismo.

"Fainting does not qualify as an emergency," Collin grumbled, waving his hand at the idea of a trip to the hospital. "I think I just need a beer."

"It's not so much the fainting episode that worries me," Sara replied, "so much as whatever caused it to happen. I mean, what if you're about to have a heart attack, or an aneurism? What if sweating and fainting are obvious signs of something worse that could be wrong with you? You don't know."

"And neither do they." Collin shuffled past her, still looking a hundred years old. "Every time, I've gone to the doctor, it's always turned out to be a big waste of time and money. Every time. Sit in that waiting room for a million years, and then they come out and don't tell you anything worthwhile in the end. They always take your blood pressure and listen to your breathing, as if that crap means anything, when you're sitting there with a broken ankle.   They're all just a bunch of sorry front-men for the pharmaceutical industry, all standing there ready to write everybody who walks through their doors a bunch of bogus prescriptions."

"Well, why don't you tell me how you really feel about it." Sara rolled her eyes and smeared her face in her hands, drawing a deep breath through her nose and expelling it through her mouth. Thank God, she wasn't a doctor or a nurse. She supposed Collin's distrust of medical professionals was pretty typical for a guy his age, but Collin sometimes seemed to take it to a fanatical level. His whole male code of honor dictated certain things.   Sara understood that, and she guessed she respected that, seeing as how so many guys from his part of the world held tightly to the exact same standards.   Eat beef, drink domestic beer, listen only to country music or classic rock and roll … it went on from there to acceptable clothing, hobbies, and automobile makes and models. Any habits falling outside these basic guidelines could constitute considerable negative pressure applied by other males of the same ilk, who seemed to constantly audit one another, inasmuch as they seemed to depend on the affirmation they received by living their lives according to the code.   The idea seemed to be that certain acceptable habits were good building materials to frame a solid structure, upon which, a sturdy American male could be built. But ironically, the code really only provided the illusion of strength and solidarity, when in reality, it fostered dependence, distrust, a commitment to weakness, and an inability to adapt to new people and situations. She loved Collin, but she found these traits to be exhausting.

"You going to come up?" Collin asked.

"Yeah," Sara replied, "but you don't look so good."

"I'm rock solid." Collin pantomimed a bodybuilder's flex, but stood rather shakily. Sara probably could've tipped him over with a good poke from her finger.

"I think I'd better come up, just to keep an eye on you, crazy man."

Collin held the door, allowing Sara past him. His face still glistened with a sickly sheen of perspiration. His gray eyes peered at her from dark hollows. Sara wrinkled her nose at the scent of his unhealthy musk, sharpened by the acrid sting of vomit.

"You," Sara pinched her nose, "will be requiring a shower, immediately followed by a very thorough tooth brushing. Holy cow."

"As you wish, my queen." Collin swept low in a stately bow, allowing the glass door to bang shut, behind him.

"... but the light to which the fish is drawn is not at all what it seems. It is in fact the lure of the anglerfish."

Sara watched as a translucent horror emerged from the blackness of the ocean depths to fill the screen of Collin's television. She drew her knees up a little tighter, where she was curled on the couch. She took a sip from her glass of ice water. Why were the narrators of these nature shows always British? She wondered if the producers of European documentaries also sought Southern American narrators in return? She considered the wild difference that such a swap of accents would impart to a scientific program, and the thought made her smile.

"Look out, little minner. That dangly ol' light ain't even what ya think. Oh, Lord, here he come. It's a mean ol' anglerfee-ush!"

Sara glanced at her phone on the coffee table. Nothing had come through, but by force of habit, just looking at it prompted her to reach out and retrieve it. Somehow, she'd lost her mood to call anyone in her family, or to post anything about her and Collin's engagement. Things had just gotten a little too strange to feel much like celebrating. They could try again, tomorrow. Maybe after the fog of tonight's strangeness cleared, their future would seem all right.

She unlocked the phone's screen with a sweep of her thumb, and then proceeded with her usual check of specific apps and emails. Nothing much was happening out there in phone land. Friday nights were always slow. Everyone was out, doing fun and interesting things. They weren't sitting alone on their boyfriend's couch, toying with a phone and watching shows about anglerfee-ush. Ah, but he was no longer her boyfriend. That was really going to take some getting used to.

Up on the flat screen, the hapless minnow ascended toward the dim globe of light, unaware of the fleshy cable that attached the dangling lantern to the broad forehead of a monster. Just inches away from the rows of needled teeth, the little fish gave the bulb a playful peck. It was the minnow's last act. As if the predator had opened a valve to a terrible vacuum, the minnow vanished into its maw in a fraction of an instant. The jaws closed. The headlamp dimmed, and the monster in Collin's living room faded into utter blackness.

"Have you ever been to the sea bottom?"

Sara shrieked, tipping right off the couch and onto the hardwood floor. Her phone went clattering beneath the coffee table. "Shit the bed, Collin!" She gathered herself off the floor, rescued her phone, and rose defensively to her feet. "What are you trying to do? Scare me half to death?"

Her fiancé lurked behind the couch, bathed in what was now the cool blue effervescence emanating from the television screen, where shoaling fish cavorted through azure abysms. Collin's eyes were dilated to weird pools. He was completely naked and dripping. Sara noticed that his shower was still running in the background.

"What's the matter, babe?" Sara's heart still hammered inside her chest. Even now that she realized the person who'd crept up right behind her was none other than the man with whom she planned to spend the rest of her life, he seemed a stranger. In this moment, she could not recognize him.

"I heard the sea." Collin raised a trembling finger, pointing at the television. A vapid smile spread across his face. A grayish tongue quested about his lips. His gaze fell upon Sara's glass of ice water, and remained transfixed.

"Do you need a drink?" Sara asked. She edged around the coffee table, keeping her eyes trained on the man behind the couch. She picked up her glass of water. "Are you thirsty, babe?" Ice chattered against the vessel's thin walls. She extended her arm toward Collin's wet and hairless chest. "Here."

He stared at the water. His gaze seemed so strangely unseeing, as if he had no real recognition of all the ordinary things around him. His lips drew back, and his teeth began to chatter, but he wasn't shivering.

"Oh, baby." Sara began to choke. Her eyes welled with tears. "I knew we should've taken you to the hospital. Oh, my God. Something is seriously wrong with you. I think you might've had a stroke or something."

Collin's hand snapped out to seize the glass from her hand. His wet fingers encircled the vessel, sliding briefly against her own, with the slipperiness of an eel. Sara retracted her hand, smearing the slimy feeling against the fabric of her dress.

"I want to go."

"Good, baby." Sara nodded her head, trying to keep from sobbing. "That's good. I think we probably need to go."

"To the sea."

"What?" Sara frowned and cocked her head. Her chest rose and fell. She wiped a tear from the corner of her eye. "You want to what? I don't know what you're talking about, baby."

Collin stared down into the glass of ice water. He appeared to be mesmerized by its fluidity, by the clinking cubes that floated on its surface. He looked up from the glass with an infantine smile. A rope of drool spilled from his lower lip to land on the back of the couch. He raised the glass, as though he were about to propose a toast, and then he poured it over the top of his head. Once emptied, he let it fall from his hand to shatter on the hardwood floor. Collin's downturned lips opened and closed, as if he were trying to speak, or trying to breathe. He lurched forward, grinding shards of glass beneath his bare foot. Blood began to pool darkly on the floor.

Sara shrieked, placing both hands against his clammy chest. "Stop! Stop, baby, stop! Let's get you dried off. We've got to go, right now."

"To the sea."

"No! To the hospital, Collin! Something's wrong. Something's really-really wrong with you. I'm calling 911, right now." Hugging her fiancé to prevent him from advancing, and further injuring himself, she raised her phone and dialed the three digits. The voice of a female operator greeted her, and then inquired about the nature of her emergency.

Collin's whole body stiffened and his head snapped back. His face stretched into a terrible rictus grin, revealing rows of loudly chattering teeth. Sara watched in horror as his neck began to swell, right before her eyes. A rising knot ballooned in his throat, as he rolled his eyeballs back into his skull. It looked as if he were about to regurgitate a tennis ball.

"Hello?" asked the voice on the phone. "What is the nature of your emergency?"

Collin's face twisted with muscle spasms that snatched and restored his humanity. His head thrashed back and forth, teeth popping, until the seizure terminated with an audible crunch that seemed to emanate from inside his head. Sara screamed, as twin jerks of blood exploded from both of her fiancé's nostrils, streaking his bare chest all the way to his navel. He teetered in place, staring confusedly down at all the blood and glass, before crashing facedown upon the hardwood floor

Chapter Three

In the glare of portable floodlights that had been positioned intermittently along a half-mile of Henderson Beach, throngs of shouting volunteers, roaring bulldozers and prattling generators contributed a noisy industrial atmosphere to the ordinarily tranquil state park. It reminded Mitch of a huge construction site. Only, it was not buildings over which the workers labored. People and equipment maneuvered around the dark bodies of beached whales. Most of the smaller pilot whales had already been rolled back into the sea, by the cooperative efforts of volunteers and heavy equipment operators. Now, the rescuers were faced with the more difficult task of moving the great whales, which were the rarest, the oldest, and arguably the most important, both to the ocean's circle of life, and to the familial pods to which they belonged. If they were not able to be saved, they would have to be euthanized by dawn's break. Nobody wanted to see that happen.

A canvass corset had been fitted above the flukes of the northern right whale, the rarest and most endangered of all the species represented. Hunted nearly to extinction in the nineteenth century, the northern rights had only managed to rebound to an estimated worldwide population of about three hundred. The stranded individual happened to be a female. Of all the whales, she was deemed most critical to be saved.

The corset contraption was designed to safely tow a large whale in reverse, by distributing the cinching pressure of the towline over a greater portion of the whale's body, thereby preventing lacerations and spinal injuries that were often associated with a noosed tow cable. Multiple cables were fastened to steel ringlets that fringed the corset. They converged behind the flukes in a common line to a winch that was mounted to the deck of a barge. Fifty yards seaward, the flat-bottomed vessel idled coolly in reverse to keep from being washed ashore. Her spotlight blazed over the back of the northern right, where half a dozen volunteers clambered around, checking all of her rings and rigging. It was a dangerous operation. If the whale panicked and began to thrash about, a person could be killed in an instant by one slap of her flukes.

One by one, volunteers slid off the creature's back, dropping soundlessly to the sand. In the spotlights, their long-legged shadows articulated with a villous, spiderlike quality. The trussed whale in their midst looked as though it had fallen prey to a colony of giant ants. The workers stepped back out of the way, when the foreman raised an arm in a chopping gesture, a signal to the barge pilot that all the lines were securely fastened. Everything was set. The moment of truth had arrived.

The moan of the barge's motor ramped up into a roar, as the slackened towline rose taut and dripping from the sea. The friction of stretching cables, tightening canvas, was clearly audible, as the motor bellowed increasingly louder, throwing up foamy jettisons like a pair of white pillars. The tension of the moment was as palpable as it was measurable in the lines. There was a certainly a sense that something was about to give, at any second. But what would it be?

Volunteers continued to step further and further backward. Water streamed from the towlines, as the fibers constricted until every drop of moisture had been released. Suddenly, the northern right lurched backward a few inches. She raised her flukes and flippers, as if surprised by this queer new sensation. Thankfully, she did not panic. The bellowing barge spewed foam thirty feet into the air, until the whale suddenly began plowing seaward through the sand, like an elephantine penguin sliding over a snowfield. She slapped her flippers against the water, as she was welcomed home by her natural element's foamy embrace.

Volunteers rushed in. The whale spouted gleefully as her tiny helpers unfastened the main hasp of her corset, allowing the device to slough right off to the sea floor. It was a rush to retrieve the mess of lines and canvas before the whale became entangled in what could quickly become an even more dangerous situation. The volunteers floundered about with armloads of canvas and coiled lines, as the behemoth continued to spout in successive bursts. It appeared as though the whale could not believe that her dilemma had been solved, that she'd been freed from beneath the weight of her own crushing tonnage, and was at last able to breathe easily, once more. The whale turned slowly, orienting herself toward the deep. With a gentle fan of her flukes, she was in motion, heading back into the Gulf. A great cheer resounded through the predawn gloom. Volunteers slapped high-fives, and embraced.

Mitch watched all of the activity from the shadow of the dead sperm whale. He was relieved to see that the corset system was working, and that the life of an endangered whale had just been saved. However, his thoughts descended with the whale, to the darker depths of the ocean. While the focus of the majority was trained on resolving the immediate situation, someone had to focus on prevention, and on why this had happened in the first place. Why had all of these whales from diverse ecologies, feeding zones and familial pods, all rushed the shores of Henderson Beach together? It was the marine equivalent of a cattle stampede, but what had spooked them?

He shouted over to Skip, who was positioned on the other side of the carcass. When Skip marked his location with a reply, Mitch tossed the reel of measuring tape over the monster's back. Mitch waited a moment, until he felt the line tighten in his hand. All of the slack left the measuring tape, as it rose through the gore to span the widest gap in the transected whale. Skip shouted back a measurement of nearly two meters.

Two meters was far too wide and the injury too clean to have been inflicted by the bite of any living shark. They were ruling out suspects, one by one. Whatever had delivered the single deathblow to this colossus, slicing it nearly in two, was a whale killer of stupendous proportions. Here lay a beast twenty meters in length, with a weight of probably eighteen tons. Its flippers were three feet wide, as long as a man's body. Its massive jaws were lined with teeth the size of railroad spikes, more than sufficient to crush a whaling longboat into kindling. Despite all of its size, and raw power, something down there had cleaved this leviathan neatly in half, as if it had been nothing more than a roll of sushi.

The reel came flying back over the whale's hump. Mitch caught it single-handed. He cranked the bloody slack back up inside it. Skip came slogging back around the head of the dead whale, arms wagging at his sides. All of the strange new activity and stimulation through hour after weird hour had mentally and physically worn him out. It had not been an easy night. Mitch had watched Skip serve as the foreman on no less than twenty of the rolling and carrying teams. He'd worked extremely hard, maybe harder than anyone else on the beach. Skip had really proven his worth tonight.

"How about we call it a night, bud?" Mitch slapped his colleague on the back, leaving a gory handprint on his shirt. He glanced down at his hands, and then wiped the remaining blood on the back pockets of his shorts. The beach was all but cleared of the catastrophe. The barge and corset team had moved on to the pair of humpbacks. A crowd of idle volunteers milled around, laughing, talking, and celebrating the night's successes. The hard work was basically finished. Already, the dozer operators were maneuvering their heavy equipment off the beach, and up into adjacent parking lots, where huge trailers were standing by to receive them. One by one, the generators were being shut down. Spotlights winked out. Extension cords were being wound back up around their spools. The regular rush and hiss of the surf could at last be heard again. What a relief it was to hear the sound of the sea, restored to its rightful place in this setting. The first blush of sunrise would tease the eastern skies in just a couple of hours.

"What did this, do you think?" Skip asked.

"Had to have been a ship. Those props on those ocean liners are the only blades big enough to have inflicted this size of a wound."

"But an ocean liner isn't going to scare fifty whales of different species up onto the shore."

"No," Mitch glanced seaward with a knotted brow, "it wouldn't."

"What about a submarine? A big one. Like, one of those huge nuclear subs down there testing out all sorts of top secret weapons and junk?"

Mitch sighed, and raised his eyebrows wearily. He still didn't care much for converting to that heretical cult of the conspiracy theorists. Blaming the military was such a lazy solution. It was just a cop-out, adopted for lack of any reasonable explanation. Mitch disliked theories that offered no chance of ever being scientifically proven or disproven. He was a scientist, after all, and that wasn't what scientific thinking was all about. It was quite the opposite, but then, he really didn't feel like he had any other options in this situation. Something down there was terrifying whales and it was sizable enough to slash an adult sperm whale nearly in half. It all suggested something like a massive sonic disturbance, or a pressure wave, such as would be created by a powerful blast of sonar, or explosives. Combine those requirements with a spinning prop blade that was large enough to propel a vessel the size of an ocean liner, and what else but the military could possibly account for everything involved in such a bizarre case?

"Ugh. How about we go get some sleep," Mitch said, rubbing his face, "and come back by here tomorrow morning with a set of fresh eyes. Maybe we overlooked something tonight. Maybe tomorrow, something new will jump out at us."

"Do you really think you're going to go home, and actually fall asleep?"

Mitch sighed. "Not a chance."

"Me neither. That sun will be up pretty soon. Want to go grab an early breakfast?" Skip reached out and thumped Mitch in the middle of his chest with a big finger. "Dude, I know this place, just up off the harbor ... buttermilk biscuits with shrimp and sausage gravy. Oh, yeah. You hit that action with a shot of hot sauce, dash of Cajun seasoning, huh. Get ready to live, Mitchy-boy. Uncle Skip'll show you how it's done."

"Long as they serve a good cup of coffee, I'm all in, brother."

"Guess we might want to stop by the center up there, and uh, wash some of this gunk off our hands first."

"Six-one-six, respond on a one. Six-one-six, respond on a one. Pediatric non-responsive. Twelfth and Locust. Respond on a one."

Kate Browning decreased the volume on her radio. Sitting in the passenger seat of her ambulance, she studied the pounding of her heart. Closing her eyes, she breathed in and out. Her mouth already felt dry, her throat tight. Her stomach churned, and her skin felt like it was going to crawl right off her bones. This little charade of hers could not last much longer. It was getting worse. People were going to take notice. With every panic attack, came a looming reminder that this little game of pretend had gone on far too long without being discovered by someone else in the company, forcing some sort of a resolution. She dreaded that moment, and deep down, she knew that she needed to be called out. The problem was, she'd become too darned good at hiding her little issue. How long before she would simply have to resign as a paramedic to begin all over again in some new line of work that would drop her all the way back down to the bottom of the totem pole? Thoughts like this only made her anxiety worse, but she could not help herself. She felt trapped.

"Six-one-six? Do you copy?"

She opened her eyes, just a crack. Inside the gas station, Quincy was paying. Kate whispered a little prayer, as she bombarded her partner with mental signals to slow down, to take his time, to give her a few minutes to collect herself, and for another ambulance to respond to the call. She watched Quincy lean over the counter. He was smiling charmingly, as he began to chat with the little redheaded cashier. Good.

"Copy, Dispatch. Four-niner-five," Kate's radio blurped, with the reply of another paramedic, "responding to that pediatric at Twelfth and Locust on a Priority One."

Kate slumped in her seat with her hand over her heart, emitting an anguished sigh of relief. The panic attack immediately released its grip on her mind and body, allowing the flow of blood to resume its normal course through her extremities. As the fog of fear dissipated, she felt the sickening weight of failure upon her chest and shoulders. No surprise, there. This was all just part of the usual cycle.

Angry with herself, Kate straightened up in her seat. She turned the volume back up on her radio. Her eyes narrowed as she glared through the windshield at her partner, redirecting some of that venom toward him. Inside, Quincy shoved off the counter and sauntered backward out of the convenience store, chatting up his favorite clerk all the way out into the parking lot. At last, he spun on a heel, grinning in the streetlight, and jogged back to the ambulance.

Quincy pulled open the driver's side door. He leapt up into the vehicle, still smiling, but his smile faded as he noticed Kate's glare. He began to twist around in his seat, searching the floor, and center console. He slapped at his hips, and then checked the driver's side door compartment, all the while, muttering under his breath.

"Looking for this?" Kate held up his portable radio.

Quincy glanced up at Kate, cleared his throat, and took the radio out of her hand. An uneasy smile returned to his face. "Thank you, thank you. You know what I want, girl. You know what I need. Sorry about that. Forgot that bad boy again. Get any calls while I was out?"

"You mean, while you were in there flirting and fooling around?"

"Flirting?" Quincy's mouth fell open in an exaggerated display of disbelief. "Flirt-ting?"

"Uh, yeah. A hundred other parking lots in our zone where we could sit and wait for dispatches, and you always manage to pick this one. Interesting."

"This one," Quincy looked around the gas station parking lot, "has everything Q needs. This one has free air. It has clean restrooms. And I do enjoy the selection of fine foods and beverages."

"You didn't buy anything, Q. And as a matter of fact, yeah, we did get a call while you were in there goofing off on the job. A Priority One." Kate looked him over. "And guess what? I had no way of reaching you. Probably just missed another chance to get some of your skills signed off."

"Naw, come on. We didn't really get no Priority One"

"Yeah, we did. And guess who took it? Four-ninety-five. How many times have we been over this, Q?"

"I had to use the restroom, Katydid." Quincy raised the pitch of his voice in contrived innocence. "When you got to go, you got to go."

"Whatever." Kate tossed the portable into his lap.

"Hey, I'm sorry." Quincy lowered his voice. "It won't happen again."

"You're putting me in a real awkward position, dude," Kate gazed out the window, biting her lip and shaking her head, "because in three short months, I've got to make a big decision on you."

"I'm sorry. For real. I want your recommendation. I need your recommendation. I messed up, but I won't mess up again. See, I'm putting it on right now." Quincy clipped the portable to his belt. "I'm putting it on. I'm leaving it on. Never taking it off. Never-ever. In the shower. In the bed ..."

"Six-one-six. Are you guys even out there, tonight?" both of their radios blurped.

Kate shot Quincy a stabbing glare as she retrieved her radio, raised it to her mouth, and keyed-up. "Six-one-six, awaiting dispatch."

"Six-one-six, status epilepticus at Third and Delaware, loft apartment number two."

"Roger that, Dispatch. Third and Delaware, loft two."

Quincy pulled his seatbelt across his broad chest and clicked it into the receptacle. He reached for the dashboard control panel, and switched on the lights and the howler. Kate flipped open her computer. Her fingertips rattled over the keyboard, as she forwarded the incident waypoint from their digital rip-sheet to the dashboard GPS.

"Ready, cowboy?"

"Ready, cowgirl. And away we go."

Quincy wheeled the bus, as they affectionately called their ambulance, out onto Walnut and bore north, sirens screaming in the direction of the River Market area. The close proximity of all the buildings amplified the howler's deafening wail as they blasted through the downtown corridor. Neon reflections of their whirling lights smeared the mirrored walls of the skyscrapers with snakelike tracers of red, white and blue. This was what it was all about. This was what turned heads, stopped traffic, and inspired more than a few young people to earn their patch, and become first responders. Not so much, for Kate. But it most certainly was, for many of the thrill seekers in the company. The regular race against time, glorified with a big show of lights and sirens, while the life of a stranger was hanging in the balance; it was the ultimate thrill ride, with the highest stakes imaginable.

Kate summarized the details from their digital rip-sheet. "Looks like we've got a twenty-six-year-old male, suffering a seizure and flu-like symptoms, delirium and severe extrapyramidal side effects." She looked over at Quincy, her trainee. "Where's your head on this one, Q? What's your preliminary diagnosis and treatment plan?"

Quincy's eyes flicked side to side as he swerved through traffic. He blasted the air horn a few times, to clear the way. "Um, twenty-something male with seizure and flu-like symptoms? I'm going with narcotic overdose. Meth, coke, smack, maybe bath salts."

"How will we verify? What skills will we use?"

Beads of sweat popped up across Quincy's forehead. Theirs was an occupation with tremendous outside pressures, with life or death consequences if you didn't keep your cool, keep your head in the game. Kate never stopped testing her Basics. She tried to apply similar stress levels, during their training, that they would experience once they had earned that coveted paramedic patch on their sleeve. "Verify narcotics with the Life Pack ... elevated blood pressure, temp, and heart rate."

"What else? You're forgetting something obvious."

"Um ..." Quincy mashed the brakes and blasted the air horn to clear a busy intersection. Once through, he glanced up at the GPS, still pondering his preceptor's question. "Drugs and paraphernalia!"

"Right. You search the premises for contraband while I'm doing skills. Check every table in every room. Check the bathroom vanity. Check the nightstands. Now, what if I run vitals and I'm not getting any verification for narcotics?" Kate glanced out her passenger window as they roared through downtown's Power and Light District, lit up like Tokyo. Her gaze was attracted to an enormous pendant in the shape of an oriental dragon, cut from brushed steel and backlit with red neon. She'd never seen that one, before. Things were popping up all over downtown. Every month, it seemed like there was some new bar or restaurant, turning heads. She'd never eaten at any of them. She didn't get out much. The attraction to glam, decadence and debauchery just wasn't in her. Although she lived in the city, she would probably always be the little girl from the rolling wheat fields of central Kansas.

"You say, you got nothing corroborating narcotics?"

"That's right."

"Epileptic, maybe."

"How can you verify, and what's the treatment plan?"

"Tonic clonic seizures … arms and legs stiff and rigid … five milligrams valium, with permission."

"Good job, Q. Anything else you can think of?"

"Yeah, don't forget to smile!" Q turned, to flash his winning grin.

Kate chuckled, and shook her head. She couldn't really tell him so, or it would just feed his ego, but Quincy would make a fine paramedic. Kate had seen enough of them come and go to see that he was Grade-A EMT material. He really had the head for it. Quincy was smart, energetic, and quick on his feet, cool under fire, and blessed with an indefatigably sunny disposition. All of those traits would serve him well in the field. He would no doubt make a far better medic than her.

Kate glanced at the columns of water jutting from the pools of Barney Allis Plaza, and her throat involuntarily tightened. All it took was the sight of water, sometimes. Or the word, "pediatric." She closed her eyes, waiting for the fountains to pass. But, they didn't. Quincy had to hit the brakes, right beside the water. He cursed, and blasted the air horn. Kate opened her eyes, just a sliver. There was a crowd of drunks in the street, blocking their way, like a horde of mindless zombies in their headlights. Kate closed her eyes tightly, again. Trapped right beside the fountain, there was no escape from its greenish odor. Her ears could not divorce themselves from the sickly lapping of its swells against the concrete retaining walls. And from some unlit corner of her mind, a hot prairie wind gusted up from that place in her past, where a mother's agonized screams expanded like the rings of water from that pale hump of a child's back, out there, where it shouldn't be, in the middle of their cows' watering pond.

Kate gritted her teeth. She balled the fabric of her pants into her fists. She could feel the icy tendrils of a panic attack around her chest and throat, threatening to squeeze the last drop of sanity from her mind. She had seen too much death. Too much trauma. It had all been such a joke. To think she could possibly build such a house of cards, on such an unstable foundation. Hard as she'd tried to run from it, she would never escape the inevitable. She was only prolonging it. The human psyche was not designed to withstand so much loss. Something was going to give. When it did, Kate's whole house of cards would be scattered, forevermore, in the hot prairie winds.

"Maybe a possible allergic reaction."

"Huh?" Kate opened her eyes and relaxed the grip on her pants. The pedestrians had cleared, and the bus was moving again. Kate's blood pressure dropped, the further the fountain traveled in her side mirror.

"Those symptoms could also be an allergic reaction of some kind. If the patient is also itching, or covered with hives. Fifty milligrams diphenhydramine."

Kate coughed, cleared her throat. "Good," Kate nodded her head and rubbed her face, straightening back up in her chair. "Very good, Q."

"I'm sorry about the whole radio-thing, back there. I swear, Katydid, I'll never forget my portable again. Never-ever."

"Relax, Q. You're doing fine. I've forgotten my radio before, too. And I've missed some big calls. I'm just trying to do my job, dude. Trying to prepare you to be the best EMT that you can be. I wouldn't be doing you any service by letting mistakes like that slide." Kate glanced at the GPS, and then searched the bricked avenues of the River Market for the address of their call.

It riddled her with guilt every time she did it, distracted a trainee from her own obvious flaws by drawing attention to theirs. It was too easy. Her position empowered her with just enough freedom and authority to avoid the dispatches that bothered her most; namely, those calls that reminded her of that traumatic afternoon that directed her down this career path. But Kate was acting as her own worst enabler, and she knew it. The more years that passed by, with her anxieties undetected, the more paralyzing they became.

She was not proud of it, and could scarcely admit it to herself, but there had been more than a few potential paramedics whom she'd washed out of the program simply because of the manner in which they'd played the keys of her anxiety. Sometimes, it seemed to Kate that they knew too much about her. They'd probed a little too deeply. Or, maybe they had looked at her just a little too long, when she was not in the best frame of mind. The truth was, Kate knew, deep down, that she had ceased to be an asset to the company, years ago. Somehow, she had learned to live with that. But when she started cutting good people down, from behind, simply because they were too close to the truth …

"We're right up here, Q, in this loft apartment building on the right."

Then, there were days when she was revalidated, when she was hailed as a rock star, and restored to her rightful place, as quite possibly the best damned paramedic to ever ride the bus for Trinity. There seemed to be two Kate Brownings, forever grappling to expose the other as a fraud. Not even she knew which one was the real Kate. Not anymore.

Quincy wheeled into the parking lot and parked the bus. Kate hopped out and threw open the side door. She pulled the Life Pack, the airway bag, and the med kit, from the lower compartment. Keying-up her radio, she alerted dispatch that six-one-six was on the scene, with a response time of four minutes, forty-seven seconds. She threw the airway bag over her shoulder and hustled after Quincy, who was already halfway up the path to the glass door, on the back of the apartment building. She looked up the side of the building. Music played, through a couple of open windows.

All of the downtown loft apartments were kind of similar. Renovated stores from the old packinghouse district, they remained raw and primal with their blackened bricked walls, their industrial age framing, freight elevators, and creaky staircases. They reeked of age and experience and past lives from a bygone heyday when Kansas City was both filthy and rich. Now, with the meat-packing industry but a distant memory, twice consumed by devastating floods, the area had become a new haven for artists and yuppies. It was dominated by kids straight out of school, whose transition into the real world was often accompanied by a willful perpetuation of the weekend partying from their college days. But it wasn't college. They were getting older, and their binge drinking could sometimes cross the line between partying and the early stages of alcoholism, which could lead good people into deep trouble.

Kate followed Quincy up the narrow, squeaking staircase to the second floor, where their patient occupied the only loft apartment. The name on the rip-sheet was Collin Stillwell. The air in his building was stale with the mustiness of old wood and plaster, maybe a hint of rodent activity. The sounds of their breathing, their shoes on the hardwood floors, were sharpened by the lack of acoustic dampening by any sort of carpet, drywall or ceiling tiles. This was a building of brick, pine and steel, that reflected all sound waves right back at their creator. Quincy banged on the apartment door.

"Paramedic!" Kate shouted. She tried the handle, and the door opened. Inside, she was drawn toward the pulsing glow of a television set, the voice of a British narrator, and the sound of a woman weeping. But all of these sounds were underscored by something else. It was a sort of rhythmic hammering, like an imbalanced washing machine. Kate could feel the vibrations through her boots. She could actually see it in the subtle trembling of a few, framed pictures on the walls that showcased the important moments in the life of a good looking guy, captured in the company of his family, his friends, and an attractive young woman.

"We're in here!" a female voice cried out.

Kate hurried toward the living area, while Quincy probed the adjacent rooms with his flashlight. He slipped into what appeared to be the master bedroom, searching for contraband. Kate proceeded toward the trauma, ahead.

The vast living room of the apartment was simply furnished, nucleated by a huge flat-screen television that was almost certainly a young bachelor's first big-boy purchase. Kate rounded the worn couch and end table that looked to be cherished relics of a recent college apartment, to find a girl kneeling beside the naked patient. He was shivering like a beached minnow. His whole body was smeared with blood, and bejeweled with shattered glass.

"It all just happened, during dinner," the girl cried, "he just started getting sick, and then he fell over in the restaurant. He didn't want to go to the hospital. I told him we needed to, but he wouldn't. Then, we came here. And now, I think he's dying!"

"Alright, let's try to calm down a little, okay? What's your name?"

"Sara."

Kate checked his eyes with a pen light. Pupils were dilated but responsive. Blood from both nostrils. She pulled up the Life Pack, and began checking his vitals. "Any illegal drugs tonight, Sara?"

"No!"

Kate nodded. They never said yes, but it didn't hurt to ask. "What about prescription drugs? Is he taking anything?"

"No, not that I'm aware of."

Kate turned to the sound of footsteps. Quincy entered the living room. He was a strong, imposing figure, who provided an immediate sense of physical security whenever he entered a room. Kate was always glad to have him along, on calls. She gave Q a questioning look. He responded with an almost imperceptible shake of his head. He'd found no evidence of narcotics in the house.

"How're his signs?" Quincy asked.

"Pulse one-hundred. Pressure and temperature good. No tonic clonic motions. No hives or itching." Kate shot Quincy a look that she knew he'd understand to mean that it was time to make the diagnosis, and to start a treatment plan.

Quincy squatted opposite Kate and Sara. "Blood from the nostrils," he noted. "Ma'am, was there some kind of a struggle, or when he fell. Is that what caused all this bleeding?"

"No," Sara shook her head emphatically, "it just happened. It just kind of … blegh, blew out."

Quincy stared at Kate with pleading eyes. When she offered him no assistance, he shook his head, and shrugged. "Going to have to go with a cocaine overdose on this one."

Kate closed her eyes and slowly shook her head. He should've known better. Never say something like that. Not out loud, right in front of loved ones.

Sara began to shout. "He's not a drug addict! He's never done drugs in the six months we've been together!" She began to sob, and buried her face in her hands. "We just got engaged tonight."

"Pass me a vial of Benadryl and a needle, please," Kate said.

"But there's no hives. No itching."

Kate continued to stare him down. Quincy opened the med kit. He retrieved the vial labeled "diphenhydramine." He handed it to Kate, along with a hypodermic needle and syringe.

"Vitals are normal," Kate repeated, as she filled her syringe with fifty milligrams of Benadryl, and tapped the patient's vein. "Normal is key. You'll never get normal vitals with a cocaine overdose. What we're seeing here is a dystonic reaction. You've got normal vitals, but extrapyramidal side effects, non-tonic clonic seizing, facial contortions, tremors, and delirium."

"But a dystonic reaction to what?" Quincy asked.

Kate glanced over at Sara. "Is your fiancé taking Haldol, by any chance?"

"Is he taking what?" Sara looked from Kate to Quincy, then back to Kate again.

Kate depressed the plunger with her thumb, piping the medicine into Collin's veins. "Haldol is a pretty common anti-psychotic."

"An anti-psychotic ..."

Kate nodded. "It's prescribed to treat schizophrenia, psychosis ... a bunch of other things. Your fiancé is exhibiting all the classic side effects of a bad reaction to a dose of Haldol. They sometimes like to remove their clothing, talk nonsense. Sometimes, you see some swelling in their faces and throats. Just prior to the seizure, would you describe his speech patterns and behavior as being slow, slurred?"

Sara's chest began to rise and fall. Her eyes grew wide and shimmering. Eventually, she nodded, and then, she could not seem to stop herself from nodding.

"I'm pretty sure that's what we have here," Kate said. She took the cotton ball from Quincy, and pressed it to Collin's arm as she withdrew the needle.

"He kept talking about wanting to go to the sea," Sara whispered.

"Yeah. The Haldol reaction can make people pretty delirious."

"But, I've never seen him take anything. Nothing except ibuprofen. He hates medicine. He's weird. He won't go to the hospital, or see a doctor, or anything. I can't imagine him being on any kind of a prescription without--"

Collin's seizure suddenly abated. As the meds circulated through his body, the contorted musculature of his face relaxed. His eyes fluttered open, a little. A soft moan escaped his lips.

"Just like magic," Kate said, with a smile.

However, Sara did not appear to be impressed. The evident validation of Kate's diagnosis seemed to bring the girl very little relief. Her hands were still clasped around her mouth. Her eyes were still bugging.

Kate took a minute to level with Sara. She'd been doing this for so many years that she sometimes forgot. She had to remind herself to empathize, to be human. Just like any ordinary aspect of any ordinary job, the emotional reactions of her patients' loved ones had a tendency to become routine. "Haldol is prescribed to treat a lot of very different things, okay? There's no need to jump to the worst possible conclusion. And, it's not something you might've ever seen him take. A lot of times, patients will go in for their Haldol injections, just a few times each year. That way, they don't have to remember to take a pill every day. Injections have really become the norm." Kate took a strip of medical tape from Quincy, and then she strapped the cotton ball securely into the joint of Collin's arm. "And, you know, Sara, if you've only known Collin six months, he might've just recently gone in for his injection. That could very well explain this reaction, and it could explain why he never brought it up to you."

Sara shook her head. "I was going to marry him. I said yes." Her wide and affrighted gaze swept to meet those of the EMTs. "But now, I don't even know who he is anymore."

"You know, I can understand why this would be a shock to you," Quincy said, kneeling down beside Sara, "but I really don't think it would be all that unusual for a guy in Collin's situation to be a little afraid of telling somebody that they were on this type of treatment. You know what I'm saying? Especially if he's had some success with it, and he'd been living a normal life. Might've not wanted to try and mess up the good thing y'all had going with some news like that. Probably planned to tell you a little later."

Kate nodded. "He's right. Clearly, he was very much in love with you, or he wouldn't have asked you to spend the rest of your life with him. You can even commend him for taking all the right steps in trying to beat this thing, to try and live normally, which it sounds like he had been doing, right up until this reaction, which was not his fault."

"But when was he going to tell me? After we moved in together? Bought a house? Started a family?"

"Hey." Kate put a hand on Sara's shoulder. "It's still the man you fell in love with, right here on the floor. You might talk to his family, if you're comfortable with that? Or, wait and talk to Collin yourself, after he's had some time to recover. This is going to be pretty hard for him, too. He didn't expect to be faced with this crap any more than you did. This was supposed to be a happy night for you guys. We're going to go ahead and load him up, okay? Take him over to Trinity."

Sara did not respond. She stared down at her crumpled fiancé in the blood and broken glass. Tears rolled down her cheeks, and fell from her chin to Collin's bare chest. Blood feathered pink, where their essences merged.

"I'll tell you what," Kate said, "why don't you give me your number. You clean up around here, maybe make some phone calls to family, and I'll text you a few good links with some information on Haldol, and dystonic reactions. You guys can live with this. In sickness and in health, right? Heard that before? Well, it looks like that vow is going to get put to the test a little ahead of schedule."

Sara was still visibly stricken, but her mind seemed to be wrapping itself around the vagaries of the new situation. She dealt her fiancé a rather sad and appraising stare, as if she were somehow disappointed in him, but perhaps still willing to forgive. On the floor, Collin's fingers twitched. His hand moved. It slid through the blood and broken glass to find Sara's hand. Slowly, his fingers encircled hers.

Sara closed her eyes, pulled a deep breath through her nostrils, and then nodded her head. "Okay," Sara replied. "I can do this. I can do this with him."

Chapter Four

"Whales." Skip shook his head, and snorted. He shoveled up a spoonful of fluffy biscuit, smothered with steaming shrimp and sausage gravy. After admiring it for a moment, he docked it flawlessly into his mouth. "We got into this racket to work with sharks, you and me. And here we are, worrying over a bunch of whales."

"Oh, you work around here long enough, trust and believe, you'll get your chance to deal with all kinds of different monsters." Mitch hitched his eyebrows as he pulled a sip from his coffee. He held his phone upright, waiting on his Shark Tracker app to load, while staring out over the tranquil mouth of Choctawhatchee Bay. "It's Saturday. They'll all be out on the prowl, later this afternoon and evening, I can assure you."

It was still very early in the morning. The narrow funnel between Destin Harbor and Okaloosa Island was not yet congested with what would soon be parade of wave runners, pontoons, party boats, and fishing charters, all loaded with the droves of tourists who swarmed down upon their beloved "Redneck Riviera," every June. As the season progressed, the invading population would steadily increase until the stifling heat and the unpredictable weather patterns of the approaching hurricane season would start to drive them off. By the second week of August, Destin would start to settle back down again. That was when the locals really started to enjoy their summer.

No longer the quaint little fishing village of Mitch's youth, Destin had come to be regarded as a rather low-hanging fruit on the Florida panhandle. It was the quintessential seaside escape, complete with beautiful water and powder white beaches that were accessible to most of the country without requiring a flight. In terms of driving distance, it was a day or two from just about anywhere in the American heartland. Over the years, Destin had become extraordinarily popular as a family destination. It was celebrated all over the Internet as the perfect place to introduce your children to the ocean for a storybook experience, looking just the way the seashore was always pictured in children's books, not murky and threatening, as the ocean typically appeared, on either the east and west coast. In addition to attracting families, it had also become a mecca for partygoers; college kids and weekend warriors, who were probably less enamored with the picturesque beauty of the white sands and emerald waters as they were drawn to the hundreds of bars, restaurants and nightclubs that rocked the beach, all summer long.

"Sure you don't want a bite?" Skip offered what was left of his plate.

"No thanks." Mitch shook his head. "I've never been much of a breakfast person."

"I'm telling you, bro," Skip said, chewing with his eyes closed, and breathing loudly through his nostrils. "You are absolutely insane to pass this up. Best 'scuits and gravy on the whole panhandle. Hands down."

And, as Skip pointed out, the food could not be ignored. Situated at the confluence of three culinary influences, Destin offered the spicy Cajun and creole styles of the Louisiana bayou, the deep-fried comforts of Southern soul food, and the fresh, tropical elements of the Caribbean. All of these styles held fresh seafood in high regard. So, if anything at all had remained the same in Destin, since the days before tourism's takeover, it was a local passion for catching, cooking and eating fish.

Ubiquitously tagged as, "The World's Luckiest Fishing Village," Destin boasted one of the largest fleets of private and commercial fishing vessels anchored in any harbor, worldwide. Mitch watched, as the hundreds of shrimp trawlers and fishing charters were being loaded, rigged, iced, and painstakingly maneuvered into the fuel docks, all part of the ordinary regimen for preparing for the day's work, ahead.

As a marine biologist, Mitch understood, perhaps better than most fishermen did, why Destin's abundant marine resources had nothing to do with luck. It was all thanks to the Gulf Stream, the most powerful natural force on earth. This current roared right up Florida's Atlantic coast, casting off incalculable amounts of plankton, fish, and every variety of sea life as it rubbed shoulders with the swirling crucible that was the Gulf of Mexico. It was the world's biggest fish trap. And every great predator of fish, including humans, had eventually found this haven, and had adapted a wide variety of unique methods of exploiting its resources. Like a gigantic eddy, forever spinning over a hole in the wings of a river's current, the Gulf was a dynamic and self-replenishing ecosystem. It would have become rather bloated from the constant influx of Gulf Stream plankton, were it not for the ranks of teeming fish, and the enormous predators of fish, that haunted its lightless depths. It was the perfect location for studying the monsters of the deep, because they were all down there in that hole.

Mitch narrowed his eyes at his phone. The digital map finally took form. The ragged coastline was first to appear, followed by waypoint coordinates, and finally, the shotgun pattern of colored blips that still brightened his eyes and made his heart skip a beat, every time he opened the app. Shark Tracker was his baby, his invention, and his legacy to the science of marine biology. Over the last four years, he'd not only managed to put over a hundred tagged sharks right into people's pockets, but he'd made a cutting edge research tool available to the general public, free of charge. By tagging sharks and uploading them into the Shark Tracker system, Mitch was giving these creatures not only names, but precise locations, enabling their movements to be viewed, graphed, and compiled, right from the comforts of a person's own living room. Sharks in real time. His intent was to create a cool research tool, which he certainly did, as well as to replace some of the unwarranted fear and mystery perpetuated by these animals, with perhaps a higher level of awareness, and understanding.

"So, who's swimming around out there, today?" Skip asked, blotting gravy from his mouth with a napkin. "Anyone new?"

Through this application, they had come to know individual sharks on a pretty personal level. There was a wide variety of species represented, but of course, it was the larger oceanic individuals that attracted a following of online spectators.

GHH017, for example, was the ID tag for a hammerhead of particular enormity that had achieved immediate notoriety for nearly pulling Mitch over the rails of the Savannah, their shark research vessel. TS004 was another favorite. This fifteen-foot tiger shark had the ominous distinction of hunting the same two miles of Destin shoreline for almost four years. He cruised the mouth of the harbor, and swam in and out of the bay, literally right under the feet of all the tourists on waverunners, a stone's throw from the hundreds of revelers that permanently occupied the hump of shallow water to the bayside of Destin Bridge, known as Crab Island. The creature had yet to cause any problem. The big shark seemed only to be interested in the schools of redfish known to stage around jetties, at the mouth of the bay. But secretly, the beast made Mitch a little nervous. If there ever came a day, when TS004 made a bad decision that compromised the safety of a tourist, there would be an inevitable backlash. Sometimes, it felt like Mitch had invented an invaluable tool of science, but at other times, it felt like he'd somehow opted-in for the highest level of micromanagement.

"Oh, boy-oh-boy-oh-boy." Mitch sighed, and pressed a fist to his forehead, frowning at the handheld screen.

Skip lowered his napkin and swallowed. "They're all moving up toward Henderson Beach, aren't they?"

Mitch had suspected as much. With all the blood and stress in the water from the mass beaching, they were answering the dinner bell. Last night's event had begun to pull them all up from the depths, the big ones, into a hunting zone that was dangerously nearer a strip of public beach than they probably ought to be. Sharks were not the coldblooded killers that society made them out to be, but they were known for misidentifying human beings, and making occasionally fatal mistakes. To make matters worse, this was happening at the onset of tourist season, as well as the beginning of summer break for all the kids in the Fort Walton Beach area. Henderson Beach State Park was a significant attraction to the locals, and to the tourists who wanted to avoid the biggest crowds of Crab Island and the Emerald Coast Parkway. The people who visited Henderson Beach, were in Mitch's opinion, the best people. They came to be educated, not to party. They came to revel in the natural beauty of the panhandle environment, not to join all the inland madness. If Mitch had been a tourist, rather than a Destin local, he would have been a very similar tourist to those visitors to Henderson Beach.

"We're going to need to call up to State, maybe shut the beach down," Mitch replied, "if this doesn't start to clear up. Look at this." Mitch turned the phone around, and showed Skip the roiling mass of orange blips. Each dot in the cluster indicated a large and potentially dangerous shark, such as a tiger, a hammerhead, or a bull. Even at full zoom, there was little distinction between the blips that converged on Henderson Beach as one solid mass. "I've never seen a mass gathering like this."

"How many do you think there are?"

Mitch shook his head, wide-eyed. "Hundreds."

"It's that sperm carcass." Skip shoveled a heaping spoonful of gravy into his mouth. A pale dollop fell from his bottom lip to the plate. "That's what's pulling them all in."

"Yep."

"Got to get that guy out of there. Couldn't they use a corset to drag it off?"

"No. It would just rip right in half. We're going to need grapples and a tug. Chunk it up into pieces and drag it all out to sea. Going to be a mess. But yeah, that needs to happen, and right away." Mitch snapped a screen shot of the converging sharks. He attached the pic to an email. "I tell you what, Skipper, if those suits up at State aren't able to see the value of the Shark Tracker system now, then they never will."

"Yeah, dude, but you're using it in precisely the opposite manner in which you originally intended."

"How so?" Mitch furrowed his brow.

"Because, right now, you're using it to inspire a greater fear of sharks, rather than removing it, as you'd hoped."

Mitch's thumb hovered over the "send" tab. Skip had a point, even if he was being a little facetious. Here it was, his first chance to impress their dark overlords with his newfangled technology, and he was seconds away from scaring the hell out of everyone. Animals were his passion, his greatest love, from the most powerful of behemoths to those teeny microscopic paddlers that frolicked through every raindrop. He loved them all. And he wasn't betraying them by using Shark Tracker as a device of terror, but it kind of felt like it. Mitch favored the survival of the animals in any fight. After all, research had shown that if all insects disappeared from the earth, all life on earth would vanish into extinction within fifty years. Total collapse of every food chain. But if all humans disappeared, all other life on earth would flourish. Humans were the plague, not the insects. Nevertheless, in any fight, despite which he favored, the lives of humans came first. If Shark Tracker could prevent the death of one human, then he supposed the lives of innumerable sharks might be spared, as a result. Mitch dropped his thumb to the tab, and his recommendation to shut down Henderson Beach blasted off to State, with the sound effect of a little jet's engine.

For the first time in eons, it was alone. Its hatchlings were gone. It was time to clean out the empty nest. Time to fill the lonely depression with manna. Time to prepare for the final stage of its life. Somehow, it knew this. It understood what needed to be done, and it was afraid. It was not ready to die.

Its vacillating trunk swept slowly, side to side, sucking up tons of mud, excrement, and shell castings from the sea floor. It did not relish the task of ingesting its own young, those who had failed to survive their first molt. Multitudes of tiny carcasses were still trapped in their castings. Their rendered flesh would be converted into manna, along with everything else. It would all be passed forward to the next generation. Once the little explorers returned from their great migration, everything would be ready for their homecoming.

Each plunge of its siphoning trunk was accompanied by an abdominal contraction that spewed a black plume of filtrate. The filtered solids, it crushed and swallowed. The muddy water, it expelled through bristled vents. Through this effort, a constant shower of filth had rained down upon its vast carapace for the last several weeks. It worked within a blinding cloud of debris that muted its blinking strings of bioluminescent lights. Virtually indistinguishable from the murky sea floor, it had come to resemble an active volcano, venting a nebula of ash and slag. This task deprived it of all but its most basic, tactile senses. It was exhausted, but it did not rest. Never had its world felt so cold, so lifeless, or so alien, but this effort was for the offspring. It had to be done. Everything had to be perfect. Everything had to be just the way that its life mate would have wanted it.

Great thrusts of its fore claws shredded drifts of accumulated rubble, as it organized the benthic graveyard of the skeletal remains of every creature, every wayward vessel that had ever dared to approach its nest. It needed more space for its final creation. It needed room to draw, filter and purge, to dab its bristling abdomen along the walls of the crater, extruding a sticky bead of manna with every touch. The columns were beginning to take form, rising from the sea bottom, one bead at a time. It paused, as the mournful ululations of some other monster of the depths keened eerily through the ocean's lightless abysms.

This was a time for reflection. It knew a few songs, as well. It began to thrum tones of remembrance, vast in resonance and bottomless in timbre, recalling bygone stages of a long and fruitful existence. Explorer, dancer, seducer and destroyer, life mate and living god ... it had lived a full life. Once the hatchlings returned, it would give itself to them, body and soul. It would turn its belly skyward, amidst the columns of manna, and wait to rejoin its life mate for an endless dance through the After.

It vibrated layered diaphragms, producing its most complex intonation, used only in mourning its life mate, who should have been here to witness their migrating brood's return. It was not fair to be deprived of one's lifelong companion at the final stage of life, when they most needed the support of the other. Had those surface dwellers, many ages ago, not grown so jealous of their god. Had they not lured, trapped, and destroyed its life mate, an act which assured their annihilation. Because on that day, those creatures learned that their god was in fact not one, but two. Their world, and every living thing upon it, had been pounded into an amalgam of blood and silt and foam, lost forevermore beneath the sea.

It stopped singing. Something was approaching. Something dared trespass now, at this final hour, perhaps to steal the manna, or to threaten its nest before its hatchlings returned. Its fore claws began to rattle a fair warning. But the droning maleficence steadily approached, trundling those trailing fitments along the bottom of the sea. It could hear the rush of water through that wall of dragged fibers. Narrowing its dorsal eye, it pumped angry jets of silt from its vents, rattling its claws ever more loudly, as the color of its carapace began to shift from black to red.

Spumes leapt like pale dolphins, from either side of the The Ballyhoo's bow, as the shrimp trawler cleaved the morning waters. The rising sun brushed a glorious impression of highlights across the dimpled seascape. From his position at the helm, Captain Spencer squinted in the new dawn's brilliance with an expression that was more of a fond wink than a frown. It never got old. Not as long as he fished the canvas of his favorite artist, whose masterpiece was always changing, and never allowed to dry.

The mass stranding of mixed species of whales on Henderson Beach, Spencer found to be most intriguing. While others worried over the how and the why, and by what means could such a disaster be corrected, Spencer's concern, like most fishermen, was simply whether or not whatever had disturbed the whales would also affect his catch. The hammered surface of the sunlit sea was beautiful. There was not a single cloud to bother the azure reflection, but just beneath the perfect surface, the sea was brooding. Something was stirring things up, down there, and the darkening waters had not gone unnoticed.

There were perhaps a number of reasons why so much silt had been turned up, over the last few weeks, creating something of an immense thunderhead, just beneath the waves. It was a localized phenomenon. Few folks inland were yet aware of it, but more than a few shrimping captains had been muttering about the dark zone around the fuel docks. Whether the depths had been disturbed by rock-hopper trawls, or by some natural anomaly, like a big pocket of methane gas, or a rogue benthic current, the consensus was that the area, through which Spencer was trawling, this morning, was apt to be some pretty poor shrimping. The other boats had been steering clear of the affected area.

But with respect to almost any anomaly at sea, there would always be polarized opinions on how the event would affect the catch. Sure, the disturbed waters might disorient whales, and frighten off schools of baitfish, but shrimp? Who knew? Shrimp were an entirely different sport. The design of shrimping trawls said it all. They were equipped with forward "ticklers" that were added to the rig for the express purpose of disturbing the bottom, stirring up debris, just ahead of the trawl openings. This proven tactic was effective because an upwelling of silt was precisely what scared the shrimp up off the bottom, and into the gaping trawls.

So, the dark zone could either be devoid of shrimp, as Spencer's colleagues supposed, or it could just as easily be the best shrimping of a man's whole career. No one knew, for sure. It was all just partly an educated guess, and partly a gamble. Every day that you made that decision to step up onto your deck, you were acknowledging that all your chips were down. You were all-in, baby, in a game of life and death where the house so often won, and maybe those odds were part of what made shrimping so addictive.

It was cold. Spencer frowned at the GPS, and tapped the screen, right where the little indicator that represented *The Ballyhoo* entered a digital representation of the dark zone. And he was surprised to see that the water here was cold. Damned cold. Based on satellite data, the heart of the disturbed area was a full fifteen degrees colder than the surrounding water, indicating a more massive upwelling from below the benthic thermocline than he would have guessed. His gaze flicked over to the sonar screen, where the billowing upheaval of silt, beneath the transducer, was wreaking havoc on the confused hardware. The fish finder could not penetrate the massive field of suspended solids. The reading showed one thick band, appearing as an enormous dome, directly beneath their boat.

Twin indicators blipped on. It was from the net sounders. These were the trawl's forward set of eyes. The horizontal sonar, positioned to look out ahead of the nets for shrimp, had just detected some extreme density, fast approaching the trawl openings. He'd found the shrimp! Spencer's eyes widened. The corners of his mouth curled gently into a smile. Some days, it paid to gamble.

When his eyes finally fluttered open, he found himself staring up at the wheelhouse ceiling. The solid tone of the automated maritime emergency alarm was buzzing in his ears. He recognized the metallic taste of blood in his mouth, and he felt bits of broken teeth. Blood in his eyes. All over his face. Staggering to his feet, he was just able to see that the wheelhouse windshield was webbed with cracks, presumably from an impact with his face. Spencer grabbed for the helm and missed, before toppling once more to the weirdly canted floor. He could hear the sound of rushing water, from below.

God, they'd struck something.

The wheelhouse door flew open. The bloodied face of an unrecognizable deckhand filled the portal, screaming something in the chaos of alarms and roaring sea. The kid seized him beneath his arms, and hauled him out onto the platform aft the superstructure, where Spencer gaped through blood and spray at a sight he could not fathom. The warps were slack and harping, from the windlass drums down to the cap rail, where both three-hundred pound, steel bollards had been ripped, bolts and all, right from where they'd been anchored to the stern deck. Two deckhands floated facedown in a widening well of bloody seawater that was being regurgitated up through the hatchway in rhythmic belches.

"What the hell did we hit?" Spencer finally managed to say, spitting sharp fragments of enamel.

"That!" the deckhand screamed.

Beyond the rail, muddy water rushed off the knobbed surface of the living mountain that rose from the sea. Enmeshed in warps, rigging, and tattered trawls, the thing glowered down upon their sinking vessel through an emotionless cyclopean eye. It was black as a shark's, and blinking, from behind a shutter-like membrane.

Spencer clambered woodenly down onto the deck. He could now see, with dread certainty, that his ship was impaled on the claws of the thing, hapless as a herring snatched in a fish eagle's talons. It emitted that usual, greenish stink, that dank and briny odor of the ocean's essence, worn by all life within it. But never had the odor been so available, and with such boundless intensity.

He staggered to the rail and gripped hold of it, gawping up into the eye of his destroyer. Although it was black as a shark's, that was where the similarity ended. There was something behind that eye. Something deeper. There seemed some unmistakable aspect of intelligence, working away in there. Spencer could plainly see that the monster was appraising him, examining him, just as a scientist might regard a weird bug in a jar.

"Please," Spencer asked, hanging from the rail, "what do you want?"

Every pane of glass aboard *The Ballyhoo* shattered, as the thing emanated a blast of deafening resonance. A great hiss of expelled gas was issued from bristled vents on either side of the monster, filling the air with the putrescence of the sea. The thing tightened its claws around the trawler, crushing it, as it began to sink slowly back into the sea.

"No, wait!"

There came the sound of splintering wood from one-quarter and low, while the slackened warps tightened and groaned on their booms. A geyser exploded skyward, from the hatch, but the pillar of fluid did not appear to be purely seawater. It was thicker than water. It was pearly, viscous, and sluicing over the bodies of the dead, like spermaceti from the head of a ruptured whale. This stuff, this was the source of the awful smell.

The trawler listed sharply, plunging its starboard boom into the sea. The captain's fingers lost their purchase on the rail. He heard the sharp cracks of the ship's ribbing as he slid, and then fell through the air. He crashed to the starboard rail with an impact that pulverized every bone in both of his legs. Spencer parted his lips to scream, but a wave of that repugnant gel slopped over his face, and into his mouth. It covered him, enveloped him, suspending him like an insect trapped in amber. He realized with the most terrible certainty that he was going to die.

Bound to *The Ballyhoo*, and to his shipmates, both living and dead, Captain Spencer was dragged beneath the waves, where the audible tension in the tangled rigging played weird strings to the creature's thrumming base. The monster pulled the vessel close, lipping the entire port rail with a long and gasping mouthpart that seemed quite interested in so many new things to taste. Spencer's last breath of air departed his lungs in an unheard scream, as the vacillating trunk descended over him.

Chapter Five

"Good morning," the triage nurse said in a sleepy, public radio voice. She offered Kate the blandest of smiles. "How did the rest of your night go?"

"Oh, just a couple of diabetics. A slip-n-fall, down in Power and Light," Kate replied. She turned in her stack of signed RUN forms. The nurse took them in a slow and measured gesture that she must have made a billion times, licked her finger and thumbed carefully through them, one at a time. Her gray eyes clicked methodically from one field to the next. If those eyes had ever held a spark of enthusiasm, it had died out years ago. However, she never missed a single detail. If there were an error, she would find it.

"Oh, shoot," Kate whispered, pinching the bridge of her nose.

"Forget something, hon?"

"Sort of, yeah." Kate realized she'd forgotten to call back that poor fiancé. She was supposed to have texted her some information on Haldol reactions. Stillwell was the guy's name. Collin. "Hey, how'd the blood work come back on Stillwell? I checked him in, probably around midnight?"

"Haldol reaction," the nurse said.

"Yes. Yes, it was." Kate shook her head. "I seriously don't know how you remember everything. I'd forget my head, if it wasn't attached to my shoulders."

The nurse smiled, and turned to her monitor. She rattled off something on her keyboard. Kate watched the nurse's eye movement, as she scrolled through the patient database, accessing the details of the Stillwell case. Her eyes narrowed and hardened, when she evidently found the information that she was looking for. "He was clean. No narcotics."

"Good." Kate brushed back a wisp of auburn hair, and breathed a little sigh of relief. This was good news. They had seemed like a nice, young couple. She was glad to hear that they'd told her the truth, and that Stillwell had not been under the influence. Sometimes, receiving a bit of evidence that corroborated a patient's questionable claim of sobriety was just enough to restore a little bit of Kate's faith in humanity.

"But, I'm afraid you were wrong in your preliminary diagnosis."

Kate lowered her hand to the counter. "Well, what his deal, then?"

"Not Haldol." The triage nurse shook her head, flatly. "No mental illness or Haldol prescription in his medical history. Not much of anything, really. Looks like he broke an ankle, once, when he was sixteen, but that's about it."

"Hmm." Kate drummed her unpainted fingertips on the laminate. She leaned in on her elbows, trying to peer around the screen. The nurse turned the monitor toward her, then leaned back in her chair, and folded her hands in her lap. "That's weird, though. The Benadryl worked."

"Might've been another type of reaction," the nurse said, "just not to Haldol."

"To what, I wonder?"

The nurse slowly shook her head. "Could be a lot of different things."

"Jeez, I kind of feel bad, now."

"Why?" The nurse cocked her head.

"You know. That's not exactly the kind of diagnosis that a fiancé really wants to be surprised with on the night of her engagement." Kate looked to the nurse for affirmation, some sign of empathy in her eyes, but the woman had simply seen and heard too much, over the years. Her well was dry. "Where'd they take him? Still up in ICU? I might stop in, say hey."

The nurse turned robotically back to her monitor. She readjusted the screen to her liking, then scrolled back up the page. "Well, it looks like ..." the nurse said, and then paused, sucking her teeth. "It looks like they moved him on over to Psychiatric. Now, that's a little strange."

"You said there was no history of mental illness?"

The nurse was already shaking her head, before Kate had finished her question.

"And all of a sudden, right now? You'd think brain tumor, or onset of schizophrenia, but it had to have been a reaction, because the Benadryl worked."

"Maybe it did, maybe it didn't."

"What do you mean?"

"Could have been pure coincidence. That happens. Or, maybe the Benadryl did work, against a different type of allergic reaction, like a food allergy. Something else. Benadryl solves a lot of different problems."

"She did say the whole thing occurred while they were eating."

"What were they eating? Shellfish? Peanuts?"

"I don't remember, if she even told me. I'm not as good as you."

"Well, you've got yourself a strange one, indeed. But the bottom line is that you did your job. You stabilized the patient with the right treatment plan, and you got him to the hospital."

Kate nodded, sighed, and stepped away from the counter. "Thank you."

"Sure, hon." The nurse then hitched her penciled eyebrows. "Say, how much time you got left on your shift?"

Kate shrugged. "About thirty minutes, I guess."

"You want to drop off a Riverside discharge, for me?" The nurse smiled, tilting her head in the direction of a disheveled person in the adjacent waiting room. He was slumped in a chair in front of the television, where a home shopping network offered an emerald broach pin that was rotating on a velvet pedestal. The guy appeared to be homeless. "He's been waiting in there for almost three hours," she whispered.

Quincy pulled the bus into the parking lot of Riverside City Mission. He and Kate assisted their discharge out of the ambulance, and onto the pavement. Delivering a homeless person to Riverside always felt a little sad, sort of like dumping an unwanted dog out into the country. More often than not, there was nothing medically wrong with their regular discharges to the soup kitchens and homeless shelters. When people found a homeless person asleep on the doorstep of their workplace, on a park bench, or on the side of the street, it was a pretty typical reaction to dial 911. They often appeared to be dead. Sometimes, these guys were inebriated or stoned. Other times, just exhausted, and sound asleep. On other occasions, it was the homeless person themselves who made the call, dialing 911 from a pay phone, all on their own. It was just a little trick in the playbook of surviving their hard life on the streets. It gave them a few satisfying minutes of control. They could call in an ambulance, and basically use it as a taxicab to the hospital, where they knew they could always get a free night of room and board if the shelters refused them. Or if it was freezing cold, sweltering hot, or if they were just lonely, scared, or starved for some basic human interaction in a world that shunned them.

"Come on, buddy. Let's get you inside, and get you something to eat," Kate said.

A lot of EMTs could become a little indignant about the regular chore of dropping off homeless discharges, but Kate was not. She understood that some people are simply more easily broken than others are. The world was not an even playing field. Who was she to judge the downtrodden, based on her own life experience, when their life experiences might have been a living nightmare. Kate saw the sorts of situations from which her discharges were produced, every single day. She opened doors to terrible, hidden worlds, where she uncovered loveless childhoods, rife with drugs, alcohol, violence, and the worst kinds of child abuse. Whenever Kate looked into the eyes of those dirty children, peering back at her from their world of needles, beer cans and animal excrement, she knew that there was a chance that the day might come when she would be driving the adult versions of these same broken children from Trinity back to Riverside. Sometimes, the sight of these little ones, who lived behind unpainted doors, was almost more hurt than her heart could bear.

Kate led their discharge up to the shelter. His steps were slow and labored. He might've been younger than her, but it was impossible to tell. Kate held open the door for him, waiting patiently for him to make the small journey across the threshold. He looked utterly defeated. Still, the man thanked her, managing a nod and a ghost of a smile that creased his grimy skin in unusual ways, exposing the clean streaks beneath deeply tilled rows of anxiety. It was no small wonder why the life expectancy of the homeless was nearly half that of the other demographics. Even when you removed the abusers from the statistics, their lives remained halved, due to the everyday stress of poverty.

"Here," Kate said. She slipped a folded ten dollar bill into the man's breast pocket, and patted him on the back. "Please spend that on good things, will you?"

"God bless you," he whispered.

"Six-one-six, are you out there?" Kate's radio blurped.

"Six-one-six, copy." She smiled at her discharge, who thanked her again before stepping inside.

"Six-one-six, status epilepticus and possible pulmonary at the law office on Front and Pine. Can you respond on a one?"

Quincy chirped the sirens and flipped on the lights. Kate's heart was already thumping. She hated Front Street the most. It was a narrow ribbon of pavement that wound along the shoulder of the Missouri River, the largest and deepest body of water in her district. It was just too close for comfort. She jumped when Quincy hit the air horn.

"Alright already!"

Of course, he was raring to go. It was a pulmonary, and therefore, a probable thrill ride. Kate made her way back around to the passenger side of the ambulance. Instead of climbing in front, she climbed into the back. Quincy frowned through the Plexiglas window that separated them. On this occasion, Kate preferred to sit in the rear medic chair, where she wouldn't have to see the river coming, or to feel her anxiety mounting until her mouth ran dry, and she was ready to faint. There were no windows in back.

"You going to respond, Katydid?" Quincy's voice crackled over her radio.

"Shit ... yes." Kate popped her radio from her belt and keyed-up. "Copy that. Six-one-six responding, on a one."

"Ready, Cowgirl?"

Kate threw up her hands in annoyance. She turned to the Plexiglas window and shot Quincy a glare.

"Alrighty, then."

Quincy flipped on the howler, and then wheeled the bus out onto the street. They were northbound at a high rate of speed, hurtling down toward the Missouri River. The ambulance wheels slammed over a series of potholes that rattled everything in the medical compartments, jarring Kate's spine and swinging overhead loops of tubing on their hooks like a crazy jungle of plastic vines. Kate cursed him, clawing for the safety strap that dangled somewhere above her.

Q was driving like a freaking maniac. The pulmonary had him all wound-up. He still needed that skill, and it wasn't one that came up every day. Kate was aggravated, but she understood his circumstances. She'd been in his shoes, once upon a time. Every EMT needed to demonstrate proficiency in a long list of skills before he or she was eligible for recommendation into the paramedic program. It was a case of necessity, given the nature of their occupation, which the trainees depended on trauma for advancement. They waited for it. They quietly wished for it. Sometimes, they even prayed for it. They needed every situation on that list of skills to present itself to them during their training. Obviously, you were walking a very fine psychological line. To wish for trauma was to wish away your compassion. It was to wish away your humanity. The higher you climbed in the gory world of trauma and triage, the less human a person could become. Some medics got it, and they could see that fine line. Others did not. They became trauma addicts, craving only those Priority One calls where you roared through traffic with lights and sirens blaring to arrive at scenes drenched in blood. By any other measure, in any other context, they would be sociopathic monsters, but in the world of triage and trauma, they fit right in. Yeah, it was a thrill. That's what called some people to the job. They were the thrill seekers, with their endless party stories, their wild adolescence, and a sort of bloodlust that only other EMTs could understand. But they didn't usually last. Not those types.

Because eventually, you were going to peg your meter for want of blood and guts. Eventually, you were going to see something horrifying, something that you would wish to God that you could un-see, and it would haunt you. After that, what was left for a thrill seeker?

Kate closed her eyes and gripped the handle on the inside of the door. Sometimes, she got motion sickness, strapped backwards inside a steel box without windows, with all sorts of swaying fitments, overhead. She'd have made a terrible sailor. The back of an ambulance was not unlike the galley of a ship on stormy seas. The ambulance slammed over more potholes, and then wheeled so hotly around a corner that Kate felt her internal organs being rearranged. She gritted her teeth. "Oh, my God, Q! You're killing me, back here!"

"Sorry, Katydid!" Quincy bellowed over his shoulder. He hooted and drummed his palms against the steering wheel, blasting the air horn long and loud at an intersection. "Going to get my tube, today! Today is the Q-man's day! Woohoo!"

Quincy referred to an endotracheal intubation. It was the treatment skill typically associated with a pulmonary case, where supplemental air was provided to a patient who was not breathing, by way of administering an emergency tracheotomy. In this procedure, a hole was carefully punched through the wall of the larynx, right between the patient's vocal cords, with a bladed laryngoscope. This opened a secondary airway, through which, supplemental oxygen could be supplied to a patient who was not breathing. Quincy had been grousing about his missing "tube" for several weeks. But today, it looked like he might finally get one.

Bad as Kate felt, with her nausea coupled with anxiety, she could still relate to her trainee's excitement. Whether you were a thrill seeker or not, priority one calls were thrilling, especially in your first six months. There was just no experience in life that really compared to an exciting shift on an ambulance crew. It was a job that bombarded your mind and your senses with constant stimuli, life and death situations, and very real consequences attached to your decisions. On those shifts, when you got it right, it was awesome.

The ambulance lurched to a sudden stop. "Three minutes and twelve seconds," Quincy's voice blurped over her radio. "We have arrived."

She could feel its presence. Even before Q had thrown open her door, filling the ambulance with its fishy odor, Kate could literally feel something of its cold and massive gravity, dragging along through America's heartland with that inexorable pull of the mighty fluid element. Likewise, it had already detected her presence, right through the stainless steel panels. It seemed to sense her fear. Although it had taken the life of someone dear to her, and had tormented Kate for twenty-five years, it still didn't seem to be satisfied. That nymph spirit of the depths that inhabited all bodies of water always seemed to be hungering for souls.

In her mind's eye, Kate saw that pale hump, out in the middle of the cow pond. It was always there, floating in the depths of her mind. Except for sometimes, late at night, when it would crawl out. It crawled out to remind big sister that she'd failed. The temperature of her dreams would drop twenty degrees, as it dragged her down, down below the thermocline, down to the frigid depths, where water beetles flitted through the lips of drowned babies, who reeked of the murk that had pulled them right out of their world, down into another.

Kate cried out as the side door flew open. Harsh sunlight exposed her in her private moment of panic. She reacted with movement, unbuckling her seatbelt, groping around, trying to appear preoccupied, focused, as a good EMT should. However, it was a poor effort, and she sensed Quincy's scrutiny of her every mindless motion. In that instant, she could not, for the life of her, remember what it was she was supposed to be doing. Quincy just stood in the doorway, gawping at her. And beyond him, the River.

"You alright, Katydid?"

"About made me frigging carsick, the way you drove here. Lot of good it does to get to a call in less than five minutes if you kill somebody else, along the way."

"I thought I did just fine," he replied, flatly, sounding just a little hurt. "I hit a couple potholes but they couldn't be avoided. I didn't take any risks."

"Well, back here, it felt like you were driving through a damned war zone."

"Sorry, sometimes, it feels like I can't do anything right."

"Oh, stop being such a martyr. I just feel sick, alright? I'm just hoping I can even make it in there without puking."

Kate groped mindlessly through compartments, opening and closing doors. The longer she tried to pretend she knew what she was looking for, the more heightened her panic attack became. And it wasn't a gradual increase, like dialing up a rheostat knob. The increases came in great and terrible spikes that gushed icily up through her core, flooding her mind with a paralyzing cocktail that numbed all but her hammering heart.

"Airway bag?"

"I know," Kate snapped, smearing her face in her hands. She sucked a big shot of air through her nostrils, and then exhaled through her mouth. The river was waiting. Quincy was waiting. Pressure was mounting. She turned and snatched the blue bag from the lower compartment, stashed beneath her medic's seat. When she moved for the door, she found Quincy still standing there, blocking her way. Kate cocked her head at his look of mild disgust. "You want to move, so we can go do this?" After a moment's hesitation, the big guy stepped aside.

Kate kept her hand on the ambulance as she rounded the fender, as if the vehicle somehow grounded her negative energy. She would not look at the river. Instead, she trained her eyes on her feet, focusing on the cool smoothness of the steel sliding beneath her fingertips. When she followed Quincy across the parking lot, she focused on his movements, matching his long stride, secretly borrowing his strength. A natural stone walkway meandered through tussocks of fountain grass and barberry islands that appeared to float on a sea of fescue that sparkled in the sunshine, wet from the last automated soaking. Kate inhaled the bucolic aroma of cut grass. She heard the whine of leaf blowers, the trumpeting of geese, the occasional blurp and pop of the radio that rode faithfully upon her hip. Gradually, her world became right again. The further she got from the river, the better she felt.

Her job kept her grounded. Without it, she had no doubt that she would be sitting in a padded cell. The familiarity of the ambulance was like a life raft on an ocean of uncertainties. Her ringmaster's role in situations of controlled chaos was somehow vital to her own brand of therapy. She tamed chaos by facing it, controlling it. She challenged death daily, forcing it to relax its grip on victims, and sending the dark angel flapping away. And on those calls where death and chaos happened to win a round, when a life was lost, that was also acceptable. It was acceptable because there was always a reason for the failure that was outside her realm of control. She was a paramedic, trying her best to save lives. If someone died, it wasn't for her lack of trying, or for her lack of attention. Their time had simply come. It was not her fault, so long as she didn't make any mistakes. Losing a patient never felt anything like that day, at cow pond. It was never like losing little Jeffrey.

"Paramedic!" Kate shouted, as they passed through the revolving doors, into a bright and lofty lobby, many floors high. Stacked catwalks bisected the open airspace, offering glimpses into conference rooms, lounges, and what appeared to be a cappuccino bar. A gargantuan chrome sculpture dangled from the ceiling, six floors up, suspended by a very thin cable.

"Up here!" A woman appeared on the highest catwalk. "They're up here! Hurry!"

"They?" Quincy murmured, as they ran for the bank for elevators. "How come you rode in back?"

"What's the difference?" They stepped onto the elevator, and Kate poked the six button. She shot Quincy a look. "I was getting a few things organized."

"Well, I'm kind of wishing you hadn't done that."

"Why would that be?"

"Because we're going into a situation that we know nothing about. You should've been sitting up front, reading me the rip-sheet."

Kate looked Quincy up and down. She knew that he was right, but her gut told her to bluff, to hold her ground. "Sometimes I need a minute. That alright with you?"

"What, did dropping off that bum stress you out?"

"You freaking kidding me, Q?" Kate turned to square up with Quincy. The man towered over her. His shoulders were twice the width of her own. A glare of conviction burned in his eyes. He knew that he was in the right. She could see that, but she could also see fear. The guy knew that he'd crossed some sort of unspoken line of respect that was supposed to exist between a trainee and a preceptor. However, this time, Quincy wasn't backing down. That was a bad sign. Maybe, he was starting to lose respect for her.

They were still staring each other down when the elevator doors opened. The hysterical woman from the catwalk was there to greet them. "Hurry! Oh, please hurry! Oh my God, please hurry!"

"We'll deal with this later," Kate hissed. She broke her glare first, and stormed out of the elevator. She felt she owed Q that much, if all he wanted to feed his hurt ego was the small satisfaction of winning a staring contest. After all, he was absolutely right, and the company would certainly take his side, if this situation turned into a disaster. There was no excuse for neglecting to read a rip-sheet on the way to a priority one call. It was a matter of life and death, and here they were, walking blindly into it, totally oblivious to all of the details. Already, their expectations had been challenged, with the news that there was more than one patient, and a sixth floor location. Regardless, Kate refused to be addled. The river was behind her. Its dark power over her had waned, leaving her burning hotly inside. She was in control. This was her circus, and she was the ringmaster. Between the airway bag, the med kit, and the Life Pack, Kate was confident that she could handle any situation that might lie ahead.

The woman ran to a set of closed conference room doors. She gripped the door handles, looking frantically back to the EMTs. Mascara streamed down her pale cheeks. She was missing a shoe. "Hurry! We can't hold them much lon—"

As though fired from a cannon, the balled body of a man detonated a plate glass window that overlooked the six-story atrium. Kate heard herself choke. Entangled in a snarl of venetian blinds and curtains, he plummeted, bloody linens flapping behind him like the shroud of a soaring revenant, until his flight came to an end with a wet impact.

Kate heard Q shout her name, not an instant before a solid wall of flesh slammed into her with the force of a stampeding bull. An elbow cracked across her face. The back of her head struck the catwalk rail. She heard several people scream. Someone, maybe the same person who'd collided with her, leapt right over her with a crash of aluminum and a spray of what felt oddly like warm rice.

When her eyes blinked open, she saw the faces of several people gawping down at her through a swarm of silvery stars. She tasted blood in her mouth. She licked her teeth and dabbed the back of her latex gloved hand at her upper lip. A couple of the men in suits helped lift her to her feet. They were all mumbling about how fast it all had happened, and thank God that her partner had stopped him.

Kate turned to see a toppled catering cart and a mostly naked man, lying in a mess of smashed salmon, crab cakes, and wild rice. Quincy was securing his wrists and ankles with soft restraints.

"You good to go after the other one?" Quincy asked. He had a rare aspect of panic shimmering in his eyes.

"Him?" Kate asked, still reeling, pointing over the catwalk rail.

"No-no-no. Number three!" Quincy shouted. "There's three! He went toward the elevators! Hurry, you can catch him!"

The crowd of suits parted for Kate, who jogged back over the catwalk in the direction of the elevator bank. She snatched her radio from her belt and keyed-up to dispatch. "Six-one-six, on call at Front Street." She was breathless, dizzy, and on the verge of what almost felt like crying. The stars in her eyes had not yet cleared. She had a terrible intuition, that as bad as things already were, they were about to get worse. This circus had just spun out of her control. "We've got a Code Blue and a runner. Need police support. I repeat. Need police support. Secure this area."

The elevator door was standing open. There was no movement on the strip of lights. He'd taken the stairwell. Kate slammed the brassy bar with both palms and practically tumbled into the stairwell. It smelled like paint and rubber. Her breaths and steps were sharp in the confined space. As she pounded down the first flight of stairs, she peered over the rail. Down through the stairwell's core, she saw him, grinning mindlessly back up at her. He was naked. His muzzle and chest were streaked with gore.

She shouted down at him, but her command only hastened his descent. She could hear the slapping of his bare feet against the concrete treads. He was already at the bottom. She heard his palms strike the exit bar with a steely whack, and he was gone.

Kate's gaze didn't linger too long at the shrouded mess on the lobby floor. She saw smears in the pool of blood, where the man she was pursuing had evidently slipped, and had fallen down. Then, a trail of crimson footprints suggested that he'd regained his footing, and had continued through the revolving doors. Bloody handprints smeared the glass, where he'd pushed his way through.

The sprinklers were misting, as Kate ran across the lawn. She could see his footprints in the wet grass. Another slip and fall, on the backside of a berm. Wet footprints across the sidewalk, out into the parking lot. There he was, still running. He was headed directly for the Missouri River.

"No!"

Arms wind milling, he scattered honking scads of Canadian geese into tumults of wings and pumping necks. A growl low in Kate's throat escalated to a screech as she dug deep to pick up speed, closing the gap between her and her escapee. Now, she knew where he was headed. She would have to add it all up later, but the three lawyers in this building all seemed to be afflicted with the same strange reaction as the Stillwell kid. Seizures, delirium, pronounced bleeding from the nasal passages, removal of clothing … and, a hydrophilic obsession. They were determined to reach deep water.

"Stop!" Kate screamed, as the man passed their ambulance. He hurtled over a decorative fence, ran across a mulched bed, and dropped straight over the riverbank's edge.

It had been a wet year. Five feet of snow in the first three months of the year was followed by another ninety days of regular rains. The ground was saturated. It couldn't hold another drop. It seemed that all the water in the world was all running downhill to join the river.

Kate leapt over the fence, landed wrong and stumbled. She picked herself up from the cedar chips and crawled through the mulch to the river's edge. She was hyperventilating, cold, lost somewhere within herself. The sight of so much raw elemental power was staggering. She didn't think that she had ever beheld a river so mighty. Swollen to capacity, it rafted whole trees with green canopies of leaves down a deluge of liquefied earth and swirling hell. They disappeared, and reappeared, their branches clawing at the sky like desperate arms.

"Please, don't move! Just stay right where you are."

Kate's runner had the kindly face of an older gentleman, beneath his mask of bloody mud. He was probably someone's husband, father, and grandfather. Long wisps of snowy hair seemed to stand on end in the summer breeze, as he waded further into the terrible water.

"Don't go any further. Please. You'll drown."

Kate dragged herself over the rim. She slid on her flank down onto a bank of sloppy quicksand at the river's edge. It was the closest she had ever been to any river, or to any body of water that was larger than the cow pond. Her combat boots were getting stuck in the mud with every step, as she followed her patient out into the current. The water sucked at her pant legs. She realized her radio was under water. Cursing, she pulled at the thing until it popped loose of her belt, but she promptly fumbled it. Just like that, it was gone. Her feet were so badly stuck that she was unable to lift them. She pulled her bare feet free of the boots, one at a time, and pushed on without them. Almost an arm's length away from her patient. Getting closer. Kate extended her arm, and clawed the air, just inches from the pale flesh of his back.

The runner was up to his chest, when he turned with the most serene expression. He extended his frail arms to either side, smiling up at the sun in what appeared to be a gesture of fond farewell to the whole surface world in which he'd lived. He blinked at Kate, and then dealt her an impish grin, as he allowed himself to be taken by the torrent. He gave himself to the river. In an instant, his smiling image dissolved, as if a strange face imagined.

Chapter Six

Mitch stood with his hands on his hips. The sea breeze shifted into his face. He wheeled away from the stench, walking a few short steps away, choking down bile. It was interesting, how with more than a decade in the biological sciences, innumerable dissections and forensic studies on animals, he had somehow failed to steel his composure against his first glimpse of a dismembered human being. After all, humans were animals. They were made of all the same biological components, assembled in much the same way as any other living mammal. But there was something horribly inherent in the sight of a mutilated human being that was substantially lessened, or even lacking in the sight of a dead animal.

The coast guard officer followed lackadaisically along. He took no notice of Mitch's nausea. He was still talking, still divulging details to Mitch as though he were totally disconnected from the horrific scene and from its obvious effects on those unaccustomed to seeing them. "We've identified these three as crew members of the *Ballyhoo*. Shrimp trawler, went missing earlier this morning."

Mitch squatted upwind of the macabre orgy of drowned sailors and rigging. One man was twisted several times around, at the waistline. The skin of his back tented over his snapped spine. His legs were jointed in strange and numerous places. His head and one arm were missing altogether.

"Shark must've gotten a hold of that one," the officer said.

Mitch nodded. He cocked his head to squint up at the officer. "There's a bunch of them stacked up out there, right now, all within a mile of shore."

"Yeah?"

"It was the whale stranding. Brought them all in, from miles around. That's the reason we closed the beach."

"Probably a good thing you did. I don't think mama and the kids would've much enjoyed finding this mess on their little trip to the beach."

"No, I don't imagine that they would have." Mitch rose, and dusted the sand off his knee.

"It's not these guys, so much as the two up there, who really have us scratching our heads. Both are evidently tourists, out of Kansas City, but we don't have any missing person's reports. At least, not yet. And, their swimming attire is a little strange."

"How do you know they're out of Kansas City?" Mitch asked. He followed the officer in the direction of the other two bodies, while blocking his nostrils with the back of his hand.

"Still had their wallets in their pockets. Both guys are in their early sixties. Both are wearing nothing except some tattered dress slacks."

"You think they were aboard the trawler?"

The officer shook his head.

"Seems like an awfully big coincidence. Maybe they fell off a cruise ship, or something. A yacht?"

"Possible."

"They could've gone overboard as far south as the Keys, and the jet stream could've delivered them here."

"No other evidence in their wallets, unfortunately."

"Have you tried to contact their families?"

"That'll be next."

The sight of the next two bodies made Mitch feel a little dizzy. The long night was beginning to catch up with him. He felt as though he had perhaps seen too much tragedy in the last twenty-four hours. It wasn't healthy. He wondered, as he stopped before the corpse, how medical professionals dealt with all of the accumulated trauma that they were called to witness. It was hard to imagine.

"You know what's strange about these two?"

Mitch eyed the officer. "Their, uh ... their heads."

The officer snapped a stalk of sea grass. He knelt, and used the stem to poke at the deflated head of the victim. It looked grotesquely artificial, flaccid, as if bad special effects straight off the set of some B movie. But this wasn't special effects. Somehow, this cranial deflation had actually happened.

"No brains," the officer said, tilting his head to squint dramatically up at Mitch. "Now, the water pressure at great depths will probably do that for you. Just, squish your head like an ol' grape. But, look at the hemorrhaging in the whites of the eyes, there." The officer poked a protruding eyeball with his stem of grass. "I'm no medical examiner, but I've watched enough of those shows. Hemorrhaged eyes are a sign that the trauma happened while the victim was still alive."

Mitch scowled at the officer. "What exactly are you saying?"

"I'm not saying anything."

"Are you saying these guys were kicked out of a submarine?"

"No, but I'm not ruling out foul play."

The officer suddenly straightened up, popped his whistle into his mouth, and blew an earsplitting trill. "Hey, you! Beach is closed!"

Mitch turned, as the officer brushed past him. He blew his whistle a second time, while marching up the beach in the direction of a lone figure, who rose eerily from the sand dunes.

"Beach is closed!"

The woman appeared not to have heard or understood the officer's order. She proceeded down the slope of the dune and continued seaward. She stepped out of her heels, and then removed the red jacket of her pantsuit, casting it nonchalantly into the sand.

"Ma'am, turn back the way you came, and exit the beach immediately! Henderson Beach is closed!"

The officer began to jog toward the woman, but she picked up her pace enough to ensure that he would not be able to reach her before she made it to the water's edge. She seemed not to notice or care about the bodies, and the wreckage, strewn all around her. She seemed as oblivious to everything as any one of the twig-legged seabirds that skittered out of her way. The surf wrapped around her ankles. She hesitated, for just a moment, turning to deliver a haunting smile, before diving headlong into the first wave. She never resurfaced.

If the dull knocking of an oil pumper was the heartbeat of the plains, then the southwesterly winds were the region's breath, unbroken by anything but barbed wire. The winds hissed daily through the barrens, until sundown quelled the breeze to a profound silence so stifling that it made the ears ring. At that hour, formless things, blanched as the dust and dry grass that wrought them, emerged from seams in the wastelands to ply soundlessly through the bluestem, while the heartbeat of the plains kept on knocking. From atop some Osage post, a meadowlark bid the sun farewell with its piercing apogee, and another day was done.

At the heart of this vast desert, situated in a common cow pasture, was a something of a dimple in the parched earth, an old landmark. Arrowheads were common, here. The Naturals learned of this place by following the dauber swallows from their colonies of mud nests, and soon enough, it became a place of slaughter. Here was a scar, where the earth itself had been scalped to the bone, so bare and so cracked that no plant grew. Most years, it remained as such. But on good years, against all odds, this slight depression in the plains became a pond.

Summer days, its surface mirrored the sparkling blue skies. Buzzing things and crackling hoppers patrolled its muddy banks, all fringed with smartweed, green tangles and pink starbursts that writhed through the pocks left by wallowing cattle. It shimmered when the breeze tousled its glassy surface. Rings expanded, as tadpoles rose to kiss the sky, and descended, waggling, back down into their cool abysms. Whirligig beetles gyrated in their endless promenades. By day, the cow pond was a peaceful place, a crucible of life and flashing minnows that came from God knew where. But by the light of a dying sun, another presence within the pool seemed to awaken. Kate encountered it, not long after Jeffrey drowned.

Surrounded on all sides by pasture, where anthills tented the aggregate shells of a bygone seascape, Kate nested in the oasis in a snarl of smartweed at an hour when the lonely pond flattened black as a shark's eye, and the stars burned coldly in the gulfs of space. This was Jeffery's Place. In the weeks following his drowning, she came here with false hopes to commune with some lingering vestige of all she'd lost to this place. This was her vigil. Her penance. Her fault that her little brother drowned.

But she should not have come here, at this hour. Kate was just a child, naïve to the world's evils, exposed in her openness to a sign, to some form of contact from the other side, and perhaps that is why Kate attracted the attention of a thing that she'd otherwise have not.

It rose in its funereal suit of oily mud, and glistened in the starlight. If this was her Jeffrey, then it was not but the husk of that sweet child, its eyes so dulled to a sinful complacence, its lips curled into a larval smile. Jeffrey was gone, but Kate could not turn away from the mirage of him. Because she understood in that moment that she was being visited by the very thing responsible. Children don't drown where water should not exist, not in the wishing pools remembered in the hearts of deserts. No, it could not be. What happened to Jeffrey was no accident. His was a willful killing, and a cruel one. There stood a mimic in the moonlight, connected by deeper roots to something else, something down in a pond beneath a pond, a grotto, where it fanned its saffron gills and waited, just as it had haunted the seas of time's beginning. It waited for a chance to lure young life to an early death. Because that's what it was all about. That's all that it did.

The nymph hooked its greasy finger, and it beckoned to her. It wanted to show her things, would only she hear its siren's song and follow this bait into the pond, as three-year-old Jeffrey had done. If she would take its slick fingers into her own, then together, they would go down, down, into the world of drowned children, down to the places where the tadpoles lay torpid in the mud, and deeper still, to the pond beneath the pond, to the dark sanctuary where older things waited. There, in the pit of pits, lived her personal demon. It could not ease Kate's burden, but it could certainly give her what she deserved.

Kate awoke with a gasp and a spasm. The dusty blades of her ceiling fan, rotating on the popcorn ceiling of her living room, provided an immediate reference that reconnected her to reality. She sat up from the couch, with a groan. She took a sip of tepid water from a glass that was probably iced-something, a day or two ago, but it still brought some relief to the dryness of her mouth. Outside, it was twilight. She glanced at the clock. She'd slept all afternoon. Her sodden work clothes were still heaped in a reeking pile, right where she'd stripped them off, by the bathroom door. She remembered taking a shower, but she felt like she needed another one, as the events of the long night shift came back to her in an agonizing crash of failures, humiliations and defeats.

She'd misdiagnosed the Stillwell kid, then forgotten her promise to contact his fiancé. She'd ridden her partner too hard, failed to follow company protocol, and maybe, as a direct result, the lives of two patients had been lost. If she hadn't freaked out about their proximity to the river, and she'd read the details of the rip-sheet, learned that they were going to face three combative patients, quarantined in a sixth floor conference room … who knew how it might've turned out? Five days of paid suspension was an insult to injury. In all her years, she had never heard of any EMT in the company ever receiving a paid suspension. She'd never felt so small. And when she'd emerged from her supervisor's office, and caught the attention of her trainee, she'd spotted just a sparkle of vindication in Q's eyes. How could she blame him? In less than twenty-four hours, her status had devolved from arguably the best EMT ever to ride the bus for Trinity, to the biggest screw-up in her company's history.

Despite the gravity of self-pity, she found her waking mind to be surprisingly active, refreshed, after the worst night of her career. It felt as though she had inadvertently broken through some barrier in her anxiety. Was it totally failing that remedied her fear of failing? Or, had her suspension simply forced her to a safe distance from the stress of the job? Maybe the job itself, which she'd believed so long to be her brand of personal therapy, had actually grafted to the root of the disorder, and they'd merged into one terrible monster in her messed-up, complicated mind.

Kate rose, finished off her stale water, and then padded into the bedroom to pull on a pair of shorts and a tee shirt. She was feeling a little hungry, so she walked into the kitchen. She cranked the oven dial to preheat, then pulled a frozen dinner from its packaging, and dropped it onto the counter, with a dull clatter. Yum-yum. Looked like it was going to be Salisbury steak and an apple crumble, tonight. Then, she opened the fridge and got herself an ice-cold bottle of beer. She wasn't a bad cook, but she rarely ever found the time, or the reason, to make the effort to cook for herself. There was no one to impress, and single women who yammered on about what they'd cooked and eaten the night before secretly annoyed her. Kate tipped back her cold beer, pretending not to hear the distant wail of sirens.

Five days off. What the heck to do?

They had even made her turn in her radio. If that wasn't the strangest feeling, being estranged from popping, blurping, little companion, her source of constant connection to the job, to the whole outside world. She checked her personal phone while the oven heated, something she rarely did. No messages. No emails. No alerts. Well, that was fun. She dropped her phone back onto the table.

Being single was boring, but boring had its benefits. She hadn't dated in almost two years, and that was a relief. She guessed that bit of information might scare a few people, but Kate didn't miss it. Not one bit. She had normal desires, she guessed. Maybe they weren't quite as dramatic as everyone else's, but they were there, and very content to remain latent, untapped and unexplored, instead of being constantly fed and exploited. Love was a messy and overrated affair. There had been a couple of long-term relationships, the longest being nine months. Nine long and exhausting months. She'd never been so relieved to learn that someone was cheating on her.

It was all due to little Jeffery, of course. Jeffery was somewhere at the root of everything, all of her hang-ups and anxieties. She didn't blame him, obviously. Not like that. That poor little guy had never done anything to deserve having his whole life snatched away, all on account of five minutes of negligence, on the part of his big sister. Kate pulled a swig from her beer, and then exhaled through her teeth. Sometimes, she wondered if normal, intimate relationships would have been possible for her, if that day at the cow pond had never happened, or if this hot mess was just who Kate Browning was, regardless of the childhood trauma? It was something of an unsolvable riddle, one that ran on a continual loop inside her head. Her brain could be so exhausting. She was just about more than she could handle, let alone, throwing someone else's baggage into the mix. No, she was perfectly happy to be single, at a safe distance from all of those unnecessary emotional risks that were so popular.

Kate picked at the corner of her beer label, considering the strange events of her last shift. Collin Stillwell and three lawyers: all four men struck down in the same twelve-hour period by a very similar affliction. Delirium, seizing, vomiting, but normal vitals … it would have to be an allergy, a dystonic reaction, a body's physiological backlash to what it perceives to be a disagreeable invading presence. That's why the Benadryl had worked so well. The effects of the drug were immediate. It couldn't have been a coincidence. All four patients were struck down during a meal.

She reopened her telephone's digital notepad, where she entered and stored the important details of a noteworthy call. Here, she'd had the presence of mind to list everything that had been catered to the luncheon at the law office. They'd had a choice of salmon or negima yakitori, pork fried rice, and crab cakes. Ryuu, that newish Japanese joint over in Power and Light, had catered the meal.

Kate toggled her phone back over to her list of contacts, and she pulled up Sara Whitney, fiancée to Collin Stillwell. Her thumb hesitated over the call button. The information on Haldol that she'd promised Sara no longer seemed to be relevant. Everything had changed, and she no longer felt like she had anything of value to offer to the girl. Collin's case had been reopened, and as things stood, he was one of the last living cases of what was turning out to be a truly baffling disorder. But, she'd made Sara a promise, and Kate always kept her promises. As unstable and unreliable as she sometimes felt, with respect to herself, she tried to make up for, by being reliable to others. She tapped the call button, sighed, and brought the phone up to her ear. After the first ring, Sara answered.

"Sara? Hi, this is Kate Browning. I'm the EMT who took your fiancé to the hospital, last night. Yeah. Well, I did. And in fact, I was wondering if I could ask you a couple of questions about your dinner, last night? Well, I guess I should begin by asking you where you went out to eat?"

Kate's smile flattened, when she heard the reply. Her eyes widened in a new and terrible feeling of expanding space. She tried to clear the knot that suddenly appeared in her throat. "Yes. Yes, I have heard of Ryuu ... look, would you," Kate glanced over at the clock, "would you want to meet me somewhere tonight, maybe talk about this in person?"

It was not surprising that the primary clientele of Stacks Coffee Shop were nurses and other medical professionals, being that the joint was located adjacent to Trinity Regional Medical Center. Stacks was a popular place to refuel, between shifts. Thus, conversations in the booths and around the high-top tables could be morbidly unfiltered. At times, those conversations could become quite grotesque. Nurses could only say so much of what they'd like to say, around the patients. Stacks was the place where they went to vent.

The culture of Stacks could be so stark, so somber, so atypical of those other cool and cozy coffee nooks that it was often surprising that the usual suspects, the readers, writers and young professionals with their glowing laptops, were still in place. They had not been driven off by the overwhelming presence of battle-hardened medics with their mint green scrubs and severe table topics. Somehow, everyone managed to get along just fine. If a person was looking for the right place to grab a cup of coffee, and discuss life's harshest realities in an open environment, without fear of turning heads, Stacks was the perfect venue.

Glass desiccators filled with rare and roasted beans followed the curve of the brushed steel bar, from the dimly curtained windows in front, to the gas-lit alcove, in back, where customers lounged on plush couches beneath rolling ladders that jutted past shelves loaded with a variety of classic and contemporary novels. Salvaged school blackboards displayed the daily menu options, as well as some pretty fantastic pastel artwork that was probably the artistic styling of a talented staff member, versus an outsourced artist. Stacks was real. It was one of Kate's favorite places to unwind, and it was just the place to meet with Sara Whitney, who happened to be right across the street, visiting Collin in Trinity's psyche ward, when Kate called.

"I'm pretty sure it didn't have anything to do with what he ate," Sara said, "because if either of us was at risk, it would've been me. I was the one eating the raw fish. Collin had steak and lobster."

Kate nodded, staring down into her coffee. She was not yet ready to tell Sara the whole truth. There was no reason to alarm her with the details of the similar cases, and their tragic ends. The girl had been through quite enough in the last twenty-four hours. Still, the coincidence was too extraordinary. Something was missing from the equation. Out of all the people in Kansas City, and out of all the restaurants from which to choose, four people came down with the same rare and deadly malady after eating Ryuu's cuisine, twelve hours apart. On the other hand, Collin and the lawyers had eaten entirely different things.

"How is he doing?" Kate asked.

Sara shook her head. "Not good."

"I'm sorry to hear that," Kate said. "Is he responsive at all?"

"He comes and goes. But he's still, you know, talking nonsense."

Kate's brow furrowed. "Do they ... do they have him restrained at all?"

Sara nodded. "His wrists have cuff things on them. Everybody does in his room. Why do you ask?"

"Well, I wouldn't want him to, you know, try to get up, and fall down again."

"Yeah."

Kate sipped her coffee and cleared her throat. "Sara, are you positive – I mean, absolutely one-hundred percent sure that all he ate was steak and lobster?"

"And a salad. And some champagne." Sara frowned at Kate. "Do you know something else, that maybe you're not telling me?"

Kate set her coffee down and stared into Sara's sky blue eyes. "Just steak and lobster and a salad."

"Steak and lobster and a salad."

"Neither of you ordered any desserts? Or appetizers? Something that might've come out before the salad?"

Sara straightened up in her seat, eyes popping. "Oh, my God!" She smacked her palm against her forehead. "A crab cake! I totally forgot about the crab cake. He asked about it, and they brought him out a sample!"

"And you didn't have any of that crab cake, did you?" Kate's expression must have belied her withholdings, because Sara reacted by becoming suddenly very intense, leaning in across the table.

"No. No, I did not. I don't eat fried stuff, and it was just one bite." Sara's chin began to tremble. "What's going on with the crab cake? What do you think is wrong with my fiancé?"

"I don't know, yet."

Sara's hand slipped across the table. She gripped Kate's hand so tightly that her knuckles turned white. Kate could feel her trembling. The girl's swollen eyes shimmered wetly from the effects of her emotional cocktail, probably combined with lack of sleep.

"You don't know what I'm going through, right now. I'm trying to hang on. I really am. But when I go over to see Collin," Sara shook her head slowly back and forth, "Collin isn't there, anymore." She leaned in closer, across the table, and lowered her voice to a whisper. "Something has taken him."

"Oh, honey. Some of the neurological effects of these kinds—"

"No-no-no," Sara barked. She cleared her throat, and licked her lips. "No. Something has taken my fiancé. It's switched places with him. When I go talk to Collin, I'm not talking to him anymore. I'm talking to something else. I'm talking to whatever's inside him."

Chapter Seven

A streetlight shimmered through the curtains in Collin's room, bathing the line of hospital beds in a bluish luminescence. All of the lights in the room were off. The patients seemed to be asleep. They were all lying deathly still, presumably medicated. Each bunk was situated exactly the same as the next, stocked with identical provisions that were aligned with military regularity. To Kate, it felt a bit like prying with a glimpse into the barracks of a sunken submarine. Even the sleeping patients appeared to conform to some code of order. Each of them slept flat on their back, wrists and ankles restrained, with their heads oriented toward the ethereal light of the window, which Kate observed was reinforced with chain-link. This was the wing for potentially dangerous psychotics.

The nurse admitted them into the room. Following Sara, Kate slipped demurely past the woman in the doorway, avoiding eye contact. Although the mental health facility was a separate building from the main hospital, Kate felt as though she were trespassing. The terms of her paid suspension had not been fully explained. It was not until she and Sara had rolled into the parking lot that Kate began to feel a mounting unease about returning to her workplace. Was this errand in violation of her suspension? It was awkward, creeping about the premises of her own workplace, feeling like an outsider in civilian clothing. She only hoped that no one would recognize her, and call her out, especially in front of Sara. If Sara learned of her suspension, the lost lives, everything else, the girl might cease to take her seriously. She might even cut their lines of communication, altogether. If she didn't already feel like a complete failure, that would be the final blow.

Sara padded over to the third bed, and she took a seat beside her fiancé in the only chair that was available. Each bunk was provided with one seat for a guest. Kate was about to steal a chair from the bedside of a neighboring patient, when she almost bumped into the nurse, who had slipped in behind her, with a second chair.

"Thank you," Kate whispered. She took the chair from the nurse, and positioned it quietly beside Sara's. As she sat down, her gaze was attracted to the padded restraints that shackled Collin's wrists and ankles to the bed frame. The sight of these manacles was a sobering reminder of the gravity of the situation. Twenty-four hours ago, this was a normal guy. Now, he was being handled like Hannibal Lector. What had happened to this kid?

"Can I bring you anything to drink?" the nurse offered. "Coffee, tea, water?"

Collin's head, and the head of every patient in the room, swiveled simultaneously. Their eyes bulged wide and unseeing. Kate jumped, while Sara stifled a squeak. Their movement was so synchronized, as if all of the patients shared a single mind. Collin's throat rose and fell. His glazed eyes seemed to stare right through the stricken face of his fiancée in the direction of the nurse.

Kate turned to the nurse, who was backing slowly toward the open doorway, hands clasped over her mouth. The woman's reaction sufficed to answer Kate's question of whether or not this was something of a normal occurrence. It did not appear so. And it didn't seem as though the nurse had spoken so loudly that her voice should have awakened every patient in the room. Her words were barely above a whisper. Kate turned back to the restrained audience of gawping eyes, slackened mouths. All of their throats rose and fell. Their sentience seemed to have been reduced to a mindless state of suspended reactivity, waiting outside stimuli to trigger a response. Had they even been asleep at all, or just lulled into a weird nirvana by their medication?

Kate rose from her chair. "Are these people—are they all suffering from the same symptoms?"

Still petrified, the nurse was at last able to break her trance. She lowered her hands, breathed, and nodded her head. "They were all combative, at first. They took meds in the first hour, and they've since gone catatonic. If you speak to them, they will usually try to communicate, but this is the first time that some of them have moved in almost a week."

"What do you have here, nine of them? And you think they all have the same type of affliction?"

The nurse nodded.

"Delirium and seizing, but normal vitals? When they came in, were any of them bleeding from the nose?"

"All of them. Yes. She was the first, back there." The nurse pointed to the patient nearest the window. "She was admitted on Monday. The rest started to filter in over the following days. We noticed the similarities, so we started transferring them here. No one has seen anything quite like this."

Kate looked around the room. "Why would they all suddenly respond like that, do you think? Is it maybe the time of day? Are they more responsive at night, or—"

"Water," Sara said.

Every pair of eyes in the room swept away from the nurse, and redirected their undivided attention onto Sara. At last, by some measure, Collin was acknowledging the presence of his fiancé. His throat rose and fell. A bubble of spittle inflated between his lips. He stared at Sara, fully aware of her, yet he did not seem to acknowledge the tears in her eyes.

"You said water, and water is all that they want. To go to the sea." Sara sniffed. She reached for a Kleenex on Collin's nursing station. With this, she dabbed the perspiration from his brow, then folded the tissue and dried the tears from her own eyes.

"Has Collin ever been to the sea?" the nurse inquired.

"No." Sara allowed a small laugh. "I don't think he's ever been but a few miles outside of Kansas, to be perfectly honest. He's a homebody."

"I thought maybe he had a special memory, there. Some kind of connection."

"No-no, but it's not just Collin. It's all of them. Look. They all want the same thing. If you took off their restraints, that's probably where they'd all try to go."

"But why?" Kate said. "What's with the sea?"

"Well, at first you'd assume that they're talking nonsense," the nurse said, "but sometimes when the body needs something, the subconscious mind will step in and override the conscious mind, in order to get the body what it needs. Like, specific cravings for certain kinds of foods. We've all had that, right? A lot of times, those cravings are the result of a nutrient deficiency, or, weirder still, an anticipated nutrient deficiency. Women will often crave foods with vinegar, like pickles, just before their menstrual cycle, and in the later stages of pregnancy. Why? Because vinegar helps with the absorption of iron into the bloodstream. The conscious mind doesn't know this, but the subconscious does. The body is anticipating blood loss."

"How bizarre," Kate said.

"So, my thinking is that this sort of obsession with water that we're seeing in these patients may be related to a subconscious perception of thirst."

"Why don't they just ask for a Gatorade, or something?" Sara asked.

"Remember, in their condition, they're not able to rationalize their craving. This sort of disorder may be tapping into the more primal parts of the brain. The old reptilian core. Somewhere in there, their subconscious minds may have flipped an ancient switch to motivate them toward water, because it perceives a need for it. They may not know specifically why they want to head toward water, but once they arrived, they would know what to do."

Kate shook her head. "But you can't drink sea water. So, why would there even be an ancient switch in the brain to send you specifically toward a water source that you can't even drink?"

"Because the sea represents a huge water source. That's all. It's simply water that they're craving. Just look into their eyes when I say that word."

"But I gave Collin a glass of ice water, at home, and he didn't drink it," Sara said. "He still just kept talking about going to the sea."

"Has anyone tried asking them why?" Kate said. She looked from Sara to the nurse, then back again. "I mean, I have to wonder what these patients would do, if you actually took them to the place where they want to go."

"To the sea."

Everyone looked to Collin, whose strangled whisper seemed filled with secrets, ghostly portents. His image swam in oceanic swirls of blue light, as the curtains swayed gently in the ventilation. Although his eyes appeared to be unseeing, they were not unthinking. They were simply focused. His mind was functioning, processing stimuli, but from a disconnected and single-minded perspective.

Kate could not help but recall the terrifying will of those patients, back at the law office. Death was no deterrent from their goal. She supposed that she already knew the answer to her hypothetical question. If you enabled these patients to reach the seashore, they would more than likely drown themselves. They were not dehydrated. They were not interested in quenching their thirst. Her lawyers were headed straight for the Missouri River, which would actually be a direct route to the sea. It was almost logical, if you were a fish.

"Why, Collin?" Kate asked. "Why do you want to go to the sea?"

Collin's eyes brightened. His throat swelled, expelling air through his teeth as the corners of his mouth bent into an oddly contrived smile that misfit his otherwise blank expression. Kate could empathize with Sara's distress. Although she didn't know the guy prior to the onset of this condition, his total disconnection from other human beings was uncomfortable to behold. There was no recognition of his loved one. No compassion. Only the longings of an exiled toad king, who once dreamt he was a prince.

"Family." Collin's voice was thick and watery.

"What family?" Kate pressed. "What family are you talking about?"

"I'm your family," Sara whispered into his ear. "You've already got a family who loves you. They're all coming, baby. Your mom and dad. Your brother, Mark. They're all coming here to see you. We're your family."

Collin's back began to arch. His shackled fists grabbed handfuls of air. It was clear that the meaning of Sara's words had been lost on him. He was uncomfortable, distracted. The weird smile that had so recently settled upon his countenance devolved into something of a grimace. He looked as though he were in pain.

Kate put her hand on Sara's shoulder. "Do you mind," Kate gestured in Collin's direction, "if I talked with him?"

"Well, no, but ..."

"What is it? What's wrong?"

"It makes me a little uncomfortable if you're going to keep asking him questions about his whole fantasy world. I mean, I don't even see how that's helpful or relevant. It only makes him dive deeper. I think we can all agree that this is a delusion, right? So why on earth would we want to indulge him? I'm trying to get him out of that place. I need him to come back to me."

Sara was right, of course. It seemed ridiculous now, actually questioning this man about his delusions of an underwater world. It was not being helpful. But if this course of action was really so ridiculous, then why did some messed-up part of Kate still believe that she was on the right track by pushing Collin to talk more about the sea, and learning more about this other family? Obviously, she was getting in the way of things.

It was her personal demon, again, still skewing her perception of the world around her. Still perpetuating old notions that if she pushed hard enough against that wall that separated her world from little Jeffrey's, then she might just be able to break through. And what if she did? What then? What would she want from Jeffrey if the child were standing in front of her? Forgiveness? Absolution? From a three-year-old? Christ, to think how her whole life had been knocked off track by that one afternoon. Her whole existence was on a tangent. To think what she might've become in life, had Jeffrey survived, had Kate retained the self-confidence to launch herself out into the world as a normal, well-adjusted human being. Somewhere in an alternate universe, where Jeffrey was saved from drowning, an unaffected Kate Browning might be a happily married wife and mother, filled with the confidence to love, and to be loved, embracing the same risks as everyone else.

"I think what your friend was suggesting," the nurse said, "was that it might be beneficial to explore those subjects that your fiancé is willing to talk about. Not to indulge him, per se. Just to get your foot in the door, and then try to work your way into his mind, from there. Maybe point out the flaws in his thinking. It's actually the standard technique, when you've got a patient who doesn't want to talk."

Sara turned to Kate. "I'm sorry."

"No, that's okay," Kate replied. "He's your fiancé. You call the shots."

"Well, at least until his mother gets here," the nurse said, with a chuckle.

"I'm just tired. Scared. I just don't know how to help him." Sara buried her face in her hands. "He's lying right there in front of me, looking right at me, but he's gone. He's gone, and I don't know how to get him back."

Evidently, disinterested in the new direction of the conversation, Collin lolled his head slowly back toward the blowing curtains. Kate noticed that the other patients had already done so. Once again, they were uniform in their absolute disconnection from the surface world.

Kate put her arm around Sara and hugged her in. She up looked to the nurse. "Um, you don't happen to know if some of these other patients were out to dinner somewhere, when they were struck down, do you?"

"Hmm." The nurse frowned, and cocked out her hip. "You know, I do believe that at least a couple of them were out to dinner when it happened. Yes, I know for a fact that she was. She was out with her sister." The nurse poked a finger in the direction of the woman by the window. "And I believe that he was out with his wife, as well. I wasn't here to speak with all of the families in all of these cases. I don't work every shift, you know, but I do recall that a couple of them were out to eat at a restaurant when things went wrong."

"Do you know what restaurant?" Kate asked, breathlessly.

"You aren't with the health department, trying to stir up trouble, are you?" The nurse wagged her finger at Kate, hitching one eyebrow, with a cynical grin.

"Oh no," Kate replied, shaking her head. "I'm just …"

"She's a friend," Sara said, smiling at Kate.

"Well, I'll tell you what," the nurse said, retrieving a notepad from the breast pocket of her apron, "you give me your name and number, and I'll see what I can find out about what all of these folks enjoyed for their last meal."

"Thank you. That would be very helpful."

"Think nothing of it. I'll leave you two alone with your friend for a few minutes while I go make my rounds, if that's alright?"

"That would be fine," Kate replied.

The nurse winked, and then slipped out into the hallway. She closed the door quietly behind her. Darkness filled the room.

Kate and Sara just sat there in the blue-black. It felt a little bit like a visitation service. Kate waited for any sound, besides the soft rush of air through the ventilation shaft. You would expect at least one of the patients to be snoring, rustling beneath their sheets, but so far as Kate could discern, these people were not even breathing. They offered nothing. They divulged no secrets. They had no interest in communicating.

"You can ask him some questions, if you want to," Sara whispered.

"No," Kate shook her head, still a little embarrassed, "you were right. It was stupid."

"But, like the nurse said, if you-know-what is the one thing that he's willing to talk about, then maybe we can use it to get a foot in the door, see if maybe a little piece of Collin isn't hiding in there, somewhere."

Kate shrugged. "If you want to, but I think that you should do it. You're his fiancée."

"Okay." Sara nodded. She reached up, and clasped Collin's shackled hand between her own. Then, she closed her eyes for a moment. Sara might've been praying, or maybe mustering some inner-strength, or just looking for a clear direction in which to proceed with this bizarre little interview.

"Baby?" Sara gently squeezed Collin's hand. She leaned close to his ear. "I want to hear about your family. Can we talk about them? Who are they? Do they live down under the sea?"

Kate heard a loud pop, one instant before Sara's electrifying scream of agony. He had her. Sara's entire left hand was clenched inside of his trembling fist. Kate lunged from her seat. "Let her go, Collin!" She grabbed his wrist, tried to pry up his fingers, but it felt as though his fist was sculpted from marble. Sara screamed again, and then doubled-over to bite his hand. Slowly, Collin's head pivoted from the window, to face them. Chain-link shadows patterned the skin of his cheek with the scales of a fish.

"Stay away," Collin gurgled, extruding a cluster of bubbles from between his lips. A map of veins rose upon his forehead.

His eyes bulged from their sockets. His throat was so ballooned that it looked as though it might split. "Keep away from our nest."

Kate then became aware of a prattling sound. It seemed to be all around them in the gloom. It seemed to be growing louder, the more frantically her gaze whipped around the room. At once, the source of the disruption was identifiable as the combined chattering of all nine patients' teeth. By the manner in which they glared, lips drawn back over champing rows of enamel Kate took the display to be some sort of a warning, like the rattling tails of snakes in the leaf litter.

At last, Collin relaxed his vise-like grip. Bloody crescents grinned from his flesh, where Sara had repeatedly bitten him, but he seemed otherwise unaffected by their brief conflict. Sara collapsed back into her seat, hyperventilating. She clutched her crushed hand to her breast. Fingers lilted at strange angles.

Kate stared at the injury, knowing full well that bones had been broken, and that this meant that she was going to have to take Sara over to the ER, the one place she did not want to be seen. Her cowardly reaction promptly disgusted her. Whatever had happened to that person she used to be, or to the woman she'd always envisioned herself becoming? She had to get a hold of herself. Get these anxiety issues under control.

Kate's cell phone began to ring. Even as she fumbled the cheeping device from her purse, she knew that it was ridiculous to answer it, given the circumstances. But, of course, she was compelled to answer it anyway.

"Hello?" Her trembling voice sounded worse than she'd anticipated.

"Hello, I didn't know if you two had already left yet, but I wanted to catch you before you ran off. I'm the nurse, who just left the room?"

"Yes?"

"I stopped by the office to grab a few things, and I just thought that while I was here, I'd go ahead and check those patient files for you, regarding your inquiry about their last meals? And, well, I think you might just be interested in what I discovered."

Kate's eyes flicked from Sara's rocking torso to the background chorus of chattering heads. Could an ambiance possibly be any more distracting? She plugged one ear with a finger and turned away from the chaos. "What is it?"

"Well, it looks to me like they ate at the same restaurant. At least, a few of them did."

"Good evening, and welcome to Ryuu. Will there be just one of you, tonight?"

"I won't be dining, this evening," Kate replied. She held up her paramedic's identification card. "I'm here to see your manager."

"Oh. Alright. Let me see if I can get him for you." The hostess returned to her kiosk, and put the phone discreetly to her ear.

Kate turned in the direction of the raucous dining ambiance. A huge portal had been cut right into the upper portion of the wall, directly above an arched entryway. Up there, gas-blue flames spewed from copper burners mounted within the wall itself, designed to backlight the silhouette of an oriental dragon that had been cut from a solid plate of brushed steel. It was the same massive piece of artwork that they had hanging outside of the restaurant. The sculpture appeared to be the same diameter as a Teppanyaki table, for twelve. The art seemed to glorify the power of the palate. That's what this place was all about. Making diners feel powerful in their choice of Ryuu as their brand. Kind of a unique approach. Strange, but unique. Beyond the arched aperture, chefs performed their clattering dance of steel and fire, to the pulsing bass of neo-tribal rhythms. This looked less like a restaurant than it did a temple, built in the honor of some forgotten pagan god.

"Alright, ma'am," the hostess said, "if you'd care to follow me, I'll take you on back to the manager's office."

As Kate trailed the hostess through the Teppanyaki pods, where juggled knives and cleavers flipped through the air, she looked upon the displays of ancient weapons, the sprays of gilded lances, the racks of gleaming katana blades. Monstrous suits of samurai armor glowered down at her from their pedestals. There was nothing peaceful about the décor of this restaurant. No koi, cranes, bamboo, or cherry blossoms. Ryuu seemed to be a restaurant on the warpath.

Kate felt a knot beginning to form in her throat. She questioned her own authority, if she had any authority at all. Had she arrived in an ambulance, instead of her jeep, and stormed this establishment in her black boots, cargo pants and vest, her web belt and crackling radio, she would have felt empowered, even entitled, to launch an investigation. She would have controlled this restaurant, and everyone in it. But, all she had was her paramedic's identification card. Her job, her gear, they were her suit of samurai armor. In civilian clothes, she felt powerless, vulnerable, a naked woman on a battlefield.

The hostess snaked through the bustling Teppanyaki dining area, and into the more tranquil sushi bar. Schools of gasping fish hovered like dim spectators in queue for the serving platter, lining the glass walls of their prison. Below, their brethren were dissected, even vivisected, on a sprawling stainless steel counter that stocked a sushi conveyer for its unending journey, over the fields of shaved ice. The lidless eyes of the aquarium fish peered down at Kate, looking without seeing, as if they awaited some sort of a door to open between her world and theirs.

This was the room where Collin collapsed. Kate looked around at the arrangement of tables, and she tried to picture Sara and Collin seated somewhere out there, almost exactly twenty-four hours ago. She imagined the champagne toast that Sara had described while they sat together in Trinity's radiology waiting room. And, of course, she had to envision Collin staggering away from the table, plodding drunkenly in the direction of the restrooms, until he'd crumpled to the floor.

The hostess pushed through a set of double-doors. Kate followed her into the kitchen, a torrid sweatshop of fire, steam and raw emotion. Slaves to the almighty pallet worried over boiling cauldrons, heaps of chopped flesh. This was it. Kate had entered the mouth of the beast. Seven confirmed cases of the same mysterious disorder, with Ryuu cuisine being the only common link. No, there wasn't a smoking gun. Not yet. If this was a coincidence, it seemed like a pretty huge one. But even the world's biggest coincidence didn't help Kate isolate whatever it was that she was looking for.

Sara had been opposed to this intrusion. The evidence had to have been just as apparent to her, as it had been to Kate, but the girl's best suggestion was to send an email to the health department. An email. Really? Her fiancé was out of his mind, probably dying, side-by-side with three confirmed patrons of this establishment, and all she wanted to do was shoot off a snarky email? They weren't but ten years apart in age, but perhaps the biggest difference that Kate could see, between the people of her generation, and all those to follow, was a growing trend to avoid confrontation. Men were becoming effeminate drones, eunuchs, while women cowered in the chat rooms of technological fantasylands, where there seemed little distinction between bravery and big talk. Kate did not subscribe to this passive philosophy. She believed that if you wanted to get something done, you didn't pick up the phone, and you sure as hell didn't send an email. You went there. You drove to the place. You walked inside, and you put yourself in their face.

She felt bad, leaving Sara in the hands of the x-ray technicians. But it was a Saturday night. Trinity was so busy that only a couple of nurses even noticed Kate in her civilian attire, which was a relief, but that fact of the matter was that it might well be morning before Sara was actually treated and discharged, and by then, how many more would be afflicted? This showdown had to happen tonight. Right here and now. People seated all around her were seconds away from possibly being infected by something in the food, and Kate was the only person in Kansas City who was in a position to save their lives.

The hostess knocked on the office door. Kate wasn't sure what she'd anticipated the manager of Ryuu to look like, but she now imagined a solidly built Japanese man in his mid-fifties. Slicked hair, impeccably dressed, with a personality hard as katana steel, but so flawless in his skills of professional pleasantry that his demeanor would beautifully sheath his razor's edge.

The door swung partly open. Leering out, was a guy who was half the age, twice the height, and without a trace of the warrior's stoicism possessed by that fictional character she'd imagined. This individual appeared annoyed. He was distracted, and already unsettled by a meeting that had not even begun. His anxious demeanor gave Kate the distinct impression that he had a lot going on in his world, at the moment, and this conversation was probably not bound to go well.

"I'm Barton, manager of Ryuu."

"Kate Browning."

"So, you're a nurse, of sort kind?"

"I'm an EMT." Kate flashed her identification card. "Could I maybe come in, and sit down for just a minute?"

Barton glanced behind him, smoothed his hair, and then slipped toward Kate through the door, pulling it shut, behind him. "It's kind of a mess in there, right now. What—what is it that you need?" He sidled up to a stainless preparation table and leaned back against it, in what he probably supposed was a casual posture, but with his arms drawn about his chest, fingering his chin, he appeared anything but casual.

"I need to talk to you about what might possibly be a health concern, and we have reason to believe that it may be traced to this restaurant."

"Wait. What?" Barton held up his hand and screwed up his face. "What kind of health concern are you talking about? Who are you? You say you're an EMT, but what's that, exactly? Are you telling me that you're an ambulance driver?"

"No." Kate hated being called an ambulance driver. Nothing brought her blood more quickly to a boil.

"Then what are you? Who are you with?"

"If you'll let me speak, I'll explain it to you."

"Speak!" Barton threw up his hands, and then drew up a sleeve to check his watch.

"I'm a licensed paramedic. Over the last week, we've seen a number of patients with a pretty serious condition. It's been difficult to diagnose. But again and again, we're coming up with this restaurant as a common link between the cases. This is the last place that many of them had eaten before becoming very sick."

"What, are you talking about that guy who passed out in here last night? He had too much champagne."

"He's one of twelve that I'm talking about, maybe more. I picked up three new cases this morning. They had all just finished a luncheon catered by Ryuu."

"Where is the health department? Who exactly is sending you?"

"No one sent me. I'm here on my own, just to warn you, and to protect your customers from any further harm until an official diagnosis can be made. But if there turns out to be a link to this restaurant, you can expect that there may be some pretty serious allegations coming down the pike. The next phase would involve the health department, independent labs, and probably some legal action, by the families of the victims."

"Victims?"

"Yes, victims."

"Well, what are you—are you wanting to check the kitchen? Here's the kitchen." Barton gestured openly, all around him. "I don't know what you're hoping to find. Obviously, everything is clean, sterile, up to code. We use only the freshest ingredients. I can't believe you'd use the word 'victims' when we have zero violations, zero unsanitary practices. And you've got a few patients who probably have some new flu strain, who just happened to eat here. So what?"

"It's not the flu."

"We've only been open three months. We're the hottest new venue in Power and Light. Of course a lot of people are eating here. Everyone wants to get a table here!"

"People are dying, Barton!" Kate shouted. "Die-ing! We are talking about a deadly neurological epidemic, not the flu. And I wouldn't be here on my own time if this was friggin' food poisoning. This is something much worse than that!"

"What is it?" Barton seemed to lower his defenses, slightly.

"Delirium, catatonia, seizures, psychosis ..." Kate said, counting off on her fingers. "This isn't exactly my area of expertise, but the way this affliction affects the mind, I'm personally beginning to suspect that some sort of a parasite may be involved."

"A parasite?"

"Now, here's where you may know more about this than I do. Is there any sort of a brain parasite that can be contracted from seafood?"

"From sushi?"

"Actually, no."

"Because all of our sushi is top grade. Premium cuts."

"In fact, the food item that seems to be the common denominator in all of these cases are your crab cakes."

"The crab cakes ..." Barton murmured, his eyes tracking a smooth pathway to the walk-in freezer doors."

"I'm not asking you to shut down your restaurant." Kate took a step closer to him. "I don't have any authority to do that. As I said, I'm here on my own. I'm just trying to help save a few people's lives until we can get this thing figured out. So, if you could just stop serving that one item, take it off your menu, then I'd be happy to vouch for you, down the road, as someone who was willing to stand up and do their part in the face of a public health concern."

Barton lurched away from the preparation table. He advanced on the freezer doors, threw the hefty latch, and disappeared inside. After a moment, he reappeared, with a white bucket cradled in one arm. He set it down on the preparation table, and put his hands on his hips. "It's one of our most popular appetizers." He chuckled and shook his head. "And it's the only item on our menu that we purchase prepared."

Kate leaned down to read the red print on the side of the sealed container. "Crabby Batter," she read out loud. Kate rotated the small bucket, scanning the list of ingredients, to the very bottom. "Produced and packaged in Pensacola, Florida, by Emerald Coast Cannery," she read out loud.

"It's down by Destin."

"By where?"

"Destin, Florida. It's right there on the Florida panhandle. Beautiful place."

Kate curled her fingers around the rim of the lid. "Do you mind?"

"No. Go ahead and open it."

Kate popped off the white lid. Beneath, was a blanched orangey mixture, with reddish bits of crabmeat. It reeked of the sea.

"Smells nice, doesn't it? They love it, here. It's seriously one of our most popular items."

"So, this stuff is premade, then? You just scoop it out and fry it up?"

"Basically." Barton nodded. "I mean, we use this as our base, add a panko crust, fry them in sesame oil, and serve them with a nice wasabi caper sauce."

Kate snapped the lid back down over the container. "You care if I take a picture of the label?"

Barton shook his head.

Kate pulled out her phone, and snapped a shot of the container, front and back. "I may need to call down to this cannery, tomorrow morning, ask them a few questions to get this headed in some kind of direction. Do you have a card?"

Barton seemed to be lost in his own thoughts, and then snapped back into cognition. "Yeah-yeah. Sure." He retrieved his wallet and removed a business card. He passed it to Kate.

"Can I have one of yours?"

Kate chuckled. "Paramedics don't carry cards, but we probably should. Don't worry. I'll definitely be contacting you in the next couple of days."

"Okay. So, we're all finished, then?"

"If you could just follow through with what we talked about? Please take this stuff off your menu, right away, tonight. And I promise, I will get back to you the very instant that I find out anything conclusive. Until then, better safe than sorry."

Chapter Eight

Mitch awoke to the quacking ringtone of his cell phone, on his nightstand. It was a Sunday morning, and after nine o'clock. Somehow, he'd managed to sleep in. Sleeping had always been an issue for him. He was awakened easily and frequently, throughout the night, and sleeping in was next to impossible for him. However, today, he'd actually managed to do so, and a damned phone call is what he got for all his unconscious effort to make that happen.

He looked at the caller ID on the phone. It was Dave, one of his supervisors up at State. Mitch's mood prickled. He supposed that this call would be in regard to the beach closing, the whales, the dead bodies, or the Shark Tracker data. Maybe all of the above. Mitch really didn't feel much like opening that whole damned can of worms with his supervisor, first thing on a Sunday morning. But, he guessed that there must be a serious reason underlying the weekend call, since this was the first time that it had ever happened.

"This is Mitch," he answered, rubbing his eye with the palm of his free hand.

"Mitch, Dave Chambers, up at State. How are you?"

"Oh ... pretty good. How can I help you, Dave?"

"Hate to bother you, Mitch, but I got an interesting call a few minutes ago. You're the one I'm going to need to forward this to, but I thought I'd better give you a heads-up first."

"What's going on?"

"Parasites."

"Parasites?"

"The caller was a paramedic out of Kansas City, name of Kate Browning. Said they've got some kind of epidemic up there in KC that they're trying to trace back to some of our local food products."

"People are getting sick?"

"People are dying."

Kansas City … Mitch could not help but recall the two shirtless bodies. Both men had happened to be from Kansas City. A strange coincidence, perhaps. All of the recent events came tumbling back into mental collation, and he began to feel a little ill. What a terrible weekend. It was one of those weekends where he felt like he needed an extra weekend to make up for it.

"There may very well be more cities involved, depending on the distribution. Could be nationwide, but this is an outbreak that's so new that it hasn't even been officially recognized yet. They've found close to ten cases, and she's managed to link this thing to a product coming out of Emerald Coast Cannery."

"Over in Pensacola?"

"That's the one."

"So, what's the plan, here? Isn't this a job for the health department?"

"It is, but it's Sunday. Health department and the cannery are both closed for the weekend, but this situation seems serious enough that it shouldn't wait until Monday morning. All she needs, at this point, is some basic Q and A about parasites and such."

"How did she get ahold of you?"

"She probed the State hotlines. Managed to get an answer from an outsourced operator, over in Park Reservations. She convinced them to help her bully her way over to a biologist. I don't know anything about parasites, Mitch. I'm aware that they exist. That's about it. And I'm pretty sure we're not talking about tapeworms, here."

"What are the symptoms?"

"Makes them go nuts. Jump off bridges, and stuff."

"You mean, these are suicides?"

"I don't know. I wish I were being facetious, but I'm not. To hear her explain it, it's like these people are drowning themselves, inadvertently."

Mitch's eyes widened. He rose from the edge of his bed, as he recalled the bodies from Kansas City, the woman with the red jacket, on the beach.

"Have you heard of anything like this? Any bugs that can get into your brain, and rewire things?"

"Wait a minute. What bridge?"

"What-what?"

"She said they're jumping off a bridge. Which one? I mean, are we talking a lake or a river?

"Well, I'd presume the Missouri River. That's what flows through Kansas City."

Mitch remembered that last haunting glance, as she'd stood in the surf in her professional attire, moments before she dove into the sea. The woman went down, but she never came up. His was an analytical mind, designed to solve problems, but its design was dependent upon a supply problems with solvability. The woman on Henderson Beach was the opposite of what his mind required. She was pointless. She was poison to his analytical constitution. She'd left him unsettled, and just a little unhinged. Now, something else was beginning to take shape. It was something lurking, just beneath the surface, and it was huge. "Does the Missouri River flow all the way down to the Gulf?"

"Flows into the lower Mississippi, and you know right where that dumps in. Why do you ask? You want to talk to her? You don't think we've got critters swimming upriver, do you?"

"No. I mean—yes. I do want to talk to her."

The blue curtains in Collin's room rippled in the current of air. The fluid manner in which they moved was not unlike the surface of a remembered pond, where she'd once kept her sundown vigil, where Kate had waited to commune with something deeper, something down beneath the surface. Sitting in that room alone in the chair next to Collin's bed, fostered a rather cathartic sensation of nostalgia, as well as the illusion of an opportunity for closure, on a bit of unfinished business.

Sara could not have known how difficult it had been for Kate to pull back, to refrain from asking Collin all the questions she'd longed to ask him, about that secret world of his, on the other side of the looking glass. But, Sara was not here, this time. She was currently in surgery, getting that crushed paw of hers put back together.

Kate felt some trepidation, coming back here alone. Sara did not exactly support the idea of probing the depths of Collin's fantasies. It felt just a little bit dishonest to be exploring this side of him, behind the back of his fiancée. It even felt a little bit crazy. Kate was sane enough to realize that she'd been teetering on the edge of something, ever since that day that Jeffrey drowned. And she was pragmatic enough to admit that the direction in which her mind had been working, lately, was a probably dangerous one. She ought to be taking better care of herself. She could not afford the cost of gazing into that lawyer's smiling eyes, an instant before he committed himself to the river's depths, but it was a cost that had been forced upon her. Old wounds had reopened, and she knew that if she picked it them, they would never heal. But she could not stop herself. The itch was too much. The bizarre case of Collin Stillwell had flipped one of those switches, way down in her reptilian core, to satisfy a craving.

Her parents had become concerned about her, after nearly a month of her evening vigil. Up until then, Kate guessed that they must have thought it pretty natural, what she was doing, because they hadn't given her any trouble. They would only smile sadly, as she walked out that screen door, and into the twilight pasture. They must have figured that it was a phase of childhood grieving that would pass, as all phases of childhood pass. But it didn't. And there came a morning when her dad asked her, at the breakfast table, who exactly she was talking to out there. He explained that the evening had been so still that her words had carried across the pasture. When she hesitated to answer, he asked her if she had been talking to Jeffrey, or to God. His face became worried when she finally shook her head, and she told him the truth. She told him about the thing.

Who knows how it might've turned out, had she lied that day. Instead of telling her dad the truth, she could have told him that she'd been praying. Sure, he might still have forbidden her from going back out there, but he might've done so more gently. It might even have strengthened their relationship. But if she'd been permitted to keep going out there, night after night for years on end, what then? That one question was what had haunted her for twenty-five years.

She was getting so close to an answer, building her strange relationship with the thing, the presence in the pond, earning its trust, while it was earning hers in return. On the best nights, it would sing to her. Not in words. It sang in complex intonations that seemed to play the very strings of her soul. While at first, she'd been afraid to venture too near the water, for fear it might seize her, she learned that if she waded into the water just a little, then she could often entice it to sing longer, if the music was starting to fade. On her last visit to the cow pond, she'd waded in past her knees, and her skirt got a little wet.

Kate never knew if her mother had insisted he do it, or if she had seen her skirt and just decided to do it on his own. Neither of them would talk about it, when Kate came home from school that day. The bus left her at the side of their rural road, staring out across her pasture at the great hump of turned earth, like the grave of some enormous dead thing, right where her cow pond had always been.

It was still down there, somewhere, beneath that mountain of dirt. When she walked upon it with bare feet, she could feel it. Her strange friend. It was still down there, somewhere beneath that monument to little Jeffrey, the cow pond, and all of its creatures, but she knew that it was never coming up again. The experiment had been cancelled. All progress, rudely interrupted. With her therapeutic diversion ripped away, she once again felt the agony of Jeffry's death.

Loss was her obsession, and it demanded a sizable compulsion. The terrors and self-loathing returned. Like a cancer metastasizing through every whorl of her brain, those demons might have consumed her, had she not found an acceptable tithing, a new compulsion through which to ground the dark energy. It was the job. A job revealed in a vision of twisted metal and shattered glass, when a howling choir of angels with crackling radios delivered those poor souls from the worst moments of their lives. They denied death. They controlled chaos. They fostered healing, and life. For the better part of her life, the job had saved her, whether she was studying, training, or performing the skills.

Now, it was gone. Even five days away from the job and she could tell that she wasn't thinking right. Just like twenty-five years ago, when her dad filled in her pond, Kate felt the maleficent presence of a personal demon starting to meddle around inside her mind.

Her phone vibrated in her pocket. She glanced apprehensively around the room, to see if the disruption had startled any of the patients. But of course, it hadn't. Motionless, flat on their backs, they all just stared at those shimmering blue curtains. Kate retrieved the phone. It was an unknown caller. She frowned and put it to her ear. "Hello?"

"Hi, is this Kate Browning?"

"It is."

"This is Mitch Poole. I'm a marine biologist with the State of Florida, returning your call."

"Oh! Oh, hi!" Kate rose from her seat. She walked out of the room, and into the hallway, pulling the door closed quietly behind her. "Thank you so much for calling me back. I wasn't sure if I'd be able to get through to anyone on a weekend, but I'm so glad you called. We've got a situation, up here, as I'm sure you've probably heard, and I'd really like to borrow a little bit of your expertise."

"So, Dave told you that I was some sort of an expert on human parasites, did he?"

"Well, he said that if it lived in the waters off the coast of Destin, then you would be the guy to talk to. He told me that your primary area of expertise was sharks, but he really gave you some high praise."

"How embarrassing."

"No, don't be embarrassed. Just enlighten me. Teach me a little bit about human parasites that infect crabmeat. Or, more specifically, do you know of any parasites that could affect the human mind, actually take a person over, alter their personalities and their behavior. I know this must sound totally ridiculous ..."

"No. As a matter of fact, it doesn't sound the least bit ridiculous."

"Really?"

"Really."

"Such a thing actually exists?"

"Most definitely. Not in humans, by this tick of the evolutionary clock, but there are a number of parasites that can accomplish exactly what you just described in other host species. Parasites are pretty simple creatures, but with very complex lifecycles that can seem totally improbable. They require specific hosts, and in many cases, transfers from one specific host to a second, or even a third, in order to complete their lifecycle. Snails play a big part in the world of parasites. Never eat a snail. They host a list of parasites as long as my arm and some of them are unbelievably nasty. But these little buggers can't accomplish their whole lifecycle in the body of a snail. They require a transfer. So, at some point in their development, they need to be relocated to the body of their secondary host, whether it's a bird, a fish, or a human being. In order for that to happen, Mr. Snail needs to be eaten. So, that's when the parasite intervenes."

"I'm listening."

"They move from the snail's gut, up into its brain, where they physically seize control and take over the snail. The parasite compels the snail to crawl out of the safety of the pond, or the leaf litter, or whatever, and send it crawling up a tree, way out to the tip of a branch, where they're totally exposed. Then, to attract the attention of a bird, they make that snail dance."

"You're kidding."

"Not at all. That snail will wiggle back and forth, wagging its eyestalks all around for however long it takes to be snapped up by a hungry bird."

"I thought I was halfway nuts to suggest such a thing to you."

"Oh, no. And the phenomenon goes beyond snails. There's a parasite with an ant-cow lifecycle that is also a brain invader."

"It takes over the minds of cows?"

"Nope. Ants. The poor little guy stops working. It walks right out of the anthill, and marches far away, out into a field of lush green grass, where it climbs to the tip of a blade of grass and just sits there for as long as it takes to be accidentally eaten by a grazing cow. All of this usually takes place within a relatively small area, so the parasites are likely able to return to their birthplace, as adults, where generations of successful eggs have been laid, and the cycle begins all over again."

"But there's no parasite that affects the human mind in a similar way?"

"Like I said, not yet. Now, I heard a little bit about what's going on up there, and I have to say, I'm intrigued. These people, they're all ... jumping off bridges?"

"No. Not jumping off bridges. But yes. Normal people suddenly becoming hydrophilic. Within an hour of their last meal, they develop an obsession with the sea, specifically. And once they decide that they're going, they have no qualms about dying, trying to get there. It's been the Missouri River that calls most loudly to them. It's the largest body of water in the area, so I guess they figure that it's the closest thing to the sea."

"But they're not attracted to the area lakes. Just the river."

"So far, that's been the case."

"Kate, I have reason to believe that at least some of these people are accomplishing their goal."

"What do you mean?"

"I don't want to go morbid on you, but ... we've found bodies, here in Destin. And they're yours. We're talking Kansas City residents with no connection to Destin, no reason whatsoever for being here. They're dressed in everyday attire, and somehow, they're ending up in the Gulf of Mexico. I believe they're taking the river downstream."

Kate gasped. "Of course! The river is transporting them back to their birthplace! And it's Destin. The Emerald Coast. That's where all of the infected food is coming from, and little invaders have found a way to get back to where they belong." Kate's eyes widened. "They're just all trying to get back home."

"This must be verified, of course."

"That's my whole reason for calling you. I think I've traced this thing to a specific product, but now, I'm kind of stuck. Do you know of anywhere in town where you could go and pick up a sample of the Crabby Batter that's produced by Emerald Coast Cannery?"

"I'm sure it shouldn't be a problem."

"Like, today?"

"Shouldn't be a problem. Here in Destin, seafood is all we do."

"I wouldn't even know what to tell you to look for."

"Of course, you wouldn't. Leave that part to me."

"What do I do in the meantime?"

"For God's sake, don't go making any accusations. Don't even tell people about this. Not until we're able to verify our parasite theory."

"Our theory?" Kate looked up and down the empty hallway. No one was in sight, but she still felt compelled to lower her voice. "Mitch, what's happening here?"

After a long and strange silence, the voice on the other end of the line replied, "Let's wait on all of that, okay? Let's just wait and see what we find."

"And if you do find something?"

"I'll call you."

"Right away?"

"Right away."

"Thank you."

"Kate, if it turns out that you're right about all of this, I'm pretty sure that a whole lot of people will be lining up to thank you."

Kate ended the call. She stood idly in the empty hallway, with phone in hand. She'd done all she could. At this point, the situation was out of her hands. Now, it looked like she was out of a good diversion. She sighed, and turned back toward Collin's door. After a moment's hesitation, she opened it, and walked inside.

Kate froze, halfway through the doorway. All of the patients were sitting upright in their beds. They were staring at her.

She was intimidated. Before entering the room, Kate had to remind herself that their wrists and ankles were safely restrained. Even so, the compulsion to back right out and call for a nurse was a strong one, but she didn't. She didn't need a nurse's assistance. Kate waited for her beating heart to slow, and then, she stepped into the room, and closed the door quietly behind her.

Every set of eyes tracked her movements, as she put one foot in front of the other, until she reached the foot of Collin's bed. She was not comfortable taking a seat beside him. It felt preferable to remain standing, to look down on them, and keep her position of higher ground. Although their facial expressions remained just as blank as they had been, five minutes ago, something about their attitudes seemed to have changed. The patients appeared to be as engaging as she'd ever seen them. They seemed suddenly connected to her. And why? She couldn't imagine what could have aroused them, while she was outside of the room. Unless, they'd happened to have heard her on the phone … conspiring against them. But no conspiracy had been struck against the patients. She and Mitch were plotting against something else. Something deeper. Something down beneath the surface of these people that had seized their control panels, and seated at the helm of their minds, even now, peering right out at Kate through stolen eyes.

"Do you remember me?" Kate asked.

Collin, or whatever it was that possessed him, emitted a low gurgle. His throat expanded and contracted. His restraints creaked under the tension that he was evidently putting on them. Veins bulged from his arms, but his muscles did not quiver, suggesting some formidable strength. Although Collin was of average build, and not necessarily developed, the will of whatever controlled the kid's body appeared capable of exceeding his ordinary physical limitations, if it wanted to. And probably at the risk of Collin's body.

"I remember you," Kate whispered. As she approached the foot of the bed, it felt as though she were wading out, as if to meet something in its own world, on its own terms. "You are a taker of people."

The thing inside Collin glared out at Kate through the red-rimmed portals of its borrowed eyes. It lowered its chin. Twin threads of drool spilled from the corners of its mouth into its lap. The veins in its arms raised higher still, as the restraints complained under the increasing level of tension. There seemed little doubt that it could snap these bonds like rubber bands, if it really wanted to.

Kate waded deeper into its world, around the foot of the bed, to the single chair. She pulled it out and sat casually beside Collin. It studied her movements, as she reached into the pocket of her cardigan, and removed her phone. She opened her browser, and pulled up a map of the continental U.S. "Where do you want to go?"

"Go to the sea," it hissed. The silvery tendrils of saliva glistened like spider webs.

"But where, specifically?" Kate raised her phone up near its shackled hand, the same hand that had so recently crushed the bones of Sara's hand. Kate saw the dark crescents of scabs in every spot where Sara had delivered a bite. She would keep her distance from those powerful claws. "Can you show me?"

Kate spread her fingers across the screen, and zoomed into the map until the city of Kansas City nucleated the center of the screen. She moved her hands closer, just a hair out of its reach. "We're right here," she said. "Can you use your finger and show me? Where is your home?"

The Collin-thing's eyes swiveled mechanically in their sunken sockets. Kate could see the reflection of her glowing screen, cast upon them. Its expression showed no sign of recognition of the device in front of it, nor any hint of acknowledgement of her request, yet, its index finger straightened. It appeared as though Collin were still in there on some level. That, or whatever had invaded the kid had full access to all of his mental files. The pad of its finger settled down upon the center of the screen, and with a stroke as smooth as a canoe paddle through clear water, it swept east, toward Saint Louis. The finger hovered here, as though disoriented.

"Need me to zoom in?"

Kate expanded the map again, drawing in tightly on the Saint Louis area. The extended finger seemed once again to find its way, touching down lightly upon the confluence of the Missouri and the Mississippi River, then sweeping southward.

"You're following the rivers downstream, aren't you?" Kate watched with amazement, as the ghostly navigator tracked the river south. It swept through Memphis, past Baton Rouge, and down into New Orleans. There, it left shore for open water, until it finally came to rest. The end of its journey was a specific spot in the Gulf of Mexico, not far from the Emerald Coast and Destin, Florida.

"Good job." Kate smiled. She sat back in her chair, pinned the location on her map, and saved it to her home screen. "Thank you so much for showing me to your neighborhood." She rose from her seat, and slipped her phone back into her pocket. Her first thought was to text the waypoint to Mitch Poole, provide him with another piece to the puzzle, but then she remembered that he'd called from an unlisted number. He must have called her from his office. Kate realized, with considerable dismay, that she had no way of contacting him. They would not talk again until he learned something conclusive, if that ever happened, and called her back.

"Go to the sea."

Kate's eyes flicked up to meet those of the thing, or at least, those through which it leered. For the first time, the face of Collin wore a distinct and recognizable expression. It was desperation. The increasing tension on the restraints made the metal framework of the bed begin to groan. "Oh, I'm sure that's what you'd like to do, wouldn't you? But guess what? You're about as far from the sea as you could possibly get, and you're never going to get there. None of you in this room, so help me God, will ever go to the sea."

Every restraint in the room seemed to tighten. Lips curled back over chattering teeth. In concert, the sound reminded Kate of a balmy summer's eve down by the cow pond, when the chorus of frogs began to sing. But this was not the rapture of tiny creatures. This was the sound of hatred.

The female patient nearest the window began to arch her back. She was the first one brought into Trinity, Kate recalled. She was one of the first in Kansas City to be infected, as well as one of the confirmed patrons of Ryuu. Tendons sprung from her neck like guitar strings, as her face stretched into a terrible grimace. Her whole body began to tremble, as her throat ballooned like a snake swallowing an egg.

Kate smacked the emergency call button on the wall to alert the nurse's station. Every muscle in the woman's body was set aquiver. Her skin tone was chilling to a pale blue. Kate recognized all the signs. This woman was about to convulse.

"Hang on. Hang on." Kate removed her cardigan. She twisted up one of the sleeves, between her hands. She had to get the packing between the woman's teeth, or else she was liable to chew off her own tongue. Placing her palm against the woman's sternum, she pushed steadily until the patient was laid flat upon her back. Now, Kate had to get her jaws pried open without getting bitten to insert the packing. Finally, get her to turn her head to one side to prevent choking, in case she happened to vomit.

"Come on, honey, open up. You've got to try and open up for me, okay?" Kate braced the woman's forehead with her arm, then used the heel of her other palm to press down on the woman's chin. She could feel some big tremors coming. They were on the way, beginning in her extremities, and coursing their way toward her core. The big show was just about to begin. "Come on. Open." Kate gritted her teeth, putting the whole weight of her body upon the woman's chin. It was like trying to pry open a stubborn oyster.

With an inhuman yowl, the patient beneath her finally yielded. Kate felt the jaw begin to lower like a rusty trap door. She continued to push steadily. "There you go. It's okay. It's okay. I know this doesn't feel very good, but we need to get this between your teeth before you seize." Maintaining pressure on the point of the woman's chin, and transferring her weight to the forehead, Kate carefully shifted her body to one side, enabling her to drag the sleeve of the cardigan toward the yawning mouth.

A rope of marmalade-colored pus arched from the woman's throat, thick and warm upon Kate's cheek. It reeked. It reminded Kate of that awful fish oil that her Granny used to spoon into her mouth as a kid. Gasping, turning her head, she fought the urge to wipe off the viscous stuff. Yellow bridges swung from Kate's face to the patient's lolling tongue. For an instant, she was sure that the poor woman had just vomited on her—until she saw the thing down in her throat, staring back at her.

Kate reared back from the bed, and spat, smearing away at the stuff that now webbed her fingers. Soon enough, she regained control of herself, slowed her breathing back down to a normal rate, and edged back up to the bedside. While struggling to salvage some semblance of her professionalism, Kate took a deep breath, and dared to steal a second peak downward. Lodged there, like the blackest of eggs in a nest of its own sallow tissue, was a single blinking eye.

Chapter Nine

Up on the big screen, a trembling stainless steel hook dragged ruts through a moist matrix that looked similar to carrot cake. Joined by a long probe, the implements worked cooperatively to rend a gaping hole in the matter. Like a hidden gem, a crimson fragment was exposed, and then carefully unearthed. The strikingly colored article was tumbled all about by the hook, this way and that, until it was at last pinned down by the probe, and rent in two. It split into moist fibers, red on the outside, snowy-white, within.

"There," Mitch said.

Skip frowned up at the digital monitor, where Mitch's dissection hook extracted what appeared to be a tiny crystal that was embedded in the fibers of crabmeat. It was oblong, and translucent, noticeably wider at one end than the other was. "So, what is it? Some kind of an egg?"

"Not an egg." Mitch lifted the ovate crystal out of the batter, balancing it on the point of his probe, and he placed it into a droplet of distilled water onto a slide. This, he returned to the dissecting microscope, replacing the petri dish of Crabby Batter. Adjusting the binocular eyepieces, he then rotated through the various lens options until he settled on one with the right magnification for the job. All it took was a little tweaking to bring the focus in, nice and sharp. The strange little treasure filled the digital screen. "It's a sporocyst."

"Come again?"

"Well, you know how a caterpillar forms a cocoon?"

"Yeah."

"Very similar." Mitch licked his lips. The Crabby Batter actually smelled pretty good. The fishmonger assured him that it was the bestselling premixed batter of its kind, used for stuffing mushrooms, oysters, and for rolling crab cakes. He could understand the popularity. The crab actually smelled fresh. It probably was, here in Destin. It probably had never been frozen. The mixture of breadcrumbs was a deeply herbal concoction with notes of sage, bay leaf, and more than a hint of creole spice. Mitch could hear his stomach growling, in spite of his better judgment. "You see, in the world of aquatic parasites, the lifecycle normally begins with an egg. Egg hatches. Out swims a little critter. These are sometimes called miracidia, sometimes larva. But oftentimes, this guy is a borer. He swims around until he finds a very specific host, whether it's a fish or a snail or a frog, and then he tunnels right into their flesh."

"Ew."

"Once embedded, it's time to build this thing. It's cocoon. After it's protected inside its hard little capsule, it can kick back and await the next stage of development."

"And what stage would that be?"

"Varies, depending on the organism. In this case, we're presuming that the sporocyst is inadvertently eaten, probably by a secondary host who devours the first. Once inside the belly of host number two, the cyst hatches. Something new emerges. Once again, it begins to bore. In this stage, they often bore into the arteries and use the host's circulatory system like public transportation to get them where they need to go. Might be the liver, or up into the brain, the eyes, the testicles … all sorts of fun possibilities. In fact, if you can even think of a weird possibility, odds are, nature has already beaten you to it. It's all been done."

Skip scratched at his arms, shifting his weight from one foot to the other. "Dude, this world is a horrible place. No two ways about it."

"Ahhhh! Here-here-here! Yes. See? Tunnels." Mitch had returned the dissected gob of crab flesh to the examination table, where he zoomed in on a perfectly round tunnel through the pale fibers. "This crab was attacked. There-there. From the outside. They did in fact bore right into this guy. Right through the chinks in his suit of armor. Poor fella. Then, to top it all off, that crab managed to get trapped and processed. And by processed, we mean cooked. So, the million-dollar question is, after cooking, are the critters inside still viable?"

Mitch switched subjects, back to the sporocyst. He struggled to pin the tiny thing to the microscope slide, but it kept popping free, whenever he applied pressure. "It's almost like a piece of broken glass. Tough to crush. Very hard. Very durable. But maybe ... maybe I don't have to open it, after all." Mitch rose from the eyepieces, blinked, and then clicked through the lens options until he reached the highest level of magnification. "Kind of tricky to focus this one."

"Here, use the fine tuner." Skip stepped in, and reminded Mitch of a second focal adjustor, located higher up on the eyepieces. A few strokes of his thumb, and every pulsating detail of the organism behind those crystalline walls appeared, stunningly focused. Amber fluids chugged through vessels, to the drumbeat of its simple heart. And atop its domed carapace, gaping up into oblivion, was a single blinking eye.

"You're alive, aren't you, you little devil."

"What is that thing?" Skip whispered. The two men stood side by side, aweing up at the vacillating life form, on the big screen. All microscopic life had an unearthly appearance, but this creature seemed somehow to be a breed apart from those garden variety flatworms and amoebas, which seemed little more than pieces of wriggly protein. The structure of this animal was so much more complex, similar to a mollusk, really. And, perhaps owed to the keen awareness of that cyclopean eye, it gave the distinct impression of sentience. It was the distant manner in which it blinked into the microscope light, as though questioning its tier in the universal pecking order, its tiny place in this great big world.

"I don't know," Mitch replied, "but I think I'd like to try a little experiment."

"What?"

"I'd like to see if we can convince this little monster to come out and play with us, all on its own." Mitch double-snapped his fingers, turned on one heel, and marched off into the lab.

The marine biology lab was not just a place of research and environmental testing. It was also something of a trophy room, displaying thousands of jars of pickled fish and other marine life, preserved for eternity in a pinkish bath of formaldehyde. It was an ichthyology student's dream come true, and Mitch's home away from home. His was more of a creative mind than an analytical one, a creative mind that was most inspired in a scientific environment. He'd always been funny that way. A laboratory setting was the most delectable fuel for his brain, inspiring him to draw, dream and design things that could change the world. The analysis itself was pretty dry. Although a wide variety of water and soil tests could be conducted here, as well as data processing on their intranet LIM system, Mitch considered it mindless busywork, best left to the undergrads and interns. They ate that stuff up. Mitch preferred the beach, the open sea. The lab was simply where he recharged his creative mind.

Mitch swerved down the aisle between the spectrophotometry station and the wet chemistry bench, and then, he came to a stop in front of the steel cabinet that safely contained all of their strong acids and bases. Mitch unlocked it, then dragged open the sliding door with a terrible squeal. He snorted and shook his head. The sulfurous-vinegar reek of all the acids was just about enough to curl the nose hairs. There. He pushed aside the glass jugs of sulfuric to retrieve the dusty vessel that he was looking for.

"What exactly are you up to?" Skip inquired.

Mitch unscrewed the cap on the jug of 1:1 hydrochloric acid. He poured out approximately twenty milliliters into a small beaker, about the size of a shot glass. Tendrils of milky steam oozed from the surface of the beaker, and hung like a miniature toxic cloud over the laboratory bench.

"The digestive juices of the human stomach are primarily hydrochloric, at a normal pH range of about one to two— depending on how many cups of coffee per day you drink." Mitch hitched his eyebrows, as he carefully transferred the beaker of acid over to a nearby hotplate, and switched the device on. He adjusted the temperature setting, then, with another heel spin, he sidled over to a drawer that was filled with disposable pipettes. He pulled one free, and tapped it thoughtfully against the palm of his hand. "Human body temp, ninety-eight-point-six, obviously, but we're going to lose a few degrees as soon as it hits the slide."

"You mean you're going to dissolve him?"

"No." Mitch paused. "Well, I mean, I don't think so." He slid back over to the hot plate, and checked the temperature. It didn't take long at all to heat up hydrochloric acid. "Think about it. If this critter has evolved toward a crab-human lifecycle, then I would think that replicating the conditions of the human stomach might be just the tune we need to play to coax this little introvert out of his shell. Know what I mean?"

Both men stared up at the wriggling monster, on the screen. It did not exhibit the random larval twitching of a caterpillar inside a cocoon. It cleaned the walls of its tiny prison with a dipping, trunk-like mouthpart that could descend to the very bottom of the cyst, where it vacuumed up particles of waste. It kept a very clean house. Every movement had purpose, belying some level of cognition.

"What the hell should we call it?" Skip said.

"I dunno."

"Well, if it turns out we've discovered a brand new species, we'll have to call it something."

"Mm-yeah."

"It looks like a Cyclops, to me." Skip snapped his fingers, and spun toward Mitch. "What was Cyclops's real name in the X-men?"

"Scott Summers."

"Nah." Skip sighed, and turned back to the screen. "Scott would be a stupid name for it." He gasped, clapped his hands, and spun back around. "Rell! The Cyclops from <u>Krull</u>! Dude, that would be so awesome!"

"How about Polyphemus?"

"Poly-who? Did you just make that up?"

"No. That's actually the name of the most famous Cyclops of all time. The one blinded by Odysseus?"

"Meh. I don't know," Skip sighed, "it's got too many syllables going on."

"Well, are we ready to do this, or what?" Mitch switched off the hotplate. "One-oh-three." He lowered his plastic pipette into the acid, and drew up one milliliter. "Ought to be around ninety-eight-six by the time it hits … and …" he brought the pipette tip down over the microscope slide, dangling a bead of acid directly over their tiny creature.

"Screw it. Let's call him Scott."

"And, go." Mitch squeezed one droplet from the pipette. It hit, with audible fizzing, and a little chuff of milky steam. Both men's heads snapped upward, to view the result of the experiment up on the big screen. At first, it was quite hazy. Billions of bubbles spewed from the crystalline casing.

"The sporocyst is dissolving, but we expected that."

"We did?"

"Imagine, it's just been eaten by a human being. Now, it's floating in the gut, immersed in a solution of concentrated hydrochloric acid. The sporocyst, probably calcium-based would naturally dissolve, and the creature—"

"Scott."

"—would be automatically released into its new environment." Mitch smiled up at the screen, where the bubbles began to clear. In a spray of whipping tentacles, a new creature gradually decompressed, fanning fluids into its new appendages like a young butterfly just emerged from its chrysalis. It seemed not surprised by the abrupt transition, as if it expected as much, and knew just what to do. Instinct, genetic memory, whatever you wanted to call it, could be downright miraculous to behold.

"It's beautiful."

The creature was pearly in color, with iridescent striations along its flanks and back. It didn't swim, or jerk about in the liquid environment. Rather, it walked, tiptoed upon its cilia, with an almost dainty, floating gait. A pair of long claws appeared to be folded, mantis-like, beneath its carapace, awaiting use. Mounted atop that armored body, like a turret on a tiny tank, was that single blinking eye. For a deadly parasite, Mitch had to admit, it was pretty darned cute.

"Turn off the lights!"

"Why? You don't think ..." Skip's eyes widened. He ran from the microscope table to the row of switches on the far wall, and slapped them all downward with a single motion. Now, the only source of light in the room was that over the microscope slide, which was projected upon the screen.

"Get ready for blackout," Mitch whispered, and he switched off the scope light. At first, the blackness within the lab was impenetrable, but after a few seconds, pulsing rows of blue lights became apparent, upon the screen. The biologists fawned up at the dazzling display, like a couple of awestruck kids, before a lit Christmas tree. Chains of lights streamed sequentially, along its flanks, while twin regions of a deeper red throbbed rhythmically in its undercarriage, like the cadence of a beating heart.

"You know that this means?" Skip said.

"What?"

"It means that Scott comes from the very bottom. The darkest depths of the Gulf."

"You're absolutely right," Mitch replied, with a smile. "There would be no need for bioluminescence, if you weren't right. But what creature is designed to withstand the extremes of travelling back and forth along either end of that pressure range?"

"Let's not forget, you can also cook Scott, freeze Scott … and, he also happens to be doing the Cha-Cha through a bath of hydrochloric acid."

"Tough cookie." Mitch beamed in the flashing bioluminescence. "I'm glad you're tiny."

"You asked me to look into all the known parasites of crustaceans, while you were out getting your crabby patties."

"Crabby Batter."

"Well, I didn't find anything remotely like this." Skip tipped his chin at the screen. "So, we may in fact be looking at an undiscovered new species. But, I did stumble across something that you might find rather interesting."

"And what's that?"

"You mentioned hydrophilic obsession as one of the major symptoms, right?"

"Right."

"Well, I ran a search on that, and I did come up with something. It's a nematode. A type of aquatic hairworm to be exact. Lives in freshwater ponds. Its primary hosts are grasshoppers and crickets. The hoppers drink water infested with their larvae. Over the summer, those larvae grow inside the grasshopper's body, until the time comes when they take over the bug's mind. See, the worms know when it's time to return to their birth pond, to mate, and to lay eggs of their own, so they squirm up into the grasshopper's brain, work their nasty magic, and cause their grasshopper hosts to become—guess what—hydrophilic."

Skip hitched his eyebrows. "The hoppers all fly back to that same little pond where they originally became infected. And once they get there, they climb to the top of a stalk of grass, make a suicidal jump out into the water, and then, the worms come pouring out of their bodies, ripping the grasshopper to shreds, as they all return to the bottom of the pond."

Mitch and Skip stared at each other in the pulsing blue light. "If you can imagine it," Mitch said, "odds are, Mother Nature has already beaten you to it."

Kate scrolled through image after image, with the pad of her thumb. The search was too broad. She knew that. But nothing specific was yielding any usable results. How could she run an effective search for the crazy thing she'd seen, peering out from that woman's throat? "Human parasite images" yielded thousands of photographs, mostly microscope slides and medical illustrations of tiny worms, along with some festering sores, swollen body parts, and other revolting anfractuosities. "Human parasite throat" resulted in some absolutely horrifying conversation threads, but it was no use. Whatever this creature was, it appeared to be unknown to the science of parasitology. Kate was beginning to suspect that she had stumbled onto a new life form.

She closed her eyes and lowered her phone into her lap. It was hard to think. She frowned at the constant clamor of breaking nurses, all around her, the fits of laughter and competing voices, popping Tupperware dishes, and beeping microwave keypads. If everyone would just shut the hell up …

Kate opened her eyes. "Sea creature," she typed, "Cyclops images."

She involuntarily lurched back from the table as the first image loaded. A bulging black eye gawped from the pale forehead of a creature purported to be a Cyclops shark. For an instant, it looked strikingly similar to the thing she'd seen. Several more photographs of the same bizarre creature followed. It was apparently a deformed shark fetus. Kate kept scrolling. Illustrations of the classic Cyclops slid by. Bellowing one-eyed troglodytes, tramping over ancient wastelands, dragging a spiked club behind. No. Not the monster that she was after. But wait.

Her thumb hovered over what appeared to be an ancient illustration. It was not a small creature in this depiction. It was huge. Far greater in size than the wooden ships it imperiled. Much of its body remained a mystery, hidden beneath the whirlpool of seawater that it nucleated, but its evil eye was most certainly depicted, even showcased, peering maleficently out from the center of the vortex. The title of the image was "Charybdis."

"Well, hey, Kate the Great! What're you doing here today?"

Kate looked up. It was Deb, one of the triage nurses. What was Deb doing over in this wing? Kate hadn't guessed that she would run into many people she knew, if anybody, up on this end of the hospital. It was a huge facility, but still, she probably should have known better. Big hospital, small world. "Just looking in on a friend," Kate replied, and then promptly flipped it around on her. "What about you? What are you doing over here in Radiology? You're not switching teams on us, are you?" Kate winked.

"It's Dr. Garrison's birthday," Deb replied. "We've got his cake hidden over here in their fridge. Sneaky, huh?"

"Aw, I love Dr. Garrison."

"You should come!" Deb grabbed the back of a nearby chair and dragged it over to Kate's table, sat down and made herself right at home. "So, I was talking to Quincy this morning."

"Oh, God." Kate glowered up at the ceiling.

"What happened?"

Kate groaned. This was exactly what she didn't want. This situation, right here. "Just had a bad shift. A real bad shift."

"I'm sorry."

Kate supposed that was the good thing about talking with other nurses. You didn't have to explain to them that someone had died. They just knew. "It is what it is, you know. I took it kind of hard, and I decided that I probably ought to take a few days off."

"Quincy said you got suspended."

"Quincy ... doesn't know everything, okay? It was a bad shift. I made a bad call. Call it what you want, but you and I both know that we've seen a hundred Quincies come and go through these doors, and we're still here to train the next one."

"I'm sorry. I'd be kind of pissed at Quincy, too."

"Why? What was he saying?"

"It was more just the way he was acting, like he's the new big shot on campus, like he was somehow vindicated, by everything. They reassigned him to a new preceptor, you know?"

Kate's hands fell into her lap with a smack. "So, they've decided that I'm unfit to train anyone now? Because I had one bad shift?" Kate felt her eyes welling up with tears, and she hated that. "Yeah, that seems real reasonable."

"I wouldn't take it that way, Kate. He's just running out of time. I think he's the one that went in there pushing for a transfer."

"Oh, really."

"That's how I understood it. Yeah."

"So, he went in there and talked a bunch of smack on me. Convinced them that I was too loony tunes to train him."

"As a matter of fact, I heard that's why you received a paid suspension. I heard Quincy pretty much threw you under the bus."

"I'm going to kill him."

"Don't tell him I told you so." Deb rose from her chair, and pushed it in. She gave Kate a quick hug, and then got her cake from the refrigerator. "You really could have heard it from just about anyone." Deb raised her eyebrows, and whispered, with her hand to the side of her mouth. "He's been kind of bragging about it."

"I … am going … to kill him."

"Kate Browning?"

Kate turned toward the sound of the voice in the lounge doorway. It was a radiology technician. She held a clipboard and a file in her hands.

"The images are up now, if you'd like to see them?"

Kate rose, pulled her purse strap over her shoulder, and wiped the tears from her eyes. She hated crying. It was only a matter of time, before someone figured her out, and exposed her flaws to the world. She knew it was coming, and she'd dreaded this day for years. But why did it have to be Quincy? Of all the trainees she'd survived, he was the loudest, and the cockiest. Everyone in the ER loved him, especially the ladies. Yeah, he was immature. An overgrown child, really, but Q was not stupid. He had the height, looks, energy and charisma that made him the kind of guy who you just knew would always win the hearts around him, and therefore succeed, without really even trying, in whatever he attempted in life, which made it all the more unnecessary for him to crush someone else as his personal stepping stone. There was no need for that. He was a golden boy. The more Kate brooded over it, the bitterer she became, until she felt like taking a hammer to his car in the parking lot.

"I didn't want to say anything, and make a scene," the tech said, as Kate followed her back to the diagnostic imaging lab, "but these images are really pretty incredible. No one has ever seen anything like this."

"Where is the patient, now?" Kate asked.

"Down in OR."

"Have they started surgery?"

"No, not yet. The surgeons are all still examining the images. It's looking pretty dicey. Hard to say where they ought to begin."

"What do you mean?" Kate asked, as they went through a set of double doors, and into the diagnostics lab, where around twenty physicians and nurses stood before the digital screens.

The tech lowered her voice to a whisper, and pointed to the set of projected x-rays. "Because of the way it's situated inside her. And because it's not the only one. She's got loads of them, deep inside her."

"Oh, my God."

The first image clearly showed the foreign body lodged in the patient's esophagus. But additional images of the woman's chest and torso, revealed that her innards were teeming. Most were of a smaller size. The one in her throat looked as large as a lemon. Those inhabiting the woman's stomach and intestines were slightly smaller, about the size of eggs. The largest and most dominant of the brood must have been the first to rise to the top of the horde, where it sealed off the esophagus with its body, and seized complete control of their common host.

By the murmuring of the physicians, all around her, Kate was able to gather that the creature had extended a pair of spiny appendages up through the sinus cavities, plunging them deeply into both hemispheres of the woman's brain. The purpose of this cerebral connection was unclear, but the barbed arms would be exceedingly difficult to remove, without endangering the life of patient. The consensus seemed to be that this organism probably had the ability to retract those spines, whenever it felt that the time was right, enabling it to depart its host with its appendages still intact. But it was not likely going to be removed any sooner, not without causing a fatal hemorrhage.

It was verified. They were looking at a species of human parasite that was completely unknown to science. The buzz in the room was so electrifying that you'd never have expected a woman's life to be on the line. Odds were that they were going to push the family to let them attempt a risky surgery. Scientists yearned to be a part of such a groundbreaking discovery. Surgeons lived for this kind of a challenge.

Kate wondered who would get credit for such a discovery. No one in the room had even acknowledged her presence. It hardly seemed fair that any one of the doctors who'd just walked into the room would probably soak up most of the credit, and she would be nothing but a forgotten accessory. However, Kate had been around the block enough times in the health care industry to feel fairly certain that that's exactly how it was bound to play out. They were all talking over each other. Every doctor in the room wanted to be the one whose profound insights would make it onto the permanent record. Kate was invisible. Nothing in the medical world had ever been named after an EMT.

Kate slipped up behind the surgeons. She raised her phone up over the backs of their heads, and snapped a few shots of the x-ray images. No one even noticed her, standing behind them. Kate liked the second image the best. It revealed the silhouette of the little invader in amazing detail.

"What about the other patients in that room?" Kate asked the x-ray tech. "Have any of them been brought up to diagnostics?"

"Not yet. This one was kind of a show stopper."

"They do realize, though, that they've probably got close to ten identical cases on their hands?"

"I don't think that they're ready to discuss that possibility, just yet. Not until they've come up with what they hope will be a plan for a successful procedure, and unfortunately, they're not anywhere even close to that point. They're still figuring out their own pecking order."

Kate's phone vibrated in her hand. She'd just received a photo by text message. It was from a phone number without a contact name. Frowning at the little thumbnail image, Kate pulled up the full message to view it. Her eyes widened.

PARASITE FOUND!!!

"Excuse me, for just a sec." Kate slipped past the x-ray technician, and stepped back through the double-doors of the diagnostics lab, into a relatively quiet corridor. Here, she turned her back to the main walkway, and reopened the text. It was from Mitch. When the attached pic sprung into view, Kate covered her mouth and gasped.

She could not begin to imagine how he had snapped the photo. It was stunning. Without question, this was the same organism that was being scrutinized over in the next room. But Mitch's pic was not a bleary, x-ray silhouette. The floating creature on her cell phone screen was alive and vibrant, staring back in the direction of the photographer with what appeared to be a keen awareness. It was impossible to discern the background or the scale. She would have to call him.

As Kate created a new contact from the incoming number, she felt her anger toward Quincy melting away. She felt the stress of the hospital setting, the humiliation of her paid suspension, all dissipating into vapor. The healing power of a new mission in life was nothing short of extraordinary, especially when that mission was bolstered by a fresh connection to a new friend, who shared your passion for the adventure.

Her phone began to ring.

"Hello?"

"Kate? This is Mitch."

"Hey!"

"Did you get the photo I sent?"

"Yes, I was just getting ready to call you."

"The product is infested. Completely infested. I'm heading straight up to Emerald Coast Cannery, first thing tomorrow morning, and I'm going to shut that place down. In the meantime, I need you to get back over to that restaurant where you found this stuff. Destroy every single crumb of it. Tomorrow morning, it's time to get the health departments involved on both our ends, get them chasing down a list of merchants. In the meantime, you might want to make a few calls yourself to other area restaurants, see who else might be carrying this product. We may have opened a big can of worms here, Kate. Emerald Coast Cannery happens to be one of the biggest distributors of seafood products in the Gulf, if not the world."

"How widespread do you think this problem is?"

"I'm afraid it could be everywhere."

Chapter Ten

"Good evening, welcome to Ryuu," the smiling hostess said. "Have you been here, before?"

"Yes, as a matter of fact, I have. I'm going to need to speak to your manager, please."

"Ohhhh-kay. Give me just one second, alright? Let me page him for you. Didn't you come by here last night?"

"Yes, I did." Kate nodded.

"That's what I thought. Hang on just a sec, okay?" The hostess slipped back around behind her kiosk. She picked up the phone, pushed a button, and shot Kate a furtive glance as she turned her back to her to begin whispering into the phone.

Kate looked away. The restaurant ambiance was somewhat more subdued on a Sunday night. Conversation between the patrons remained a low murmur. The obnoxious electronic trance music that had been so pervasive on a Saturday night, had been replaced with a waterfall soundtrack that was overlaid with the tranquil strings of a koto. You could actually hear the clink of silverware against plates, the tinkling of ice, and the hiss of gas flames flickering behind the Ryuu pendant. Kate glared up at the dragon. She could smell the aged reek of natural gas, and could feel the radiant heat of the metal. Though the restaurant seemed tranquil on the surface, it felt as though there were evil roiling at its core.

"I'm sorry," the hostess said, her upper lip curled into a sort of apologetic sneer. "But it sounds like Barton is going to be stuck in meetings for the rest of the night. He said he'd be happy to call you back, though. What was your name again, ma'am? And a number where he can reach you?"

"Oh, that's alright. I really don't even need to speak with him. I just swung back by to pick something up that I forgot. I know right where it is." Kate winked, and gave the edge of the kiosk a friendly pat. "I'll just be a second."

"Ma'am?"

Kate ignored the thin plea of a hostess, already behind her and forgotten, as she marched through the flaming portal, and out across the dining area. This time, she was not distracted by the clattering steel and spumes of fire, nor was she the least bit intimidated by the racks of ancient weaponry, or the hollowed suits of samurai armor. She saw none of these things. Her eyes flicked only from table to table, plate to plate. She was going to control this restaurant, and everyone inside it, with or without her paramedic's uniform. None of that superficial façade really mattered to her anymore. Because, for the first time in twenty-five years, she understood that it was never the cow pond, never the medical schooling, or the job. None of these outlets had ever really served her all that well as sources of therapy. It was never even about being on a mission to save lives. Death was simply her obsession. And controlling it, her compulsion. That's all it ever had been. And that's why, no matter how many lives she saved, how many times she snatched death's prize right from its skeletal grip, it would never be enough. Not until she had the strength to free herself from her obsession.

Despite all she'd done to convince herself otherwise, death controlled her. It was never little Jeffrey, haunting the unlit corners of her mind, and making her life a living hell. No. It was always Kate Browning, obsessed by the uncontrollable truth, weak and proud, a gutless coward. So afraid of pain and loss that she'd willfully traded away the best parts of life for an illusion of control in a lifelong battle to protect that worthless heart of hers from the risks of love and loss, which everyone else around her was somehow strong enough to bear. Suddenly, Kate hated herself. She hated the lie, the great and empty shell that she'd allowed herself to become.

Her gaze fell upon a plate. The sight of it stopped her in her tracks. It did not surprise her. Not really. Somehow, she knew she was going to find this tonight. Kate reached out and smacked the fork right out of the diner's hand. She swept his half-eaten crab cake right off the plate and onto the floor. She felt disgusted for having even touched it, the unassuming source of so much evil. There were two more at the next table. Kate smeared the grease from the edge of her hand, grabbed both plates, and flipped them onto the floor. The indignant cries of the diners, and a resounding crash of shattering plates, ceased all conversations throughout the restaurant. Heads turned, on gawking necks. Teppanyaki chefs stilled their sideshow racket. Servers froze with armloads of entrees beside tables.

"Everyone stop eating!" Kate shouted. "The food here is contaminated! You're all being infected with parasites! This is not a joke! Put down your food, right now!"

She continued prowling from table to table, pitching every crab cake that she encountered, or what was left of them. Kate was thoroughly revolted. She could not believe that Ryuu had completely disregarded her warning, and had continued to serve a potentially deadly meal to innocent and unsuspecting people. Then again, maybe she could believe it. That arrogant manager, Barton, had disregarded her simply to be stubborn. For that, he deserved to pay the highest price for his negligence. If anyone else wound up in Collin's room, as a result of consuming Ryuu's overpriced garbage, Kate couldn't wait to testify. She approached an eight-top table, where crab cakes were present in front of all eight diners. One of the patrons was just a small child, strapped helplessly into a high chair. Her small hands were covered with the same greasy crumbs and pinkish fibers of crabmeat that were slathered over the lower-half of her face. What once was a crab cake had been mangled to a pulp across her tray. Enraged, Kate swept the pulverized remains off the toddler's tray. She seized the adult table's edge, and overturned it with a horrendous crash. Diners leapt to their feet. The baby began to cry.

Kate knew that by tonight's end, she could easily find herself rotting in a jail cell for what might be months before any convictions were made against Ryuu. Those sorts of allegations against a corporate giant would require extensive research, panels of experts, independent laboratory testing. But, when it came to disorderly conduct, or disturbing the peace, an offender could probably be wearing an orange jumpsuit in less than an hour. If they caught her, that's what would happen. But Kate could not afford to be arrested. Not now. There was too much work to be done. They were going to have to catch her.

"Have you lost your mind?" Barton burst through the kitchen doors. "Shelby, call the police!" he shouted up to the hostess. "What in the Sam Hill do you think you're doing?"

"Saving lives!" Before Barton could lay a finger on her, Kate had already grabbed two fistfuls of his shirt. She swung him over her hip, and shoved him with such force that he stumbled sideways to collide headlong into a two-top. The male guest at the table had the strange presence of mind to snap out with one hand and save his beer at the penultimate moment, just as their table went toppling beneath the flailing manager.

Kate was already through the kitchen doors before Barton had hit the floor. Once inside, she seized a four-foot stainless steel paddle from a giant kettle of miso soup, and she rammed it through the inside handles of the double doors. No one would be coming in or going out. The kitchen was sealed from the inside. She snatched a fire extinguisher off the wall, yanked the cotter pin, and unleashed a yellow plume of retardant all over the griddles and grills. Cooks ran choking into the depths of the kitchen, as the room filled with the swirling fog. She made her way down the kitchen line, blasting every kettle and steamer that she passed, until she came to the walk-in cooler, where the supply of contaminated batter was stored.

"Get back!" she shouted at an encroaching chef, releasing a jet of retardant into his face. His little hat went flipping into the air. "Health department is on the way! This kitchen is being shut down!"

Kate backed into the freezer. There it was. She seized the wheeled rack that supported close to twenty white tubs from Emerald Coast Cannery. She dragged the cart out into the main aisle, locked down the rolling casters, and pushed the entire contraption over, right in front of the double doors. Barton's seething face sprayed motes of spittle against the other side of the little window. Tubs tumbled, rolled and split. Orange rivulets of crabby mixture spilled like guts from their ruptured sides. It gave Kate immense satisfaction to stomp every one of those white containers, until she was sure that they were all burst open and exposed on the kitchen floor. The fishy stench of the sea filled the kitchen. God, how she loathed that smell. As she stomped, her footprints squished wetly into the mix. Stringy morsels of contaminated crabmeat smeared the greasy kitchen tile, and dangled like hair from the bottoms of her shoes. Disgusting. She could not even imagine what life forms were squirming all over the soles of her feet. The sight and stench of the infested batch, exploded all over the floor, was just about enough to make Kate vomit, but she managed to keep it down. Aiming the fire extinguisher at the floor, she blasted the entire mess until the thing was spent. Cursing, she threw the empty canister across the steaming griddles, and then snatched up a two-gallon jug of bleach, from where it was housed on a shelf beneath one of the stainless counters.

Somehow, the fire extinguisher just did not seem sufficient. She couldn't bring herself to quit this place until she was certain that Barton couldn't produce another usable crab cake from this stock of inventory. The microscopic creatures were killers. They'd taken innocent lives, robbed families of their loved ones. Kate wasn't leaving until she was sure that every last parasite was dead. She spun the cap off the industrial sized jug, and upended it over the mess. Liquid death rained down upon the unseen monsters with every glug and spurt of the huge container. Astringent fumes burned Kate's nose and throat. She choked, but did not stop, until she had soaked every square inch of the mixture in concentrated bleach. Satisfied, jug emptied, she headed for the back of the kitchen.

It was almost impossible to see six feet ahead. Yellow reefs of flame retardant hung in the air like clouds of mustard gas. This was a war zone. It was a war against the worst side of nature, and its slimy corporate allies. Cooks scurried around her, or flattened against walls, as she stormed by. It felt good to be in control. She imagined that this was how guys like Quincy must feel, every single day of their lives, just walking around parting crowds, wherever they went. How great would that be? And how unfair, that all too often, it was the abusers of power who were entrusted with it.

She followed the glowing exit signs. Noticing a fuse box mounted on the wall, she paused to open the door, and to drop the main breaker. A collective scream rang out, as the restaurant was consumed by utter blackness. By feel, she yanked breakers, one at a time, and pitched them in all different directions, all around the lightless kitchen. She could hear them clattering against steel and sliding across the wet tiles. That ought to take them a while to sort out. Mission accomplished. Without so much as a backward glance, Kate slipped out the back door of Ryuu, and vanished into the balmy summer night.

It plunged its claws into the muddy sea floor, and dragged itself forward, another body length. It had been travelling in this manner for almost two days. By repeating this same cumbersome motion, it had managed to plow a wide track, from its empty nest all the way out to the volcanic vents. There was something wrong with its legs. They would no longer support the weight of its body. It was certain that it could still swim at its usual velocity, by pumping water through its gills, but that seemed like a waste of energy, when it had so little energy left. For weeks, all of its resources had gone into the production of manna. It still had a small reserve, but it intuited that it had better save that last bit until the very end, just in case the need would arise to defend its nest one last time.

This would be its final journey. The brood would be returning soon. And when they did, enveloped inside the protective bodies of their hosts, the time would come for it to give itself to them, body and soul, as its last parental sacrifice. Already, its faculties had begun the process of shutting down. Its vision was blurry. It was difficult to think. Its cognition was disrupted by emotional glitches, snippets of memory, and strange patches of blackness, from which it repeatedly emerged, angry and disoriented. It was as if some internal mechanism had been switched, one which triggered some sort of an irreversible countdown toward a sequence of events that had probably evolved, over untold millennia, to ensure that returning broods would be provided with a lasting meal.

It paused, drawing water through its vents. This was it. At last, it had arrived at its secret destination. Although it could not clearly see the remains of its life mate, it could detect the higher levels of ammonia in the water. It could sense the electric signatures emitted by the multitudes of crabs and benthic worms that had swarmed the gargantuan carcass for nearly three thousand years. They scuttled everywhere, these maggots of the deep that had been its only companions since its mate was slaughtered.

Once it located the body, now just a hollowed carapace, it extended its sensitive trunk. Tenderly, it explored every recess of the abandoned shell. Even after all these years, it could still detect familiar vestiges of its bygone friend. Through the caustic clouds of ammonia, there remained traces of the magnificent creature that its mate had once been. Powerfully nostalgic tastes and smells endured, prompting memories to flash through its mind with dazzling clarity. For fleeting instants, it perceived ghosts of lost youth, virility, and it how loved to taste the sweetness of those days, when their road ahead seemed to race to infinity.

Now, it was as if their formative years in the deep, their courtship dance, were but wonderful stories etched into the walls of time. It seemed so long ago. How had it all slipped by so quickly? Even though there were only the two of them stranded here in the lightless seas of this hostile alien world, its mate had still played hard to get. Although frustrating, at the time, this admirable trait was fondly remembered. For two thousand years, their dance endured, until at last, its mate had accepted their union. Together, they constructed their nest. They'd bred, and guarded their millions of precious eggs against those hordes of voracious crabs, defending their territory from larger creatures foolish enough to venture too near. They were a perfect pair, fearlessly devoted. Together, they became an island. Nothing beyond their intimate sanctuary mattered. They shared their emotions through songs, lights, electric pulses, until they were no longer two creatures, but one.

It crooned a lasting eulogy to such basal depths that no other creature of this world had the capacity to hear its private song. Its trunk caressed the empty shell of its mate, tracing the familiar scars and contours. It lipped the subtle grooves that had once pulsed so beautifully with fantastic shows of light. It recalled the favored array of colors produced by its life mate, that unique signature of intense emotions, projected throughout the depths. Even their unborn brood had understood this ancient harmony of light, song, and electric pulses, right through the walls of their shells, and they learned to pulse back, to communicate in that complex language that was unique to their kind since the beginning of time. It retracted its trunk, and it ended its song. Its underbelly pulsed slowly, with the deep violet light of mourning.

It did not want to go back to the nest, where it was going to die alone. It preferred to remain here, near the warmth of the vents, alongside the remains of its life mate. But if it did not return to the nest, if it failed to sacrifice its body to their brood, then their combined life's work over so many thousands of years would amount nothing. It could not remain here. Their bodies could never hope to be enmeshed in death, the way that their souls had been conjoined in life. Their carapaces would never lie hollowed on the sea floor, side by side, the way it was meant to be. No, they would be denied that rightful end to their life's story. Their reunion could not happen on this world. It would have to wait for the After.

With a blast of anguish that resounded through ocean trenches, stirred unseen avalanches throughout submerged mountain ranges, it imparted its last goodbye to the best and only friend it had ever known. This was its loudest, most passionate emission of its life, a sonic eruption that reverberated through the depths until its layered diaphragms were utterly compressed. And then, a moment of silence.

Violet waning to blue, the sorrowful pulses surged back into streaming sequences of light. It rotated its failing body back in the direction from which it had come, realigning itself with the track in the ocean floor. Raising its claws, it plunged them into the muck. A low pulse of red indicated its commitment to the direction of the nest. The brood was near. It could sense them, reaching out with its consciousness to connect with theirs. When it detected them, it experienced a new emotion, for the first time in its long life. It was fear—fear of its own offspring. They were not endowed with emotional attachment, or compassion for their single parent. Larvae were savage and selfish creatures, equipped with only the most basic instinct: the drive to feed. When they arrived, they would expect a large meal. The time had come to prepare for a slow and agonizing death, and for its journey into the After.

Chapter Eleven

Somewhere deep in the bowels of the building, a thermostat hit a programmed set point. A circuit board emitted a soft click. A tiny, yellow bulb illuminated. An electrical relay was activated. Inside an enormous air handler, the drum of a blower began to turn. As it picked up speed, its aluminum fins pushed chilled air through the maze of ductwork that spanned four floors, three wings, until it gushed through the grate in the ceiling of a darkened room. Blue curtains rippled in the new current of air, wimpling the glow of a streetlight through its folds, like the reflection of a full moon upon rippling water.

All of the patients lay still. Only the rise and fall of their throats betrayed the life inside their bodies. They were not sleeping. Their eyes were open. They seemed to be hovering, not unlike insects in that torpid state of inactivity that was not exactly sleep, not exactly wakefulness, but a sort of suspended animation between explosions of motion. Although their bodies remained utterly still, signs of internal activity belied their vegetative state. From beneath the bed sheets, came subtle pulses of light.

The living dead conspired. Connected by a thread of ghostly chatter, they exchanged unheard plans, and opinions, with respect to their situation. Their host bodies had been immobilized by those strappings upon their limbs. Dependent upon the moisture of their enveloping tissue, they could not abandon their fleshy vessels, or they would swiftly desiccate and die, but it was time to go. Every cell in their bodies cried out for the sea, for the nest, where a great feast awaited. Their rapid rate of growth required sustenance and more space. They were outgrowing their fleshy prison. The pulsing lights beneath the covers steadily synchronized, to a common hue and cadence. They had reached an agreement. If they did not rise tonight, then they would never rise. A sacrifice was required.

The head of the patient in bed number five swiveled from the window. Facing upward, toward the ceiling, his mouth fell open. The sheets that covered his body seemed to move with a life of their own, crawling and undulating. His eyes rolled back into his skull, as his neck arched back into his pillow. Trembling, swelling, his jaw seemed to unhinge as his chin dropped clear to his chest. Dark rivulets of blood rolled from his nostrils, down his cheeks, to drip from the lobes of his ears. Rosettes blossomed on the pillowcase where they fell. His throat ballooned. His cheeks tented. A glottal popping sound preceded the emergence of pale articulated legs. They hooked outward from the corners of his mouth, establishing secure footing, as more legs rose, flowering over his face, and around his chin. Like an elephantine spider, the parasite employed its legs as levers to drag its bulbous body up over the trembling man's tongue. Freed at last, the creature hitched forward to plop wetly upon the patient's chest, webbed with mucous and blood.

It rose shakily, on untested legs. The air was so dry. The environment, so hostile. Already, its flaccid skin was beginning to tighten. It did not have long. Blinking its cyclopean eye, it gazed back in the direction of its host's open mouth from which it had emerged. The jaws were already closing, as one of its brethren assumed the commanding position, and closed the gates. The newly birthed creature understood that there would be no return.

Lurching down the man's chest like a crushed insect, it dragged a dark trail of gore and slime all the way down his belly to his groin. The creature paused here, gills palpitating, as it studied the bonds around the patient's wrists and ankles. After a moment, it hitched weakly toward the nearest wrist. Engaging the padded strap, it unfolded its mantis-like forelegs, wielding pincers that sprung open like sets of razor shears. In one swift motion, a snipped restraint fell to the tiled floor.

Stacks coffee shop was slow, Sunday nights. Kate clasped her coffee cup in both hands. She sat with her back to the wall, one leg folded beneath her, while the other jiggled fitfully under the table. She'd chosen a corner booth, where she could remain partially hidden in the shadows of ferns and curtains, while utilizing a commanding view of the interior of the establishment. Here, she could watch both entry doors, as well as the parking lot. There were just two baristas on duty. The girl behind the counter sat on a stool, humped over her glowing tablet, while her coworker had remained in back for almost a half-hour.

Kate didn't know where else to go. She was afraid to go home, and she didn't want to go back over to Trinity. It wasn't Quincy or anyone else. She was just feeling a little paranoid, after sacking Ryuu's kitchen. On her first visit to the restaurant, she was pretty sure that she'd given Barton her full name. He'd seemed so agitated and distracted that she was almost certain that he wouldn't remember it, but without a doubt, he'd remember that she was a licensed paramedic, and that narrowed down his list of suspects. She had no idea how many licensed paramedics resided in Kansas City. However, whatever that number was, once you cut it down by around seventy percent to eliminate all the males, who dominated the physically demanding field, you weren't left with a whole lot of females. If there were a critical thinker amongst the investigators that were sure to be on this case, they would be able to track her down. It probably wouldn't take them very long to identify her, once they'd pulled up a list of names and photographs from the certified paramedic registry. All she had going for her was her change in appearance, hair length and color, since that photograph was taken.

She had no doubt that her buddy, Barton, would be looking to mount her head on his kitchen wall. He was a kind of loose cannon, hotheaded enough that she guessed he could make a pretty formidable adversary, if you ever gave him reason to decide to make you his pet project. He was nasty, proud, stubborn, and arrogant as hell. All of these qualities pretty much assured Kate that she would be facing assault and battery charges for laying her hands on him, as well as destruction of private property, trespassing, disorderly conduct … to name but a few. She could be in a whole lot of trouble. From a legal standpoint, Kate guessed that she wouldn't be pardoned for her actions, even if Ryuu was found guilty of serving contaminated food. The courts would look at the cases separately. And if she was caught, and found guilty of those charges, she would not only lose her job at Trinity, but she would not likely ever be hirable anywhere else. Like teachers, and cops, paramedics were held to a pretty high standard when it came to background checks.

Kate pressed her knuckles into her forehead, and sighed. She hadn't thought her actions through. She'd reacted emotionally. When she'd heard Mitch confirm the presence of unknown parasites, jumped into her jeep, and rushed straight off to Ryuu, she'd never considered how she might react if she found that they were still serving that stuff. She'd hoped that all the product would still be in the freezer, and that she would be able to talk Barton into destroying it, or waiting for a confirmation from the health department before serving it again. But that crap was sitting on people's plates, an infant's tray. People were shoveling it into their mouths right in front of her. The reaction she experienced to the sight of this blatant disregard to her warning was never in her playbook. Had she seriously considered the possibility that she might lose her cool, she could've planned a better strategy— although she had no idea what that strategy would have been. If someone was consuming poison, it was her job, as a medical professional to slap that poison out of their hand, but perhaps she had gone too far. Especially, by pushing Barton into that table.

Right now, he was probably sitting in his office, surrounded by police, who were photographing every bruise or chafe on his body. Kate hoped that he hadn't injured himself in that fall. Not just for her own sake, but for his, as well. She never meant to hurt anybody, but he was coming straight at her, hard and fast, and she was sure that he was a split-second from putting his hands on her. She just beat him to taking the initiative. Man, if only she'd let him grab her, push her around … what a game-changer that would've been. Rather than making her look like a psycho, Barton would have demonized himself. She felt like such an idiot.

Worst of all, by going berserk in that restaurant, Kate knew that she had just eliminated herself from any further involvement in this case. She could not even call the health department. They would require all the right information and that would lead directly to her arrest. Nope. She had officially bumped herself out of the loop, at least, on the Kansas City front. From this point forward, the ball would have to be carried by Sara.

Kate straightened up in her seat, as Sara's car rolled into the parking lot, and pulled into a slot next to her jeep. She could actually feel some of the weight sliding off of her shoulders. Kate had laid the groundwork, and now Sara, with her close emotional attachment to the case, could be the one to bring down the hatchet on Ryuu. Sara would have to begin working with Mitch, chasing down leads to other local merchants, closing off all of those potential valves that might still be spewing parasites into the populace. Kate had to admit, it saddened her a little bit to be passing the torch, stepping down, but what was done was done. Sara would understand. And Kate could still assist her with all of the research and the footwork, just so long as she remained off to one side of the stage. She just hoped that Sara would have it in her. Someone had to finish this.

Sara leapt out of her car without killing the headlights, and ran toward the front doors. Kate smiled, once she could see that Sara's poor right hand was now bound in a cast. Hopefully, her surgery had gone well. But as Sara ran closer, Kate noticed the tracks of mascara streaming down her cheeks, the sheen of hysteria in her eyes. Kate's expression slackened. The blood drained from her face. This did not look good. Something unexpected had happened. Kate's heartbeat picked up, as dread filled her chest like a cloud of caustic gas.

"Oh my God! Kate, come on!" Sara shrieked, as she burst through the side door. "Hurry!"

The barista behind the counter nearly leapt right out of her skin. Her coworker came skidding out the kitchen door, gawping one way, then another. Kate rose from the booth, feeling a little mortified by the glare of the spotlight that was suddenly blasting away every shred of her anonymity.

"Collin is gone! They're all gone!"

"Hey-hey-hey-hey …" Kate rushed to meet her at the door, if only to encourage her to lower her voice. "What the heck is going on?"

"All the patients in the room are gone!"

"No-no-no, they've probably just moved them." Kate urged her out the door, and into the parking lot. "One was already getting booked for pre-surgery, the rest to follow. Honey, they found this thing in their—"

"No!" Sara screeched, grabbing Kate by her shoulders. "They. Are. Gone. Gone!"

"What do you mean?"

"They've escaped! Broke their restraints and escaped the hospital. All of them are gone! Oh, my God, Kate! Where could Collin be?"

"Get in my jeep," Kate whispered, "I know where they're headed."

It was a lot easier with lights and sirens. Kate swerved through traffic like a professional stunt driver, flashing her bright lights and hammering her horn. A sudden stop. Brake lights everywhere. Squealing tires. Sara flew forward into the dash. Kate cranked the wheel hard right, and punched it. Her old CJ-7 hopped the curb, and with a rusty growl, took to the sidewalk. At least the sidewalks were clear at eleven o'clock on a Sunday night. Not a living soul anywhere, except at bus stops.

From Trinity Regional, Kate knew that the patients would orient themselves north. It was thirty blocks to the Missouri River, and they would travel just as the crow flies, straight, fast, and right over every obstacle in their path. Kate would never admit it to Sara, but she knew that there was a very good chance that one or more of them would be injured, even killed, during this insane migration. They would not stop for an oncoming bus, any more than those lawyers had feared a six-story fall from that catwalk. Again, thanks to the day and the hour, traffic was sparse. Nobody but Kate was in any kind of a hurry. Hopefully, God willing, they would survive this transit, and allow enough time for Kate to intercept them.

"How do you know they're going to the river?" Sara cried.

Kate shook her head, biting down on her bottom lip. She hadn't wanted to discuss this. It led to dark places, terrible ends. "That's just where they go, Sara."

"But how do you know that?"

Kate shot Sara a glance, and then looked away.

"What do they do once they get there?"

Both women screamed, as a transient lurched out of an alley, pie-eyed and reeling in their headlights. Kate mashed the brakes to the floor and leaned on the horn. It was only then that she realized her windshield wipers were running. By the time she'd figured out how to switch them off, the homeless man had vanished back into the shadows. Kate floored the accelerator and swerved off the sidewalk, back onto the road.

The most direct route to the river from Trinity would be Campbell, or Charlotte, but unlike the runaways, the jeep would not be able to run along the shoulders of the expressway, or bisect the River Market through the turnstiles and closed lots. They would have to get around all of it, somehow, and hopefully head them off, down on the riverfront. Kate was already contemplating what she might have to restrain them. Without her ambulance and her usual gear, she was limited to whatever crap might be in her jeep. She knew that there were a set of jumper cables in back.

"Hey, look behind you," Kate said. "There's a tool bag behind your seat. Check and see if it has any plastic cable ties in it."

"Any what?"

"You know, those—those plastic zippy ties."

Sara struggled to unbuckle her safety belt with her crippled right hand. She winced a couple of times, while fighting the buckle with her badly swollen fingers. Once freed, she turned around in her seat. "Well, aren't you going to tell me? What do they do once they get to the river?"

"Sara, please! We just have to catch them before they get there, okay?"

"How much about all of this do you know that you're not telling me?"

"I haven't had time to tell you! I'm trying to drive at a high rate of speed, right now, but I swear to God, I will tell you everything that I know just as soon as we get through this!"

Sara returned to her seat with a handful of the plastic zip-straps. "Are these what you were wanting?" she asked, as she buckled herself.

Kate nodded. Who would've thought she'd ever use that tool bag. It had been a gift from her father. When she left home, transferring from Barber County Ambulance up to Trinity, her dad had worried terribly. He was a farmer, master of all things that walked, crawled or grew upon his land, but he was completely cowed by the city. Her dad was a great mechanic, and he'd put in hundreds of hours beneath the hood of her jeep. God only knew what the man did under there, but he'd always kept that motor purring like a kitten. In the years since she'd left home, it never sounded half as healthy. The day before she left, he'd given her the tool bag, assuring her that he'd stocked it with just about anything she'd ever need, for any roadside emergency. But, even Dad couldn't have seen this one coming.

Went ahead and stocked her all up with cable ties, Katydid, case you ever got to wrestle down a danged mer-zombie, 'fore he gets to the river.

The river …

Kate's knuckles tightened. Booted out of the moment, her focus was gone. Her mental maps, her self-awareness, even her sense of identity, it all dissolved into a sort of cold, viscous goo that always preceded an anxiety attack. It was a condition impermeable to rational thought, a cognitive barrier that inhibited quick decisions, delayed responses. Her right foot unconsciously lightened. The speed of the jeep began to drop. She could sense that Sara was going to look at her, questioningly, moments before she actually did. Kate dreaded that moment of scrutiny. When Sara's head turned, as she knew it would, sweeping that stare her way, her anxiety skyrocketed into terror. A private attack was bad enough, but when she was being watched, thereby increasing the outside pressure with another person watching something go horribly wrong with her mind, it made her heart slam against her sternum until she feared she might go into cardiac arrest.

"What are you doing?"

She heard Sara's voice. It was piercing in her ear, but she could not verbalize a response. Her whole body was going numb. Not by degrees. It was plummeting. She felt hollowed, then like she was shutting down, lips tingling, going into shock.

"What's the matter? Kate! Why are you stopping?"

Kate didn't even realize that she had allowed the jeep to roll to a stop, but now that she saw that she'd stopped alongside the curb, there was nothing she could do about it. She could only gasp for breath and try to still her thudding heart. Her arms clung woodenly to the steering wheel. She felt utterly disconnected from her body, as if she were sitting on someone else's lap, looking at the outstretched arms of another being.

"Kate!" Sara grabbed her by the forearm.

"Something's wrong ... can't breathe ..." Kate whispered. She was disconnected from her own voice. She couldn't tell if she was actually talking or just hearing herself think. Somehow, her lifelong phobia of deep water had just gotten worse. Much worse. Kate was no psychologist, but she'd hoped that her recent riverside incident might have forced some exposure to her greatest fear, even lessened it. Obviously, that was not the case. Probably because of the fatal outcome, the experience had only validated her terror, amplified it.

"Do you want me to drive?" Sara asked. "Seriously. You're panicking. I'll drive." Sara popped her passenger door and bailed out.

That rush of night air helped, the open door, the change in the terrible direction of things. Kate's level of terror dropped by a substantial margin, and some rational thought crept in. Those strange manikin arms became hers again. She loosened her grip on the wheel. She reconnected to her body, and at last, she could breathe.

The driver's door opened. Sara was there, bathed in streetlight. "Come on. Hop out. I grew up in KC, you know. You want the fastest route down to the river?"

"But, your broken hand ..."

Sara snapped her left fingers. "Scoot over."

Kate shifted the jeep into Park, and then clambered over the console to dump herself into the passenger seat with a grunt of relief. Sara climbed in. She slammed the door, dropped it into gear, and swung back out onto the street. This was strange. Kate didn't think that she'd ever sat in the passenger seat of her own vehicle, let alone watch someone else drive it. It was more than a little disorienting, but it seemed to be taking her mind off of the anxiety attack.

Kate allowed her eyelids to close partway, and leaned her head in the slack of her seatbelt harness. The darkly villous forms of trees, and blinding streetlights, lulled her into something of a trance. She had failed. Completely failed. This thing, this personal demon of hers, it seemed as though it would always find a way to win, to beat her down, to make her feel sub-human and crazy. This was why Kate was kind to homeless people. She understood what it was to be powerless, trapped like a buzzing fly against a windowpane, forever able to watch that world of normal happy people flowing by, but forever prevented from joining it. She understood how the demoralizing effects of poverty could irreparably break human beings, and that's why she never judged them. Not even the raving ones, shuffling down the unlit allies, or the ones who slept in parks, snuggling with a bottle, forever trapped in a world and in a mind that never quit trying to destroy them. She didn't begrudge the ones who dialed 911 in the middle of the night, when they reached a point of absolute despair, when pushing those three buttons was their little prayer, their Hail Mary, for just a taste of that caring human contact that was, through no fault of their own, forever denied them. It was Kate's greatest fear, that despite all her efforts, her personal demon would ultimately destroy her.

"Are you alright?" Sara asked.

Kate felt the rough weight of a casted hand upon her shoulder. She felt the warmth of swollen fingertips. She was able to come up from the depths again for a single breath. But could she remain at the surface or would she sink back down again? Her failure was like a pair of concrete boots. Only Sara's broken hand was holding her head above water.

"I need you to please stay with me, Kate. I can't do this alone. Please."

Kate turned toward Sara. Her own throat suddenly choked her. Tears spilled down her cheeks. "I'm afraid of water," Kate cried. She fell forward, sobbing into her hands.

It was the first time in her life that she had ever told anybody. It was the first time in her life that she had ever said it out loud. Now, hiding behind her hands, she could not stop crying. "My little brother drowned."

The hard casted hand rubbed her back, until she at last stopped heaving, and was able to suck shortened breaths. She wiped her eyes, and apologized. But the casted hand did not leave her, or judge her for her breakdown. It stayed.

"You were trying to keep it a secret, Kate, and that's why you panicked. Now that you were brave enough to tell me, and I know about it, it's okay. Right?"

Kate breathed deeply, staring at nothing. She blinked her eyes. Sara was right. Now that she'd told her, it seemed better. Not gone, but so much better. She almost wanted to smile, and oddly, even chuckle about it. Instead, Kate just nodded. It was going to be alright.

Sara wheeled onto Twenty-Second. She gunned the jeep eastward, toward the expressway overpass. As she passed beneath, she cranked left onto the northbound ramp.

"Wait-wait," Kate said, wiping her eyes, straightening up in her seat. "These people are travelling on foot. We're going to lose them downtown."

"No we won't. They're going to run right into the loop on the north side of downtown, before they ever make it to the river. There's only a few ways across. The nearest is up here at Locust."

Kate hadn't even considered the loop as a barrier to northbound pedestrians. The loop was a confluence of several major highways that roared through a common funnel around the north end of downtown. It was a fifty foot drop from street level, down to the converged highways, that separated downtown from the River Market area. Sara was right. Based on a direct route of travel, from Trinity Regional to the riverfront, the Locust overpass would be their only safe route over the five lanes of roaring traffic. Presuming, of course, that these runaways would choose a safer route over a more direct one. Kate could not bring herself to admit to Sara that there was a distinct possibility that instead of using the Locust overpass, they would leap from the railing, and to their deaths.

"Just hurry," Kate said.

Sara floored the accelerator up the ramp onto the expressway. Traffic was light. Beneath the shoaling clouds, twinkling reefs of skyscrapers rose into view. Streetlights winked on and off in the dark trenches that rifted the structural ridgelines. At the heart of the city, shimmering streams of cars encircled the domed downtown arena, like a colony of microscopic life forms, orbiting a great polyp.

Kate retrieved a handful of plastic zip-ties from where Sara had dropped them on the floorboards. She stuffed a wad of them into the back pocket of her jeans. Kate alone knew what they were up against. She'd witnessed firsthand the indomitable will of the infested, their surprising speed and strength, and their fearlessness in the face of death. They would stop at nothing to reach the river.

Now, empowered with her knowledge of the organism that was propelling them toward the river, and then, to the sea, Kate was of the opinion that these people were not drowning. They were swimming. Somehow, they were managing to swim all the way to the sea. Because if they'd drowned within minutes, or within hours of entering the water, their bodies would have been turning up along the shores of the Missouri River, anywhere between KC and Saint Louis. But they weren't. None of them was. They were turning up in the Gulf of Mexico, near Destin in the exact place where Collin—or, at least, the entity within Collin—had pointed out to her on the map.

Based on all the imagery that she'd seen in the diagnostics lab, the creature lodged in the throats of these patients was blocking their esophagus and their airways. The organism was in complete control. It controlled their minds, their bodies, and everything that entered and left it, including air, food and water. It permitted them to breathe and speak, only when it saw fit. When they did speak, it was the creature that was speaking, accessing their mental files to borrow the vocabulary that it needed to communicate. Kate hadn't had time to carefully examine the photograph that she'd snapped, but it seemed only logical that these creatures must utilize their own diaphragms, or vents, to open and close their victim's blocked airways to enable them to inhale, exhale, and to speak. Since this monster was designed for life in the open ocean, those vents would also contain gills.

Kate's eyes widened. It was all beginning to make sense now. Once those creatures had prompted their hosts to make apparent suicidal plunges, they were breathing for them. They would have to. They would have to breathe for them with their gills, transporting oxygen to their host's brain. All of the necessary biomechanics were in place to perform such a feat. All it required was just a little imagination.

"We can't take him back to the hospital," Kate said.

"What? What are you talking about?"

"That's why I wanted to meet with you, tonight. They've discovered something, Sara. Collin doesn't have a psychological problem. None of them do. They all have something inside him. It's a parasite." Kate was failing miserably at stifling the wavering inflections of fear and revulsion in her voice, and she knew it. "It's something new. It's something no one has ever seen before. And there's no surgical plan to remove it."

"What do you mean no surgical plan? What kind of parasite is this?"

"I'm not trying to scare you, but I think it's time you need to know what's ahead of us. It cannot be safely removed, not without losing the patient. It has to decide come out on its own."

"What are we supposed to do then? Where are we supposed to take him?"

"I've found a—a sort of specialist, for this sort of thing. He's down in Florida."

"Florida?"

"I think it's his best chance. It's the only real chance Collin's got right now."

The jeep roared down the city's flank, and into the first convergence of highways. Traffic thickened. Kate knew this area all too well. They were approaching a dangerous interchange, where drivers faced short distances between splits in the confluence to make their decisions, where cars sometimes had to cut across three or four lanes in order to make critical exits, or else be washed downstream in the flow of traffic before being able to turn back around. The downtown loop could be a deadly place. Due to the high speeds and logistical chaos, it was the site of a lot of fatal accidents. Kate looked up the racing walls to the guardrails fifty feet above. If anyone was looking for a place to make a suicidal jump, she could think of no better place than this one. With the height of the fall, the river of congested traffic below, there would be no chance of survival.

"Oh, my God!" Kate cried, pointing up to the rail. "There they are!"

The jeep swerved wildly across the lanes, as Sara panicked. Another vehicle yanked out of their way. The angry blast of a semi's horn filled the corridor, followed by the downshifting growl of air brakes. Sara punched it in a deranged effort to beat the massive machine to the next exit ramp. With only inches to spare between the semi's chrome grill and a concrete piling, she squeezed the jeep through the tightening gap for a roller coaster ride of an exit down into the River Market.

"What are you doing?" Kate cried. "They're over there on the other side!" She cranked her head over her shoulder to see the pale forms of a pack of strange runners. Some trailed their flapping hospital gowns. Others wore nothing at all. But thank God, they weren't jumping. They were following the curve of the upper frontage road, following the guardrail right down to the head of the Locust overpass.

"I'm going to head them off up here at Locust. Did you see Collin? Was he with them?"

"I don't know! I couldn't tell." Kate unbuckled her seatbelt, and then grabbed the handle of her passenger door. "Just get me up near the intersection and let me out."

"I'm getting out, too!"

"You can't! Your hand is broken, Sara!"

"I don't care!"

"You'll only pressure them. Trust me, if they see us, if they know they're running toward a trap, then they might to do something stupid. We've got to let them make it safely over the loop before we approach them."

"But we can't let them make it to the river, Kate!"

"I know. Just let me out, up here. You head right. Get down a couple of blocks and cut off the headlights. If he gets past me, you'll be the safety net."

Sara slid up next to the curb at the four-way stop at sixth and Locust. She turned to Kate, with a look of absolute desperation. "Don't let Collin get away. Please!"

Kate popped the passenger door, dropped out onto the street. She slammed the door and took a last look at Sara's tearful face as the jeep turned and sped away into the darkness of the River Market.

Kate hustled off the pavement, and onto the grassy shoulder. She goose-stepped through the shrubbery that bordered the rail, overlooking the streaming chaos of the loop far below. She hunkered down in the mixture of cypress mulch, spat gum, and cigarette butts, and listened to the dull moan of traffic down in that trench. Ghostly tendrils of steam slithered up into the night around the seal of a manhole cover. She reached around behind her, checking to make sure that the handful of tie-straps were still protruding from her hip pocket. They were. She'd perhaps had stranger nights, but there were not many.

If the whole pack of runners poured past her all at once, it might be difficult to single Collin out. She wished that she could save them all, but she could only save one, and he was the one who mattered the most. He appeared to be the youngest of the infected. It made sense that the demographic appeared to be mostly older, wealthier victims. Ryuu was extremely expensive. In fact, Collin and Sara would not likely have ever dined there, had their dinner not been for such a special occasion. Collin was Patient Zero, so far as Kate was concerned. He was her first encounter with that hidden puppet master, from the Gulf. It was through Collin that she had spoken with something else, something unnatural. That's what was beginning to trouble her now, more than anything else, about this bizarre case. There was an intangible, yet identifiable, aspect of intelligence involved. However, it was an intelligence to which she could not relate. It was otherworldly, this dark mind hiding behind the screen, pulling all of these people's strings from the other side of some barrier, between its world and the world of humans that it manipulated.

Kate peeked up from her shrubbery and stared across the trench to the other side of the loop. There they were. Kate's heart began to drum inside her chest, chugging blood through her carotid arteries, pounding inside her ears. Her mouth went dry, and her hands began to shake, as the pack of runners followed the flow of the urban map, out onto the overpass.

Kate ground the balls of her feet into the mulch and put her knuckles on the ground. They were coming. Her lungs drew shots of the humid night air, and her whole body began to quiver, but this was no anxiety attack. This was pure adrenaline.

All at once, she could see him. Collin. He was at the head of the pack. Being the youngest, most physically fit, it should not have surprised her that he'd be leading the charge. His gait was stiff and strange, as though whatever controlled the movements of his body was not accustomed to maintaining the balance and fluidity of motion required by the upright human form.

Twenty feet and closing. Kate's eyes narrowed like those of a jungle cat, poised to spring. Ten feet. She grit her teeth and bore down hard against the mulch, as the roar of an oncoming CJ-7 jeep engine blazed down upon the intersection with blinding highway brights.

Kate lunged.

She collided with her star-struck target with such force that she heard the crack of ribs as Collin folded clean over her at the midsection. He went down hard, flat on his back. His skull whacked dully against the pavement. The other runners split around them. He was fighting her. He too strong to hold, preventing her from retrieving a zip-tie from her hip pocket. Kate could only hug tightly to his waist, her legs intertwined with his, as he bucked and flailed on the warm pavement like a fish out of water. As the other runners disappeared into the night, from Collin's throat came the most lugubrious wail, an unearthly, indignant howl. Kate was losing him. He was pulling free. However, when his lovely bride's silhouette suddenly appeared, backlit by blazing headlamps, she dealt him a casted right cross to his gaping jaw, knocking Collin out cold.

Chapter Twelve

Home. The only home it had ever known. Exhausted from the labors of its last excursion from the nest, it managed to drag itself to the crater's rim, where it collapsed to the sea floor in a cloud of mud. This had always been one of its favored perches, overlooking its massive graveyard of fallen enemies. These were its trophies. All encrusted with benthic life, masts jutted at strange angles from the ribbing of ancient ships and bygone creatures, ensnarled like the petrified forests of some moonscape. It had always performed its expected duty to defend its territory and its mate, to collect and amass war trophies all around its nest as a symbol of status, as a display of strength, and as a warning to those rivals that might have challenged its dominion, had any rivals ever existed. However, in this world, no challengers had ever come.

Hundreds of sharks circled overhead. They sensed something. Compelled by that strange certainty innate to all scavengers, they lurked, with their morbid sense of entitlement to an impending feast, whenever something majestic begins to stumble. Their shadows slithered over the bramble, over the hulls of steel ships that it had wrestled into the depths, the aircrafts that it had swatted right out of the sky with focused blasts of sound. It had dragged them all back here, sometimes from places that were oceans away. It had been a tremendous lifelong effort, but as it gazed out over the wreckage, it felt a deep sense of satisfaction.

Its breathing was erratic and labored. There was no doubt that its life was slipping. Soon, it would depart this dark and lonely world, following its life mate, and those thousands of lives that it had vanquished into the After. As it looked out across its collection of trophies, the balance of its entire life, it began to wonder, what did any of this matter in the end? Every triumph and agony of its whole existence was about to be reduced to so much fodder for scavengers. In the end, it was to be only a great heap of flesh for the crabs and benthic worms. And just like this jungle of bones, on the sea floor, it would be hollowed and forgotten, a barnacle encrusted carapace, indistinguishable from the rest of this mess. It would simply rot away, alongside those thousands that it had destroyed. No one would miss it. No one would ever come to honor it, just as no one had ever come to mourn or avenge its thousands of victims, and why not? Suddenly, it felt not pride over its collection, but rather, an empty empathy. None of the surface dwellers had ever seemed to care that it had destroyed them, which seemed to mean that it had never been any better than them. Not in the end. None of it had ever mattered in the grandest sense. For all of its show of power and dominance over the millennia, its war against the surface dwellers had somehow gone unnoticed. None of it had ever amounted to anything. It had lived undiscovered, unrecognized, and would die unnoticed. This world would simply go on without it, as if it had never been here at all.

As its breath slowed, it noticed something undulating down through the gloom. Its pupil dilated. They were returning. Its great eye widened and the pace of its breathing increased. Its children, enveloped in the flesh vessels of host bodies, were coming home. And the bodies that its offspring had chosen were none other than those of the surface dwellers.

The creature rose from the sea floor, trumpeting a welcome to the brood. Like a hatch of descending souls, they wriggled downward, flickering with joyful strobes of the life within them, the twinkling stars of the next generation. The unexpected choice of host body brought it so much pleasure that its entire carapace radiated with bluish effervescence, a beacon that set the whole graveyard aglow. And there came another, and another ... dozens of surface dwellers, their thin appendages wimpling like flagella. Of all the possible life forms on this planet that its brood might've overtaken, it would be these reviled things that were chosen to host their own destruction, elected as the unwilling ushers of a new beginning, a glorious dawn in the wake of their erasure.

One of the sharks took a sudden interest in a descending host body. The great fish wheeled about in the crimson ribbons that unfurled skyward, from the eye sockets of the surface dweller's collapsing skull. These ridiculous creatures were not designed for the pressures of the deep, nor could they likely withstand the bite of a shark. They were frail and weak, and they would not provide much protection for their precious cargo. As the shark flanked the swimmer, unhinging its jaws for an exploratory bite, the creature reared up from the gloom, finding new reserves of strength in its devotion to the brood. A barnacled claw lashed out to transect the body of the shark in one effortless snap. Two halves of what had so recently been a whole predator pirouetted down into the boneyard, billowing plumes of blood.

The creature spread its diaphragms, filling its bladders with seawater. Pulsing with red strobes of hatred, it rotated skyward, aiming its frontal vents in the direction of the hundreds of scavenging fish. It then compressed itself, emitting a deafening blast that left every shark stunned and shivering. They fell, all of them at once, fatally damaged by the sonic shockwave. Nothing that sought to bring harm to its brood would be tolerated. Pulsing like a thermal vent, the creature pumped black clouds of silt and rattled its saber claws. It would not die. Not yet. It would live to protect its children, to see that every one of them made it safely down into the reservoir of manna that would feed and house them until they were large enough to defend territories of their own.

As it watched them, its children, bucking down through the gloom, it understood that its existence had not been for nothing. Its lifelong efforts would have purpose. The collection would be its legacy. This place, this vast field of wreckage, would be its lasting message to the next generation. Its offspring would leave this sanctuary before they were old enough to understand or appreciate it. They would leave to wander the seas of the world, seeking mischief, and mates. However, when their breeding time arrived, they would return to this site of their hatching, just as their kind had always done. Then, they would look upon this collection with their matured eyes, and they would at last understand these ancient customs, scribed upon the sea floor like sacred passages. They would behold this field of wreckage as an unmistakable message, left by a bygone elder to its offspring, and they would know something of their mighty parent. They would understand what it meant to be one of their kind. The brood, as one legion, would then depart this place of learning to spread throughout all the seas of this world. They would battle for territories, amass trophy collections of their own, excavate nests, and fill them with billions and billions of eggs.

Drowning in a wheat field was all that Kate could remember of the dream that jolted her awake on some nameless stretch, to the strobe of highway lights that rushed by with blinding regularity. Nowhere was safe in a world where babies drowned in the hearts of deserts, where a woman's worst fears would always find her. No matter how far she ran, solid ground could always yawn wide to receive her, to draw her down through that rip in the vast flaxen carpet, that tear in her reality, to drag her screaming from a world of wheat and sunshine, down into lightless depths that sucked hungrily at her legs, filled her lungs, and crushed her skull. And although it hadn't revealed itself in the dream, Kate knew what was down there, lurking, biding its time, waiting for her, at the end of the ride.

She was literally on a highway to Hell. She knew it. And in the end, the demon was going to win. There was no alternate route. No way around destiny. No detour. No matter how hard she struggled to believe otherwise, when life's ride ended, her worst nightmare would be waiting for her, ready to receive her immortal soul like a dark groom in some prearranged marriage.

Kate's state of mind was deteriorating again. She recognized the signs, like a drop in temperature, just before a storm. She was disconnecting, able to hear Sara's words, but unable to understand them, the first, second, and sometimes the third time. It was the strangest feeling, going insane. Numbed, distracted, detached from the present, because the better part of her was already clenched in the future's icy grip. They were travelling further than she'd ever been from home, over the borders of one state and into the next. With every stream they forded, every river they crossed, all swirling darkly in that fluid network to the next confluence, where systems merged roiling into greater systems, the dread inside her grew. Despite her commitment to Collin and Sara, and her resolve to perform whatever functions were demanded of her role in this situation, she could not escape the gravity that drew her beyond herself, beyond the jeep, her partner, and her patient, inexorably toward the end. Distractive tactics were pointless in this situation, because Kate knew that by dawn's break, she would be thrown up against the earth's greatest reservoir of water. For the first time in her life, and under the worst possible circumstances, she was going to face the ocean.

They rarely stopped. Driving through the first sleepless night and into the next day's traffic, they passed through tollbooths, some automated, some manned. In those places, watchful sentinels dealt appraising stares that always seemed to drift toward the back seat, where Sara clung to her betrothed's growling husk, whose restrained wrists wore bracelets of exposed meat and blackened blood beneath folds of shed hide.

These were the longest miles, accompanied by inhuman howls and worsening odors, which forced them to shun public areas, to fuel quickly from the furthest pump. Loathe to remain in sight of a stranger beyond those couple of terrifying minutes, they were soon back on the road again. Back roads were a worse prospect than the major highways, which at least afforded them some degree of anonymity. They could not be stopped or questioned, being so soiled with the gore of their screaming captive.

They pulled alternating shifts. One took the wheel, while the other wrestled with the thing that never ceased to writhe, wail and fight a gruesome battle against plastic bonds that sliced deeper and deeper into flesh with every twist of the wrists. He never rested. He nearly brought their journey to a tragic end, during their terrible crossing of the Mississippi River, south of Memphis, where his bucking became so violent that Kate could hardly contain him, where the button eyes of a small child gleamed through the window of a passing van, as their jeep swerved across the center line to the far shoulder, and back again.

The nearer they drew to their destination, the more combative it became, the thing inside him, twice emerging from his throat in the town of Tupolo, thrashing pale tendrils and squalling like a cat until Sara fit him with a gag fashioned from a wadded sock and her bra. Despite these measures, his howls were so earsplitting that an escape hastily made from the sliding window of a drive-through line, where an acne-spangled teen gaped down at something that he should never in his life have beheld. A spray of blood bejeweling their rear window, they quit that place, tires smoking, with the women's crazed eyes all awash with the dread paranoia of new murderers. Unfed, they pushed onward.

By the Alabama border, knobs of bone were exposed. They were stark and pale in the widening channels of rent flesh. They exited to wash in a creek, and to fashion new and padded restraints from ripped strips of their clothing before attempting to sever the plastic bonds that had disappeared beneath flaccid cuffs of skin. However, the headlights of an approaching pickup found them grimacing like sinners before the baleful eyes of God. By arms and legs, they dragged him, abandoning their efforts, to reload, crank the wheel, and drive hard the way they came. Nevertheless, their pursuer gained, headlamps electrifying their mirrors with blinding light as the pickup tailed them so closely as to fill them with terror. Nosing their rear bumper, snaking from side to side, the driver seemed a deranged lawman, some backwoods vigilante with a vendetta against women, or vehicles with out-of-state tags. The midnight game persisted, with flung bottles smashing, and vehicles fishtailing through the dirt, until the truckload of drunken cowboys forced their way alongside them, tongues fluttering between fingers, whooping heads of men, crazed with alcohol and the thrill of the chase, the race they thought they'd won, until they left the women cursing and sobbing in a billow of dust.

The first light of the second dawn found them on the road to Mobile, filthy, hollow-eyed and knotted from twenty hours of misery. And still, the thing in the back seat continued to scream. It screamed and it screamed. Restrained facedown with crossed belts, it screamed through the sodden rag that reeked of its nameless fluids. It screamed into the bend of Kate's arm. It screamed at the filtered light of the rising sun. A storm was brewing. The face once worn by young Collin Stillwell had devolved into the most hideous mask, encrusted with blood, twisted with its alien emotions into an unrecognizable countenance of pure misery. It wanted out. It ballooned his throat and tented his cheeks with its pressing tendrils. The eyes once owned by Collin were hemorrhaged red as the liquid that dripped from his wrists, bubbled from his nostrils. He was dying.

Kate rubbed away tears as she sent another text of their whereabouts to Mitch Poole, the only person in the world who could possibly validate her decision to bring this patient here. It had seemed the best treatment plan, back in Kansas City, but she could never have imagined how his condition would so dramatically deteriorate over their journey. He didn't even look human, anymore. God, if Collin died, and those hospitalized back at Trinity actually survived their surgeries, Kate would never forgive herself. Her career was over. She could never go back to Trinity. Whether or not Kate had ruined her life in addition to her livelihood, remained to be seen. The whole gamble depended on a person she'd never met, a person whose credentials and expertise she'd never once thought to question.

Now, it all seemed so insane. How could she have talked Sara into this? It had to have been little Jeffrey again, still manipulating her, from afar. She knew now that she could no longer trust herself or her judgment as a medical professional. Because in any life threatening situation, little Jeffrey would be there, affecting her decisions, prodding her to break every rule, every code, if only to prevent a single death on her watch. When a patient's death couldn't be prevented, it was Jeffrey who consoled her, assuring her that every Code Blue was just an accident beyond her control. In this case, if anything went wrong, there was no higher power to which Collin's death could be neatly attributed. It was all her. She'd eloped with this patient, against the advice of the region's brightest surgeons. If he died, this was hers to own. The trouble was, after all she'd spent owning little Jeffrey's death, the loss of Collin Stillwell was going to come at a price that she couldn't afford.

"Please, God," Kate whispered, as they merged into Mobile's morning rush, "please don't take this man." The red slit of a rising sun glowered hotly through skeins of mist that floated beneath the leaden skies. "Please let him live. Oh, God, let him live."

When Collin's visage went feral, the air was dank and heavy. Veins jagged his flesh like bolts of lightning, and his sanguine eyes rolled in their dark hollows. Fat droplets of rain spattered against the windshield. One seatbelt snapped, at the first thunderclap. Before Kate could look up from her phone, a bloodied pair of hands was clenched around her throat.

Horns blew as the jeep swerved, sliding two-wheeled through sheets of rain. Trundling thunder muted their screams. Kate was forced down to the floorboards, growling like a mongrel and pushing back against the monster with both of her feet. At last, she kicked free from his grip, pinning against the roll cage what looked for all the earth to be a flesh-crazed zombie, backlit by the wild play of lightning. His head snapped forward, jaws unhinged. Ropes of sallow mucous swung from his chin, as some sight, just ahead transfixed the monster. Seizing the unexpected opportunity, Kate threaded a zip-tie between his lowered wrists. With one quick jerk, she affixed the new bond to a loose seatbelt buckle, securing those eager hands to the seat.

Enraged by the trick, he thrust his pelvis skyward, trying to snap the fetter. He pulled so hard against those makeshift manacles that Kate was sure he'd strip the hide right off his hands like a pair of disposable gloves. She dove, hugging him tightly around his waist, trying with all the strength she could muster to drag the bloodied maniac back down, and out of public view. The monster began to beat its head against the rear window, striking the glass with such force that it webbed, stamping the pane with prints of ruddy gore.

"Pull him down! He's going to break the glass!"

"I can't!"

She'd no strength left in her limbs to wrestle a body that was so empowered by indomitable will. The thing inside him never tired, never slept, and required no food or water beyond that which it borrowed from its host. It rationed nothing, burning every last calorie of energy in its Collin's body, as if there were limitless reserves. But Kate knew better. She could see by the darkening skin of his ankles that Collin's organs were shutting down. But his puppeteer thrived, harping its host's strings like a devil's fiddle until Collin's head smashed backwards through the glass. Turtling his neck through the jagged aperture, the beast howled up Collin's throat into the tempestuous sky. Sprayed by invigorating rains, the creature whipped its writhing tendrils around the gag. Kate moaned when she spotted what had the monster so excited. The jeep roared up onto the bridge that crossed over Mobile Bay.

"Kate!" Sara shrieked, "Do something!"

Kate had slid down into her seat, paralyzed with terror. The horns of following vehicles blasted. Collin was arched backwards through the window, as far as his harness would allow him, oscillating his trunk from side to side, as if he were swimming through the rain. Pale tendrils flowered from his mouth to splay permissively over his forehead and cheeks, as though the monster inside him was relishing the torrent. Beyond, on all sides, the sea's rolling black abyss raced to every horizon.

"Kate! It's the sea, isn't it?" Sara reached back between the seats and clenched Kate's hand. "I've got you, if you've got him. Please! I've got you and I won't let go."

It was no use. Kate could not, by any power, owned or borrowed, break free of her paralysis. It felt as though she had a great weight upon her chest. Her breath would not come. She was drowning in fear.

Collin's head whipped back and forth like a dog shaking the life from some small animal. Blood streamed from his nostrils back past his ears, when the gag was snipped free. The halved bra and wadded sock flew off into the downpour, and a smile could almost be seen, crimping the corners of Collin's gaping mouth. A dark and blinking eye rose from his throat, to peer over the lipped rim of its hollow.

"Hey, you!" Sara shouted. "You, in there. If you can hear me, we're taking you home. Don't you realize that? We're taking you back to the sea!"

Sullen and dripping, Collin slumped with a grunt back into his seat. His head cocked. Those bloodstained eyes blinked at Sara. With a squelch of wet suction, the dangling monster withdrew back into his throat. The last curling tentacle retracted between his lips, and his sprung jaws slowly closed.

Sara smiled uneasily over her shoulder. "You didn't know? That's all we're doing. We're just taking you home. To the sea."

For the first time in two days, the thing quietened. Even Kate was able to break her trance enough to take notice, and turn her head in Collin's direction. She could hardly believe what she was seeing. The fight in him was gone.

"The sea," he croaked.

"Yeah. That's right. We're all going to the sea."

Kate straightened up in her seat. She could see land just a few miles ahead. They were almost across the bay. At last, the weight lifted, and she could breathe again. Filling her burning lungs with air, she stole a glance at the ocean's rolling vastness. It undulated like a wheat field in the prairie wind. She heard Sara laugh, as she felt something of a smile begin to spread across her face. The sea, it was not really alien to her life experience, after all. It almost reminded her of home in its flat and unbroken expanse.

"We're going to make it, Kate." Sara squeezed her hand. "One more hour, and we're in Destin."

Kate looked from Sara's jubilant face to Collin's mask of dripping horror, and she couldn't help but to allow a small chuckle. She squeezed Sara back, and then clambered off the floorboards, and into her seat. It was true. They were actually going to make it. With a breakthrough in the final hour, Sara had somehow found a way to calm the upset thing. After all their attempts to gag, bind, and wrestle it into submission, just like a couple of stupid guys, all they ever had to do was reason with the creature. It was almost funny.

The morning sun blazed through the breaking clouds, to glisten warmly upon Collin's drenched face. Kate smiled at him. Yeah, he was looking a little scruffy. Rode hard and put away wet. But his injuries all appeared to be survivable. After his ordeal, he'd need rehydration and rest, but he would live, so long as the little monster left peacefully. For the first time since they'd left Kansas City, Kate had a good feeling about that, and about her decision to drive him all the way here. It was going to leave him without putting up a fight. She had to believe this. She needed something to believe in after all they'd been through. Things were going to work out. There would be a happy ending.

"Want to come sit up here?" Sara asked. "I think he's all good."

Kate squeezed through the space between the front seats, and plopped into the passenger side. Still awestruck by the new cards they'd just drawn, she could not bring herself to look away from the sea. It was so huge. The biggest thing she'd ever seen. Too huge to be measured, or compared in scale to anything else but the open plains. The biggest difference was that the plains were two-dimensional, while the ocean had that hidden third dimension of depth. But Kate was alright with that. She felt as though she were filled with the amazement of a child she'd once known, a little girl she'd left behind twenty-five years ago, on the banks of a cow pond, and she could not quit smiling. She rolled her window down, filling the cab of the jeep with an exhilarating rush of briny air that seemed to promise faraway islands, new menus of delicious foods, lurid culture, and a new world of experiences. It was all there, infused into one breath of ocean breeze.

The road to Pensacola swept inland, and Kate missed the sight of the sea. She texted Mitch as they bisected lush marshlands that stunk of methane and scum. Rising, they rolled over ridges where encroaching trees, draped with moss, which formed a gauntlet of glossy umbrage, surging in the breeze like shaggy beasts at their tethers. Strange birds swooped across the gap. Small reptiles scurried on the sunny shoulders.

"I told him we'll be there in about fifteen minutes," Kate said, grinning. "He says he's going to meet us by the jetty, just off Destin Bridge. Do you know what a jetty is?"

Sara laughed and shook her head. "I think they're like, those rocky things that stick out in the water?"

"Like, a river wing-dam?"

"Yeah, kinda. Are you going to tell him we don't know what a jetty is?"

"I don't know." Kate and Sara both had the giggles. They were completely slaphappy from so many long hours deprived of sleep. Everything seemed quite funnier to them than it ordinarily would be. They were aware of their silliness, and somehow, that made their silliness even funnier.

"You should tell him we're just a couple of Kansas hicks, and we don't know what the heck a jetty is. How are we even supposed to know him when we see him? Have you seen him before? Is he hot?"

"I have no idea." Kate could feel herself starting to blush, and didn't know why. "No, I've never seen him."

"You haven't even creeped his profile?"

"No! I'm not on—any of that social stuff." Kate fanned the air dismissively.

"Are you seeing anybody at all? You're not, are you?"

"No. I'm kind of a homebody. You want to know a secret? This is actually the first time I've ever left Kansas."

"Are you freaking serious?"

"Well, aside from the Missouri-side of Kansas City, but yeah."

"Kate!"

"I've just never had that whole compulsion in me to run around and be crazy."

"Not at all? Not even in college?"

"I went to paramedic school, but that's probably not even the same thing."

Sara looked Kate up and down, twisting the steering wheel between her hands. Kate didn't look over, but she could tell that Sara was perplexed, having difficulty figuring her out. She'd received the same looks from people before, like they just couldn't wrap their mind around the fact that some people just prefer their own company, and the comfort of home to the thrills of night life, dating and travel. Back home in rural Kansas, everyone lived her way. She fit right in. Back there, she never got those kinds of dumbfounded stares. But now, maybe for the first time in her life, it did make her a little curious as to what she'd been missing, and how the other half lived.

"So, tell me more about this fear of water. How bad is it on a scale of one to ten?"

Kate glowered over at Sara.

"An eleven?"

"Eleven-hundred, maybe."

"This was all because your little brother drowned? How long ago was that?"

Kate sighed, and rubbed her face in her hands. She was surprised and revolted at how greasy she felt after two days on the run without a bath. "He was a toddler. I was a little girl. His name was Jeffrey." Kate cleared her throat of the sudden lump. She had no idea how many years had passed since she'd last spoken his name out loud. "I was supposed to have been babysitting him. We had a little pond out back of the house. It was a watering hole for the cattle out in the middle of our pasture. Jeffrey and I used to really like to walk out there, play by the pond. And that day, things went badly." Kate had to bite her upper lip for a few seconds, until the mist cleared a little. "I was looking for seashells, and he must've wandered in. It didn't take but thirty seconds. I just turned around, didn't see him, and then, there he was, out there in the middle. Gone." Kate's voice cracked. Her eyes began to fill. "Happened so fast. There, one minute, gone the next. Gone forever."

The shaggy trees yielded all at once to an open view of the ocean. The Gulf of Mexico glittered like an enormous hammered mirror, sprawling as far as the eye could see. Kate stared out to the furthest point on the horizon, and wiped her eyes with the backs of her hands.

"I'm sorry," Sara said. "That must have been really hard for you."

Kate nodded, but could not yet speak.

"Does it help? Saving lives for a living?"

Kate was taken aback, by how quickly Sara had psychoanalyzed her. Was she really that transparent? "I don't know." Kate shrugged, clearing her throat and wiping her eyes again. "Yes. No. Maybe. I used to think it was my personal form of therapy, but here I am, almost thirty-four, and I guess I'm no better off than I was twenty-five years ago. Still scared to death of water. Scared of death. Scared to be intimate with anybody on any level, for fear I'll turn around and they'll be gone. You know? So no, I guess no, saving lives for a living doesn't actually help. It's just the best thing I could think to do. More of a distraction, than anything else, while I'm avoiding relationships and avoiding myself."

"I think it's awesome that you can admit all of that."

Kate snorted. "Up until two days ago, I couldn't have."

"What changed?"

Kate shook her head, at a loss. "I guess I had to face a few things. I don't know. You've been a big help. I know that much. The things you've said. You're obviously caring, and that's helped a great deal."

"What was your mother like?" Sara asked. "Was she very caring?"

Kate shrugged. "Maybe before, you know. It's hard to even remember life before that. I think it just changed everybody, and not in good ways."

"She wasn't very loving toward you after that, your mother?"

"No," Kate said, softy. "She was pretty distant. And detached."

Sara nodded. "I'm really sorry you had to go through all of that."

"Thanks." Kate sighed, fiddling with her fingertips, and glancing out the window. "But check me out. I can ride right beside the ocean, and look right at it, without totally freaking out. That's got to be a step in the right direction."

"Course it is. You probably spent your whole life avoiding water, and look at you, just chilling, right beside the biggest body of water in the world. You're a rock star, Kate! Next thing you know, you'll be out there surfing."

"Ha!" Kate laughed. "Let's just take this thing one step at a time."

"You don't think you'll be out there by the end of the day, hangin' ten, rippin' the waves? Cowabunga, dude!"

"I'd say that rippin' the waves is highly unlikely. But, assuming everything goes well with Collin, I just might be talked into going down and sitting on the beach. I never imagined it could be so beautiful, you know?" Kate pointed at the ocean. "All that water. It's gorgeous. I can totally see why so many people are attracted to it. The sea, I mean. It's just—wow. Hard to find the words. It's awe inspiringly huge. I had no idea that anything could be so immense. But yet, it really kind of reminds me of the wheat fields and pastures, back home."

Sara smiled, and reached over to pat Kate's hand. "Well, for what it's worth, I think you're doing really great."

"You're not doing too bad yourself," Kate replied. "Seriously. You're sitting there counseling me, while your fiancé is the one back there behind us with a sea monster stuck in his throat."

"Jesus!" Sara screamed, seizing the rear-view mirror, as she mashed the brakes and swerved the jeep onto the side of the road.

Kate whirled around in her seat, and covered her mouth with a gasp of air.

The thing. It was coming out.

Chapter Thirteen

Mitch crossed the Destin Bridge, swerving cars, pushing his State Park pickup to ninety-miles-per-hour. Beside him, Skip clung to the overhead handle with one hand, bracing the other arm stiffly against the dashboard. Another text came through his cell phone. Never taking his eyes off the road, he tossed the phone over into Skip's lap. "What's it say?" he shouted.

"They're just east of Navarre, on the beach. I'm guessing Wynnehaven Beach."

Five minutes away. However, it seemed like hours, as they pushed through the early morning traffic of Fort Walton. Mostly sightseers, gawking down at the scads of revelers who were already anchoring around the popular flat known as Crab Island, and at the parade of ships motoring out of the harbor.

Mitch's heart had skipped a beat, upon reading Kate's last text. The parasite was emerging. It was leaving the body of its host. Evidently, the creature intuited that it was home, and it was desperate to reach the sea. Eleven more bodies, or what was left of them, had washed ashore over the last two days. Two more from Missouri. A few from Mississippi, Louisiana, and several more lacking any form of identification. All within the distribution network of the Emerald Coast Cannery. All within easy access of the Mississippi River basin. All scavenged by sharks.

It was clear enough that some sort of a hatch was underway. A brood was returning to its nesting grounds, and as was the case with every sort of aquatic hatch, the local predators had quickly become aware of an easy food source, and they'd gathered for a feeding frenzy. This was a terrible situation for a scientific enthusiast of sharks. These predators of the deep would of course bear the brunt of the bad press, which had already caught wind of what was currently being viewed as a rash of unprovoked shark attacks. Henderson Beach had remained closed for four days. As the foremost shark expert in the area, Mitch had barely found the time to pay a quick visit to the Emerald Coast Cannery. He'd managed to get the errand done, despite the fact that his desk phone had been ringing off the hook. The cannery conceded to shut down production of their contaminated product. But of course, before agreeing to release an official statement, they had requested more time to examine the evidence that he'd brought before them, to call in their own experts from local laboratories to cover all of their bases.

Their lagging was understandable from a business standpoint, but still infuriating. There was one critical element of evidence that Mitch's case was still lacking: proof-positive from an infected human host. And this morning, that missing link was being delivered, by jeep, all the way from Kansas City.

"They're right up there!" Skip pointed, bouncing in his seat. "I see them!"

Mitch floored the accelerator up the Navarre coastline in the direction of a stalled Jeep CJ-7, on the side of the road. Already, a couple of other vehicles had pulled over to assist.

"Hang on!" Mitch said. Through a blast of angry horns, he swerved his pickup across oncoming traffic, and onto the seaward shoulder. "You get the net and be ready! I'll get the pole!"

They rolled onto the dunes, nose to nose with Kate's jeep. Both men bailed out of their doors. The women had already exited their vehicle with the infected patient. Flanked by half a dozen strangers, they were dragging the man toward the sea.

"What the hell are they doing?" Skip said.

"I don't know! But they're going to lose him if he gets any closer to that water." Mitch reached over the bed of the pickup and grabbed the shark-tagging lance. He had already tipped it with the smallest electronic tagging device that would communicate with his floating network of Shark Tracker receivers. The tag itself was a barbed needle, with a short tail of detachable sonic transmitters that were designed to break loose at preset intervals and float to the surface, where they emitted a data beacon for several days.

Mitch sprinted across the sand, lance in hand, swiftly gaining on the staggering pair of women and their band of followers. The women had one of their patient's arms over each of their shoulders. They looked awful, bruised and battered, matted hair swinging in their faces, smeared with what appeared to be dried mud, blood, or maybe a combination of the two. They had been to Hell and back, and they'd managed to drag the devil himself back with them.

"Stop!" Mitch cried, as he approached within shouting distance. A few of the bystanders turned to stare, but the women kept right on going, dragging the man between them toward the waves. His legs plowed limp furrows through the sand, but as they neared the surf, it was obvious to Mitch that some small reserve of strength was on the verge of being tapped, by their patient. The man's legs pushed drunkenly at the ground. He was attempting to stand, to walk with them, and soon enough, Mitch knew that he was going to try and swim. "Kate!" he shouted.

The woman on the left stopped. She turned, pulling her companions to an awkward halt. The dangling patient swiveled his lolling head. From his gaping mouth flopped an oversized version of the same organism that Mitch had examined back at the lab. Blinking its cyclopean eye in the morning light, it writhed its mass of tentacles like a hydra, affording its host the appearance of having a living beard. Gawping through bloodstained eyes, the man's filthy carcass quavered on unstable legs. It was a wonder that there was any life left in him at all.

"Mitch?" The woman on the left smiled weakly. She made a halfhearted attempt to brush back the hair that clung to her face.

With a spray of sand, the patient sprung toward the waves, dragging both women down to the ground. He wrenched his gory arms from their grips, and he began to crawl mechanically, like a crushed insect, right into the surf. Mitch dropped his shark-tagging lance and dove full upon him, wrapping him up in one of his old, high school wrestling holds. He was not getting away. Not this one.

The patient hoisted his head and unleashed an earsplitting squeal, while the parasite whipped its tentacles spastically in the foam. Blood sprayed from the man's nostrils. It trickled like crimson tears from the corners of his eyes, changing the color of the surf to a sickly shade of vermillion. His whole body undulated like an eel, while his hands clawed ruts through the wet sand.

"It's letting go!" Kate shrieked. "It's coming out!"

Mitch could feel the man's guts churning, beneath his weight. With an audible crunch and a fountain of blood, the parasite wriggled free, to plop wetly onto the sand. Immediately, it began to lurch forward with shrimplike kicks into the waves. "Don't let that thing get away!" Mitch cried. "We need it!"

A dark shadow passed over Mitch, as the ample body of Skip sailed over him, lance in hand. He drew back like a javelin thrower, and drove the barbed tip of the shark tag directly into the parasite's rump. The thing reared and squealed, snapping at the lance with its razor shears. The tag slid free of the pole, dragging behind the escaping creature like a mechanical tail. A wave rushed over its domed back, and when the foam receded, the thing was gone.

"Thought you'd get away, didn't you!" Skip bellowed, pointing at the sea. "But I got you, didn't I? Ha-Ha!" He raised the lance over his head and whooped with triumph.

"Wait a minute, I think there's more coming," Mitch said.

The patient's head wagged with sickening purpose, whipping a tendril of crimson mucous from the cusp of his chin. The man emitted the unmistakable retches of warning that always preceded regurgitation. His neck straightened. Veins stood out on either side of his throat, as his whole body stiffened. A torrent of parasites rushed from his gullet in a massive torrent of squirmy little bodies. Emptied, the patient finally collapsed facedown into the foam. A wriggling brood of pale creatures hitched determinedly toward the sea, but before they reached the water's safety, they were splattered against the sand, one at a time, by the flogging handle of Skip's lance. Each departed the surface world with a squeal and a little spurt of yolk-like innards.

The glow of the computer monitor bathed the faces of the marine biologists in technical effervescence. The laboratory smelled of brewing coffee, a fragrance that mingled queerly with the tartly sulfurous reek of hydrochloric acid. The coffee pot percolated, while stir plates whirled their mesmerizing funnels through beakers of amber fluid. Up on the digital overhead, dozens of parasitic organisms grappled for crumbs that had settled to the bottom of the petri dish. Claws jabbed and clattered, as they shoved, tiptoed and slid across the slick surface. The winners of these skirmishes dipped their trunk-like proboscises to vacuum up the precious motes of debris.

"The little squirt hasn't moved in three hours," Mitch said, tapping the orange blip on the monitor with the butt of a pen. "I think it's safe to say that he made it home."

"You gotta wonder how many more are down there," Skip said. "People, I mean. Think, how many people go missing, every single day."

"You'd like to think this is a recent phenomenon, and we're right on the cutting edge, but then, you never really know, do you? This cycle could've been going on for a long time, and it's only now being discovered."

"Dude, the only reason this whole thing came to light is because when people in Kansas City start jumping into rivers, people tend to take notice. But, you know in a seaside community where these blue crabs were always eaten, who's to say that people just didn't wake up in the middle of the night and walk right out into the waves? If this bug was rare, that kind of thing could've been going on for centuries, one sailor jumping overboard, one lighthouse keeper drowned ... nobody would've jumped to this conclusion. When you live on or around the ocean, people drown. Fact of life."

"But that's just it. Why so many, all of a sudden, and why now?"

"Modern industry, bro." Skip shrugged. "Like I said, used to be, eating a mess of blue crabs was a local custom. Now we've got corporate monsters, overfishing the waters, freezing and shipping our products all over the globe. In some ways, this infestation is our own fault. Humanity's, I mean. It was human greed and gluttony that made this possible, on this kind of a scale."

"Maybe, but look at them." Mitch swiveled in his chair, and pointed to the battling beasts, up on the monitor. "Let's say you just got dropped onto an alien planet, and you discovered these things. Using your biological background, what conclusions can you derive about this species in a glance."

"Uhhh, not predators, really. No teeth. Look to be opportunistic filter feeders. Bottom feeders."

"Right. What else?"

"Well, they're obviously very territorial. Voracious feeders. And they're heavily armed, and armored. Designed to fight."

"Exactly. They have obviously evolved for a very long time to contend with what I'd guess to be intraspecific violence, amongst each other. This tells me that what's happening on the bottom of the Gulf right now is no freak occurrence. These things are tailor made to deal with massive population explosions, territorial disputes, high fecundity rates, the works. You typically see this sort of population model in temperate insects, more than any other life form. Mother Nature knows that these creatures have a short window of time to find their mates and breed in a very hostile environment, so she arms them to the teeth, and hatches them by the trillions, every spring."

"What's your point?"

"My point? I'm just drawing attention to a contradiction in what we're seeing and saying. Here, we have what appears to be a brand new phenomenon, but it's arising from a species that is designed to do exactly what they're doing. They are designed to swarm, to plague, to—take over! Their life cycle has to happen this way. As a massive explosion. We should have seen this before."

"So, what? You think they rode in on an asteroid from outer space?"

Mitch rolled his eyes. "I'm saying that these things have always existed, but they've been geographically isolated from humanity, until now. Bottom of a trench. Or a remote valley, between undersea mountain ranges."

"Yeah, and then an undersea earthquake set them all loose!" Skip nodded. "I like where you're going with this, bro."

"The sea is a huge place, and almost all of it, unexplored. All we've basically got is sonar mapping, but human eyes rarely behold what's actually living down there."

"Check this out. I heard that during World War II, a German ship dumped a bunch of depth charges overboard to take out an

Allied submarine, right? So, after the charges went off, the Germans circled their ship for a while, spotlighting the kill zone, waiting to see what debris was going to float up, and see if they hit their target, you know?" Skip cleared his throat. "But what came floating up instead—and this is in the Captain's log, bro … like, a German captain ain't going to make this crap up, and write it in the friggin' log—but he said that what came floating up instead of debris was something like a giant crocodile, except it had some long flippers instead of legs."

Mitch's eyes widened. "A mosasaur."

"Danged right, a mosasaur." Skip grinned, and chuckled. "They're still down there, dude. Mosasaurs! And who knows what else?"

"Obviously, these little critters." Mitch nodded at the digital screen, and then swiveled back to his computer monitor. He tapped his pen thoughtfully against the orange blip that represented their new friend. By the topographical overlay, it was clear that the creature had made a beeline for what appeared to be a bowl formation in the substrate. It had been situated at the center of the crater for the better part of the afternoon. "And if that doesn't look like a geographically isolated nest, then I don't know what does."

"Have you called up to the cannery, today?"

Mitch sighed and rubbed his face. "They're still waiting to hear back from a few independent labs. I don't expect they're in a huge rush to get their butts in a sling, but there's no way around a nationwide recall. I'm sure they've already reached the same conclusion. The outside lab work is just a dog and pony show. Convince the American consumers that Emerald Coast Cannery cares."

"Well, in the meantime," Skip pointed at the computer screen, "are you thinking what I'm thinking?"

Mitch looked to the screen, then back at Skip. "No. What?"

"Let's take the boat out, run the camera down."

"Well, if we're going to do that, we probably ought to more than sightseeing."

"Go trawling for bugs?"

Mitch drummed his pen against the desk. "I was actually thinking rotenone."

"You freaking serious?"

"As a freaking heart attack."

"There's no way they'll approve dumping a bunch of poison into the Gulf."

"Who ever said we'd be waiting for an approval? Hello? People are dying in real time. This thing can't wait." Mitch gestured to the scrabbling monsters, on the overhead. "We're talking millions, maybe billions of deadly parasites, all derived from this hatch, alone. How often do they breed? We don't know. When's the next hatch going to hit? We don't know that either. But when it does, we know that we can expect an epic increase in proportion of the epidemic we're seeing right now. Just think about it. If every one of these things that made it back into the sea, mates and lays eggs ... whatever barrier has managed to contain them, has obviously been breached."

"Undersea earthquake, bro."

"Whatever. They've found a way out. But the good news, if there's any good news, is that they're returning to their nesting sight. They're predictable. They're contained. And what better scenario could you ask for, for a rotenone application? We weight a bunch of drums, puncture them, and sink them to the bottom of this crater, that chemical will be neatly contained inside that bowl until it breaks down over the next few days. Nothing else will be affected—except for whatever happens to be living in the bottom of that crater. Really, it's perfect. I couldn't imagine a better situation."

Skip shrugged. "Sounds solid."

It was solid. However, for Mitch, the biggest problem would be his ethical dilemma. If this undiscovered species had been geographically isolated inside this crater for untold millennia, then they were talking about a rare and endangered lot. Like island life, these organisms had evolved and adapted to survive the trials imposed by their narrow ecological niche. They had become specialists, surviving within their little domain. They were unique, unlike any other creature, anywhere else in the living world. Their taxonomy was a total mystery. Mitch could not tell by looking at them, which order of the animal kingdom they would possibly belong. Were they mollusks, arthropods or fish? Or something else, altogether. This was a biologist's dream. To actually consider exterminating them, erasing a new species from existence before it could be documented was an unthinkable sin, the worst crime against nature that could possibly be committed. Preservation was paramount in the biologist's creed. Not to mention the fact that he would be passing on a once-in-a-lifetime chance to achieve immortal recognition in the scientific community, by discovering and naming a new species.

Protecting humans came first. There was something almost sickening about that fundamental ethical precept in a situation where the greed of humanity had unleashed a deadly plague of parasites that were innocent in the grand scheme of things. They were just critters being critters, fulfilling their little roles in this world, just as God and Mother Nature intended.

Mitch narrowed his eyes at the battling bugs, on the digital overhead. They were perfect. All animals were. They had no capacity for good or evil. They knew nothing of malice. It had always bothered Mitch a bit that world religions often placed humanity up on a pedestal, over animals, even going so far as to reward humans alone with everlasting life. And why? When humans were so flawed, so filthy, so foolish … we were the worst plague to ever float to the top of the primordial soup. Humans appeared to be destined to destroy this planet, one plant and one animal at a time. And we were supposed to believe that the soul of a small child would go straight to heaven, but the soul of a butchered whale, a creature with higher intelligence, and greater emotional capacity than the human child, would not? Arrogance was one of the precious few attributes that separated humans from animals.

"I'm going to have to agonize over this for a while," Mitch said.

Skip nodded and sighed. "Want to go agonize over a beer and a plate of oysters? That's how I agonize. And, coincidentally, that's also how I like to mentally prepare to nuke bugs with rotenone."

Mitch shook his head. "I need to run a couple of bench studies, first. You go ahead. I'll call you later tonight if that's the final decision."

Skip gave a thumbs-up. "This probably needs to happen sooner than later. Once the cannery goes public with this, and lets the cat out of the bag, we're going to get a flood of calls.

Eggheads from all over are going to want to learn everything we know about this species. We won't be the only boat out there."

He was right. The announcement of an undiscovered species would be blood in the water within the scientific community. A wide variety of interested parties, with a wide variety of agendas, would soon be crawling all over the Emerald Coast, sticking probes into things and canning samples, snapping photos, dragging nets. If there were to be an extermination, it would need to happen tonight. By tomorrow morning, it might already be too late.

"Let's do this," Mitch said. "Go grab some dinner, do whatever you need to do, but, don't you dare drink too much. Which do you want to do? Pilot the *Savannah* out of the harbor, or run up to Greyton, and load four drums of rotenone onto the skiff? Either way, we'll meet out at receiver-transmitter number four. Say, stroke of midnight?"

"Skiff."

"You sure? That's the hard part."

"No way I'm driving the *Savannah*," Skip said, raising his palms and backing slowly away. "That's all you, buddy."

The Savannah was a multi-million dollar research vessel, leased through the State for a limited time for Mitch to finish compiling all of the data from his Shark Tracker program. It was a bit of a beast to handle, with its twin Caterpillar diesel engines, especially in the close quarters of the harbor. It was festooned with crane arms and winches, all protruding from its A-frame, where anything from submarine cameras, samplers, biological trawls and CTD scanners could be deployed for scientific data collection. It had two functional on-board laboratories, a full service galley, and a bridge equipped with GPS, wireless fleet broadband, and the latest radiophone technology. The Savannah was an awesome vessel, and Mitch knew that they were very lucky to have it at their disposal, if only for a few more months.

"You know where the rotenone is, yes?" Mitch asked.

"Those four leftover drums from when we restocked the lakes? They're at the back of the machine shed, up at Greyton."

"Get those. Bring a bung wrench, a drum dolly, a cradle … a hammer and a sturdy punch. What else? Rope or tie-straps, cinderblocks …"

"Jeez, bro! What the hey? You're going to sink my skiff!"

Mitch shrugged. "You can always drive the <u>Savannah</u>. I told you, you had the harder job of the two."

"Midnight, then?" Skip asked. "Rendezvous at RT-4?"

"Midnight, RT-4. Call me, if you run into any trouble up at Greyton."

"Oh, I'll call you, alright. I'll call you all sorts of things." Skip turned, delivering a got-my-eyes-on-you gesture to the tussling creatures, up on the overhead, as he strode out the door."

Mitch rose from his chair. He walked across the lab to the row of light switches, and flipped them all off. After walking back across the room in the new darkness, he stopped, folded his arms, and stared thoughtfully up at the organisms on the screen. The rows of twinkling lights were red, instead of blue. He supposed the switch in hue had something to do with their emotional state. Despite all he knew of them, and didn't know, he still found them to be kind of cute. It was that blinking, black eye. Totally the eye. It gave it—personality. Without that endearing feature, it would be just be a new variety of squid-crab, wired with Christmas lights.

"Okay, boys," Mitch whispered, "time for your medicine."

Mitch turned, and walked back to an adjacent room, where they conducted their fish toxicity testing. No studies were currently underway. The rows of aquariums were cleaned and empty. The laboratory counters were immaculate. One of the most difficult aspects of a toxicity study was cleaning up, afterward. Every trace of the product or byproduct being tested had to be meticulously scrubbed from every aquarium, and from every piece of non-disposable equipment that was used in the study. It could take weeks to determine a precise lethal dosage for a given species of fish, and even longer to determine the minimum acceptable level, where the percent mortality was just a hair above normal levels of mortality in the population. It required flawless care of the fish to eliminate the possibility of any outside variable contributing to the mortality rate. Fish were tricky, especially the highly sensitive species. The death of one individual in the study often created a domino effect, if the dead individual was not immediately removed from the experimental population. One fish carcass rapidly produced ammonia at a level that was oftentimes immeasurably more lethal than a part-per-billion of the product being tested.

Mitch slid open the door to a lower cabinet that contained a variety of toxins that were often used as controls, against which, the experimental populations would be tested. Rotenone was one of these. A colorless, odorless ketonic compound derived from jicama vine extracts, rotenone was a deadly piscicide that was typically applied to contained bodies of water, such as lakes and ponds, when they became overrun by a nuisance or an invasive species of fish. When applied at the proper rate, rotenone would wipe out all aquatic life in a matter of hours, and then break down naturally in a matter of days, so that the lake or pond could be restocked with more appreciable species. In the lab, it was used to wipe out the experimental and control populations, at the end of the study. It was quick, painless, lethal and clean, leaving no harmful residues in the tanks or on the equipment. Mitch bent, and retrieved a small bottle of the toxin, and an eyedropper.

He never felt good about using it. Taking life was taking life, but in every rotenone application, he took some consolation in knowing that it was being used for some greater good. It restored the natural balance in lakes and ponds. It controlled the spread of unfavorable species. And it closed the laboratory studies that provided the necessary data to regulate byproducts and pollutants in the environment. For every minnow that died on his laboratory bench, millions more aquatic lives were saved from the potentially lethal effects of harmful contaminants that would otherwise make their way into the local water systems, untested and unregulated. Sometimes, there were days when he just had to keep reminding himself that he was one of the good guys.

Poised before the dissecting microscope, he dipped the disposable eyedropper into the bottle of rotenone, squeezed the bulb, and drew up one milliliter of the toxin. With a steady hand, he hovered the dropper over the petri dish. His gaze flicked up to the overhead screen, where the microscopic bar brawl continued. "Sorry, guys, party's over." Mitch squeezed the bulb, releasing the contents into the little container of synthetic human digestive juices.

Immediately, the fighting stopped. The tiny creatures appeared disoriented, drunk. The hot hues of their battle colors waned pale, and then flickered out, one by one. In a matter of seconds, the armored soldiers were all strewn lifeless across their miniature battlefield. Predictably, the rotenone proved highly effective. Mitch sighed, closed the cap on the bottle, and switched off the microscope light. Darkness settled over the laboratory.

"Hello?"

Mitch turned toward the sound of the female voice in the entryway. "Yeah, just one second." He pitched the disposable dropper into a nearby wastebasket, and walked over to the row of light switches, restoring the bright hum of fluorescent lights.

It was Kate. Showered and cleaned, she looked far different, and immeasurably more attractive, than the bedraggled mess he'd last seen being loaded into an ambulance, back on the beachfront near Navarre. She was wearing a fresh set of hospital scrubs. If she was wearing any makeup at all, it was so minimal that he couldn't tell. Hers was a very plain and natural beauty that seemed to shine, free of synthetic coatings, right from what appeared to be her very kind and sensitive soul. His gaze fell upon her left hand, where no wedding ring banded her naked finger.

"Hello, there." Mitch smiled at her. "You clean up pretty well."

"They let me run off with this outfit. Free of charge. Women in the medical world, we're sort of a big sorority."

"Nicely played," Mitch said. "And, how's your friend?"

Kate nodded, smiling more with her eyes than with her lips. "He's going to be just fine."

"That's great news. Really great news."

"They'll need to keep him there for a while, of course."

"Of course."

"Follow-up neurological testing, blood thinners. But he was so dehydrated. Just getting an I.V. in him seemed to help bring him around, as much as anything else."

"And how about his wife?"

"Fiancée. Sara's staying there with him. She hasn't called or texted. I'm guessing they're getting some much needed rest."

"I'd expect so. Sounds like they'd been through quite an ordeal."

"Yes. Indeed."

"And how about you?"

"No rest for the weary. I checked into a hotel up in Destin, and got cleaned up. It's got a beautiful view of the ocean." Kate's eyes glimmered. "I just couldn't quit looking at it. I think I could sit there on that balcony and watch the ocean for days. I've never seen anything like it. I'm sure you're used to it, though. You probably don't even notice it anymore."

"Are you kidding? Every time I look out at the ocean, I'm looking at it with the same wonder and fascination that I did as a kid. It's my whole heart and soul. Always has been, and always will be."

Kate shifted her feet. "So, there's not a Mrs. Poole competing with the ocean for your whole heart and soul?"

Mitch smiled and shook his head. "No. No, I guess I just haven't met anyone yet who shares the same passions. Most of the women around here are just tourists, you know. Party-party. Here one weekend and gone by the next. Makes dating kind of difficult for a local."

"Yeah, I guess I could see how that would be."

"So, what are your plans? Will you be staying in town for a while? Until your friends are both back on their feet."

"Yeah. I don't know if we'll be riding back together, though. I mean, they both have lives to get back to when this whole adventure is over. So, I don't know. They might decide to fly back, rather than spend another two days in that jeep with me. I think they've both probably had enough of that."

"Quite a trip?"

Kate rolled her eyes. "You have no earthly idea."

"Well, how long do you plan to spend in town, watching the ocean from that balcony of yours? If you want, I'd love to show you around town, take you out to dinner, and maybe go shopping for a—couple more sets of scrubs?"

Kate laughed. "That sounds awesome. I'd love to run around with you, if you can stand to put up with me. First, I was really kind of hoping you'd show me around your lab. I'm kind of a science nerd too, you know."

Mitch's eyes widened. He straightened up. "Absolutely! Welcome to my home away from home. Or, maybe this is actually my home. I'm not sure. I don't get out much."

"Neither do I." Kate shook her head and smiled. "I was hoping I'd be able to catch you here tonight. Sign said you were closed, but the door was open."

"Yeah, well ... I kind of run my own hours, around here." Mitch turned awkwardly on his heels, first one way, and then another. He'd never given a lab tour before, and wasn't sure where to begin. Most of his tours took place in the visitor's center, where all of the aquariums full of aquatic life served wonderfully as props, and conversation pieces. The lab was decidedly more sterile. He settled on a direction, and led Kate over to his computer monitor. He wiggled the mouse to bring the screen back up, where the little orange blip was still blinking, at the center of a virtual undersea crater.

"What am I looking at, here?" Kate asked.

"This," Mitch gestured with both hands, "is my life's work. It's the Shark Tracker system. We tag sharks with a little string of transmitters. They break off periodically, and float to the surface, where their homing beacon and data are picked up by a network of floating receivers, anchored in place throughout the Emerald Coast. The receivers pick up the data and bounce it off a satellite, enabling us to watch the movement of our sharks from home. There's even an app. You can watch them right from your phone."

"Kind of like one of those virtual aquariums."

"Mmm. Kind of. Except you're not actually seeing the fish. You're just seeing the data. How deep they went. The paths they're taking. Water temperature. That sort of geeky stuff."

"I was kidding. I like the geeky stuff."

"Oh."

"So, where are they? I only see the one."

"Well," Mitch cleared his throat, "it's because I've got all of those other icons hidden at the moment, so that we can keep our eyes focused on this little guy." Mitch tapped the orange blip on the screen. "He's not a shark. He's the critter that you delivered from Kansas City."

Kate gasped and leaned in over the desk. "Wow! That's really him?" She covered her mouth with both hands. "He was just in the backseat of my jeep!"

"Yep, and now, he's at the bottom of the Gulf of Mexico. He doesn't realize it, but he's under government surveillance."

"That's amazing!" Kate grinned, her eyes shining. "That's so cool! And this? What is this here, this blue circle that he's sitting in?"

"Well, we don't know, for sure. That's part of a topographical overlay that helps show sea bottom features, so we—"

"You think it's a crater?"

"That's—what we were just talking about, before Skip left, just a minute ago."

"He's a live one, isn't he?"

"Skip? Oh yeah. He's something special, alright."

"So, you think this is where they're all going? This crater?"

"We think so. Your critter, he sure didn't waste any time getting there, and once he arrived at this point, he stopped, and he hasn't budged since. So, yeah, I believe that what we're looking at here, is …"

"Their nest site."

"Exactly."

"You've got their breeding ground pinpointed." Kate rose, folded one arm around her chest, and hooked a finger around her lips with the other. "Seems like we've got them in a pretty compromising position, here."

Mitch nodded, eyeing Kate uneasily.

"So, what do we intend to do about this, Mitch, before we're running around dealing with a second hatch of human parasites?"

Mitch cocked his head. "Do you get seasick?"

Chapter Fourteen

Kate watched from the relative safety of the bridge, as Mitch winched four drums of rotenone from Skip's bouncing skiff up to the main deck of the *Savannah.* The size of this floating laboratory was sufficient that she didn't much feel the toss of the waves. The vast fluid element underfoot seemed more of a whimsical notion than a physical reality. At least, it felt that way from inside an air-conditioned room, dimly lit by the sprawling panels of glowing instruments and switches. She clasped a warm mug of coffee in both hands, standing firmly and quite comfortably upon the roof of the sea.

She wasn't exactly sure what had changed. Kate Browning? Sailing over the most enormous body of water that the planet had to offer? With anxiety, the period of waiting prior to the point of exposure was often worse than facing the phobia, itself. She'd confronted her deepest fear, and what she'd found instead of horror, was unimaginable beauty. Sara had been a godsend. The validation of saving the life of Collin Stillwell was absolutely a key element in her therapy. All the lives that she'd saved over the course of her career would not amount to the good that his saving Collin's had done for her. There had been so many twists and turns along this road toward conquering a lifelong fear, and she owed her success to every one of them. Sara's kind companionship had coaxed her over each of those hurdles of greater and greater levels of exposure, until at last, she'd stood in the surf of the Gulf of Mexico. And that, was positively awesome. It was a moment she would never forget, standing there in the sunshine, right on the hem between worlds, with the froth of nature's mightiest element lapping at her ankles like a friendly old dog. She had never in her life felt closer to God. Kate smiled. At last, she felt that she had completed her penance. She could let her little Jeffrey rest in peace.

Mitch dollied the final drum over to the base of the A-frame, where he chained it into place beside the other three. It helped that Mitch was here, this confident man of the sea. She trusted him completely. She supposed that of all the things her mother might've done wrong as a parent, she'd certainly done a few things right. She'd instilled her small town values into her daughter's heart. They had perhaps remained latent over nearly three decades, but they were still in there. Kate recognized that a fundamental devotion to one's family, friends and home, was one that should far surpass and suppress any desire for material rewards, and personal gratification. Kate didn't need much. A clean set of scrubs, a place to call home ... and maybe someone to love, who would love her back, just as hard, forever and ever.

It was this last item that had eluded her for the greater part of her adult life. She'd mourned so hard for her brother, suffered so deeply in so many ways that there had simply not been any room left in her heart for anyone special. Now, with her penance complete, there seemed a new void in her life. There was hollowness in her heart that ached to be filled.

She liked Mitch. They were similar in so many of the right ways. It didn't matter if you liked the same music, the same entertainment, movies, or TV shows. All of that stuff that had seemed so important, back in her younger years, had never really mattered at all, not when it came to finding a lasting relationship. No, what mattered was that your hearts were in the right place. What mattered was that you shared the same sense of your place in this world, this universe, and maybe a similar sense of humor, for a little bit of icing on the cake. The solid points of connection between two people were attached far deeper in the soul than that which pleased the eyes, ears and taste buds. It was the difference between attraction and connection. With Mitch, she felt both, and she felt it in a very good way.

Never in her life had Kate ever felt a burning desire to start a family. That, she attributed to fear. That was more of little Jeffrey's influence, from afar. She'd avoided intimacy out of her fear of loss, and now she realized that was a shame. Nothing in life was free. The price of love was perhaps the most exorbitant of all. The cost of investing your heart into love was the eventual and inevitable loss of the one you loved, but it was not a risk. It was an absolute certainty. There was a difference.

Looking down at Mitch, hard at work on the deck, she could understand why the cost of loving another human being, despite the certainty of loss, was worth every penny of the investment. What was life worth, apart from those intimate connections, apart from love, and its collective cost? The amount of love in your life was essentially your net worth in the end. She had loved little Jeffrey, and she had lost him. But she now she knew that she still had love left in her heart to give. She could actually feel the possibility for what might be an eventual yearning for motherhood, for a family of her own. These were uncharted waters, for her. But she didn't fear the journey. Not anymore. Her readiness for love was a powerful emotion, and one just as natural as bare feet. Not unlike the standing before the sea, for the first time.

Skip anchored the skiff beside the buoy, and then clambered up the ladder and onto the Savannah's deck. Kate watched the men talking through the plate glass of the bridge windshield. She saw Mitch gesture subtly in her direction. Skip's head turned her way, then back to Mitch. His shoulders slumped in a stunned expression of body language that was all too clear. She hoped that her tagging along wasn't going to drive some sort of a rift between the men. When Mitch finished speaking, Skip rubbed his head, threw up his hands, and slogged off to engage himself in deck work. Mitch watched him walk away, then turned, and headed back in the direction of the bridge.

Guys will be guys, Kate figured. She sipped her coffee, and gazed out over the rolling black fields of water. Somehow, even at the stroke of midnight, there was still a faint distinction between the sky and the sea. The stars above seemed to glimmer with hope and possibility. The sea below glowered back, with an air of indomitable autonomy. It needed nothing. It borrowed nothing. It refused even the light of the stars.

"I believe we are just about ready," Mitch said, as he entered the bridge.

"Everything alright down there?"

"Sure," Mitch said, turning toward her. "Why?"

Kate smiled, took a sip of her coffee. "Is your friend Skip upset that you brought me along for your adventure?"

"No, well … what we're doing here is—" Mitch weighed the air with balancing hands. "It's ethically questionable."

"Ethically questionable? To exterminate the breeding grounds of a deadly human parasite? How is that a questionable course of action in any sense?"

"Well, you're a paramedic, right?"

"Yes."

"Sworn to save human lives by, what's it? The Hippocratic Oath?" Mitch moved to the instrument panel, and began shifting gears. He engaged the twin diesels. They came to life with a growl. "Well, Skip and I are wildlife biologists. Marine biologists. We don't swear to an oath of any kind, but there's definitely sort of an unspoken code that we're kind of violating big time, right now."

"And what code would that be?"

"To preserve and protect the sanctity of animal species in much the same way that you live by an oath to protect ours."

"But all species? Even nuisance ones? Do you live by a code to protect rats? What about roundworms? Or mosquitoes carrying malaria? Are you obligated to protect them?"

"What about murderers, thieves, crooked politicians? If they're injured in a car accident, wouldn't you treat their injuries?"

"Yes, actually, but you avoided my question. Do you honestly feel ethically obligated to protect a deadly human parasite?"

"Well, it's more complicated than that, because there's something special about this case. Yes, we're talking about a human parasite, a nuisance, a deadly threat to human life. But it's undocumented." Mitch rotated the helm, and eased the throttle lever forward. The Savannah moaned, as she reeled starboard, and began plying the black ocean water, leaving the anchored skiff bobbing gently in her wake. "It's an undiscovered species, brand new to science. We don't know anything about it. We don't have any understanding of its place in the animal kingdom. Its taxonomy and lifecycle are a mystery. If it offers benefits to science, medical or otherwise, then we're talking about knowledge that will be lost before it's ever gained. Specifically, that's where I'm struggling."

"Look at it this way." Kate placed in hand on his shoulder. "We're talking about a creature whose microscopic brood can be easily seeded into a food source. They can survive freezing, cooking, and a trip through the human digestive system. The effects on the host are immediate and deadly. What beneficial knowledge could possibly be gained from this species that would offset its obvious potential for being weaponized?"

"I hadn't even considered that possibility." Mitch glanced at Kate, with a measure of fear in his eyes. Then, he turned back to the open water.

"This is a threat to humanity that has got to go, Mitch." Kate squeezed his shoulder. "Don't second-guess yourself. We're doing the right thing here, and for all the right reasons."

Kate was jolted awake at three a.m. by a dull impact that slopped cold coffee from her mug over the back of her hand. Kate jerked upright in her seat. It was a terrible awakening, from a dream that had just begun to materialize. Her eyes felt swollen and red. She rubbed them, shaking away residual images that felt like twisted snippets of older dreams, childhood nightmares, snapshots from some old trunk of forgotten worries that had remained locked away in the attic of her mind, until just now, only to find that reality looked not much better. Another jarring thump against the Savannah's bow was succeeded by a long and raking scrape down the side, all the way to the stern. She rose to her feet. Mitch and Skip were scrambling for the control panel, decelerating the motors, flipping on the floodlights, checking instrumentation and sonar.

"What was that?" Kate asked, her voice cracked from exhaustion. That was the first uninterrupted hour of sleep that she'd had in who knew how many hours. But somehow, she felt far worse than if she'd had no sleep at all.

"We're in some sort of a debris field," Skip replied.

"Are we alright?" Kate asked. She was still wrapped in the blanket that Mitch had given her, and she was stiff as all hell. Every muscle in her body ached, probably from her two-day wrestling match with Collin. She popped her neck, wishing she'd just stayed awake. She approached the windshield with caution, her hands drawn protectively to her chest, ready to catch herself in case the ship struck something else.

"Lot of stuff floating around out there."

Kate blinked her puffy eyes. Sheer curtains of mist curled around the prow. The sea was as black as the devil's shadow. Not a ripple on its surface. But scrolling by, on either side, was an eerie collection. Splintered planks of wood, fabric, and loops of rigging, were all enmeshed in floating islands that were glommed together by what appeared to be a glistening substance. The goo spanned the gaps between obstacles with slimy bridges. Looking forward, floating junk just kept emerging from the darkness, floating soundlessly by. Something struck the Savannah low with sufficient force to redirect their prow. A terrible squeal of wood against wood howled up from the lower laboratories.

"Is this a shipwreck? Have you guys ever run across anything like this before?"

Skip shook his head slowly.

"We're here," Mitch said. "We're right over the nest."

Kate stepped over to his console, where one of the four monitors displayed the same Shark Tracker screen that she and Mitch had examined, back at his lab. What was portrayed on the screen, with its neatly organized technical overlay, and the single orange blip, fell decidedly short of capturing the foreboding scene beyond the plate glass windows.

"Whoa!" Skip exclaimed, pointing to a big swell in the black water, just off the starboard bow.

"What was it?" Mitch asked.

"Shark! And a big one! There's another one! Hey, do you have the shark icons switched on?"

"No," Mitch replied, rattling away on the keyboard, "but I can in just a sec."

Kate gasped, as the Shark Tracker monitor turned suddenly into an orange matrix of blips. She could hardly see the map through all of the shark icons. Every shark in the Gulf of Mexico appeared to be convened and circling, directly beneath the Savannah's keel.

"Is that what keeps hitting us? Sharks?" Kate's hand rose to her lips. "Do you think this is safe?"

"We should lower the camera!" Skip said, grinning insanely at Mitch, his face aglow by the yellowish light of the instrument panel.

"I think we should probably do what we came here to do, and get out of here," Kate replied, flicking a stern gaze back and forth between the two men. Their eyes were shining like a couple of middle school boys who'd just found a pack of cigarettes.

"Tell you what," Mitch said, pointing a finger at Skip, "Why don't you get started rigging the first drum for delivery, while I lower the camera." He glanced at Kate, and shrugged. "Couldn't hurt. I mean, there's no reason why we can't do the job, and still watch just a little bit of the shark researchers' Super Bowl."

"Totally!" Skip smacked Mitch a high-five, and hustled out the bridge door.

"Don't you think that the rotenone could hurt your sharks?" Kate asked.

The question gave Mitch a moment's pause. "Yes and no. We're dropping them fast, right to the bottom. I don't think we'll lose much of anything until they get down below two-hundred feet, where the water pressure will start to squeeze some out. It's heavier than water, so it's going to sink right down into that bowl."

"What kind of crater is this? Is it like, a volcanic crater, a meteor crater, or what?"

"Hard to say, really," Mitch said, softly. "Sometimes, sailing over all of this water, it's easy to forget where you really are." He rattled away on the keyboard, until the sharks all disappeared. The lone blip was back, blinking forlornly in the eye of the crater. "The whole Gulf of Mexico is now believed to be a crater. I'm talking, THE crater. The actual site of impact left behind by the meteor that wiped out the dinosaurs, and most all other life on earth, around sixty-five million years ago. Boom. Right here, this is Ground Zero for the greatest apocalypse in our planet's history. It's just covered with water. Sometimes, I like to walk out onto deck, on nights like this, and just stare up at the stars and try to imagine what that must've looked like … something that gigantic, falling out of the sky. It was big enough to have left a thick layer of iridium all over the whole surface of the entire world in a permanent sedimentary layer."

"What's iridium?"

"Meteor dust."

Kate pulled the blanket a little more tightly around her shoulders. "Do you ever think that some things happen for a reason?"

"What do you mean?"

"Well, if you're a believer in God, or a higher power of some kind, do you believe that He or She can intervene, if the path of evolution goes too far off course? You know, just to kind of nudge things into a better direction?"

"Well, for one, if that were true, then He or She certainly took their sweet time in intervening. Dinosaurs ruled the earth for around two-hundred-million years. Two-hundred-million. Humanity, by contrast, has only been around for two-hundred-thousand. Consider that for a minute. One-fifth of one-million, compared to two-hundred-million. This is still, and probably always will be, the planet of the dinosaurs."

"And not the planet of the apes?"

"Exactly. We're a flash in the evolutionary pan. And we're not meant to last a fraction as long as those dinosaurs ruled the earth, when you consider the fact that we've done our best to destroy the planet in just one hundred years of industry. So, no, I don't believe that we're the product of divine intervention. We're the worst creatures ever to walk the earth. You yourself admitted that we're better off exterminating an undiscovered species because of its potential as a weapon in the hands of humans. That's a reality. And what does that say about us? About human beings?"

"That we are capable of extreme acts of evil. Yes. But also, we're capable of extreme acts of good. Altruism, sacrifice, unconditional love, appreciation of art and music ... you don't see any of that anywhere else in the animal kingdom." She stared into Mitch's eyes.

"I could argue some of those, but I see your point. We have our moments. Humans do."

"Do you think it's possible for a medical professional and a wildlife biologist to ever see eye-to-eye on a philosophical level?"

Mitch cleared his throat. "Well, we've managed to agree on the urgency of tonight's little mission. Quite honestly, I couldn't have come up with a pricklier dilemma ever to be posed between our two professions, even if I'd been paid to invent one. So, I believe that the answer is yes." Mitch smiled, then reached out and switched on yet another monitor, which revealed only a bright sort of blackness. "Will you be okay up here for just a few minutes?"

"I'd imagine so."

"I'm going to run down to the deck, get that submarine camera deployed while Skip finishes up. Come on down, if you want?"

Kate smiled, shook her head, and shifted her feet. "I don't know if I'm quite ready for that."

"What do you mean?" Mitch gave her a puzzled look.

Kate shrugged. She had forgotten that she still hadn't told him anything about her lifelong phobia. Much as the fear had lessened, over the last twenty-four hours, she still preferred the confines of the bridge, the plate glass, and all of the comforts of her technological surroundings. Here, she could sit in the chair, and almost pretend that she was in an aircraft, a radio studio, VIP box seats at a sporting event ... anywhere but in the middle of the Gulf of Mexico. "I'm kind of a Kansas girl. Don't quite have my sea legs, yet. But, don't give up on me. I'll get there."

"Alright. Well, if you need anything, help yourself. I'll be right back, okay?"

Kate nodded and smiled, as he closed the door. Despite their attraction, it was becoming obvious that they did have some fundamental differences to overcome. They weren't deal breakers, by any means, but they were enough to temper her initial attraction with a solid ground to reality. Kate had managed to make her peace with the ocean, but she was a far cry from the salty she-dog that Mitch was probably waiting for. And they came from too vastly different worlds for that to ever be a fair compromise. What exactly would he be giving up in that kind of an arrangement?

In overcoming her fear of the ocean, Kate strangely felt as though she'd simultaneously made her peace with the windblown prairies of her childhood. At least, certain aspects of it. She'd left that place carrying a burden of directionless resent. There was still a twinge of pain associated with her self-imposed exile, and there probably always would be, but for the first time in forever, she felt that the weight of the cross she'd been carrying had been lifted.

She missed the boundless simplicity of the plains, and she might even want to be a part of them again. The ocean was beautiful, marvelous, but she doubted that she could ever feel as passionately about the sea as Mitch did, because unlike him, she hadn't grown up here. She could appreciate his love affair with the Emerald Coast, but she doubted that she could ever mirror his passion when it was so far removed from her own life experience. Childhood fostered powerful connections to formative places, whether that place was an entire mountain range, or just a rock garden in Grandma's backyard. It would always be his world, not hers.

The camera monitor screen flickered suddenly to life. Mitch's face filled the screen. The camera wobbled crazily for a few moments, then oscillated gently back and forth, offering a panoramic view of the debris field, where the threshing fins of sharks whipped the water into foam. Mitch was winching the device down into the water, using a handheld control. The camera itself was a torpedo-shaped contraption, forged from what appeared to be yellow-painted steel and fitted front and back with racks of angled spotlights.

Skip had fitted a fifty-five-gallon drum of rotenone with a ratcheting safety strap. To this strap, he'd secured a couple of cinder blocks. Now, he was wrenching loose the bung cap. Once freed, he picked up a hammer and a metal punch, of some sort, which he used to pierce a second hole, opposite the bung. Kate watched him wrestle the punctured drum to an open gate in the bow's rail. He pushed it overboard. Seawater leapt into the air as the drum of poison plunged beneath the surface.

Kate hugged her arms tightly around herself. What they were doing felt like delivering a sort of air strike on her lifelong enemy. Not the sea, but the very essence of water, that lurking spirit that had taken people since time's beginning. Kate stared at the little orange blip on the Shark Tracker screen. That was her little friend, down below. It had turned her life upside down, and would soon bring about the extinction of its species. Somewhere below, a drum of death was falling, tumbling slowly through the lightless abyss like a cataclysmic meteor through the depths of space, hurtling toward the unsuspecting inhabitants of a doomed world, a world they'd mistakenly believed to be safe.

Skip punched a hole through the lid of the second drum. He shoved it overboard with his foot. The pale belly of a shark rolled away, as the drum of toxin struck the water. The sharks appeared to be irritated, as though the rotenone residual was enough to annoy them, perhaps burning their eyes and gills.

Kate turned to the monitor, where a view through a lens captured the submarine camera's descent. Seawater lapped at the monitor, then swallowed it whole, affording the disconcerting impression that the ship was sinking. Kate noticed her breathing and heart rate increase, as the camera plunged beneath the waves. Flashes of baitfish, streams of champagne bubbles, and then a void of utter blackness. It was not long before that lonesome abyss was visited. A large and streamlined form sliced eerily through the gloom. It vanished, as a flash of steel might be remembered from a nightmare, only to thrust suddenly back into view. A blunted nose slashed at the camera, serrated with rows of pointed teeth. That bullet hole of an eye gaped soullessly through the monitor, before the killer wheeled away.

Kate felt herself backing away from the monitor, just a couple of steps. It was too close. She had loved the ocean view from her hotel balcony, but beneath those glimmering waves, laid a hidden world, haunted by terrible things.

Mitch was missing his big show. This wasn't the movie she would've picked, and he'd left her to watch it all alone. Kate peered through the glass, just as the third drum of rotenone went over the side. Mitch and Skip were working together. Nearby, the camera cable spooled steadily from the reel. The camera, evidently, was making an automatic descent. She wished Mitch would hurry up and come back up to the bridge. If the camera crashed into the bottom, or became entangled in a mess of debris, she wouldn't have the foggiest idea what to do. Not that she could do much of anything from up here, or anywhere on this boat, for that matter, but watch any number of possible disasters unfold. Kate suddenly regretted coming along. She was a fish out of water.

Kate cocked her head and frowned at the monitor, where a mass of that gelatin stuff seemed to rise from the depths, as the camera descended. Its fluid contours reflected shimmering nuances of light. Impaled by masts and twisted in rigging, the great glob pirouetted through space. The snarl of lines in which it was entangled was taut, and pointing downward, as if the whole mass were snagged onto something at the ocean bottom. It rocked like a grotesque balloon upon its tether.

Kate covered her mouth and emitted a strangled noise with a voice that she didn't recognize as her own. Emptied sockets, fringed with pale flesh, gaped through the camera lens. They were less a pair of eyes than watery tunnels in a lifeless head. Although badly scavenged by every creature of the deep, odiously reminding Kate of thawing chicken in a sink, she was still able to recognize the spectral face that gaped back at her, through the monitor. She knew this man. This was none other than her runaway lawyer. Still leering with that same queer smile that he'd once delivered her, on the banks of a swollen river, at the very moment he'd departed the surface world. Now, he hung gelled into an agglomeration of debris, webbed in frayed rigging, sentenced to stare forevermore through those tenantless sockets at the lonely world he'd chosen. No longer did he strike Kate as being anyone's husband, father, or grandfather. This was a ghastly phantom of the deep.

Kate had seen a lot of things. On the front lines of triage, she'd beheld the effects of gruesome accidents, committing every victim of violence, collision, fire and boiling liquids to the hospital morgue. Both in all her years in the field, nothing had prepared Kate for the sight that gradually unfolded across the screen. There stood a necrotic forest, anchored by trunk-like pedestals to the ocean bottom. There were hundreds of gelatinous trees bearing bulbous, cauliflower heads, all reaching for that dark and starless sky over their eternal nightscape, and their canopies were fruiting human forms.

The camera panned slowly downward, past knobbed and glistening trunks, until it came gently to rest on the sea floor, disturbing a chuff of swirling filth that obscured Kate's view of the environment. The camera rocked back and forth, as the murk settled. It suddenly spun, forty-five degrees, panning drunkenly around the understory of the gelatin forest, and then it flowed, sliding sideways across a wriggling sea floor that seemed to flow in every direction with the most sickening motion. Parasites. The sea floor was alive, with thousands upon thousands of parasites.

As Kate stood trembling before the monitor, both hands clasped over her mouth, she noticed some movement in the background. Tumbling end over end, from the black skies above, a cylindrical form descended, plummeting upon this secret world like a chunk of space debris. Unspooling streams of bubbles, it hurtled down toward the center of the parasite colony, impacting at the heart of their strange forest with a billowing dome of debris. The cloud of death was still expanding when the second drum followed the first, unfurling ribbons of poison all the way to the bottom, where it delivered a shockwave that rocked the camera. But the device continued to film the live coverage of the holocaust, an entire species writhing together in their throes of death.

The bridge door opened. Kate swung her head up from the monitor to glance wildly at Mitch and Skip, who entered the room trailing ghostly capes of mist. "It's happening," she said, "and it's working!"

The men fell all over each other in their haste to be the first to reach the monitor, where by now, vast reefs of poisoned larvae already lay stilled. The camera rocked to and fro, as the third and fourth drums of rotenone slammed into the sea bottom, jostling lifeless bodies into corporeal avalanches. A wave of swirling toxin and motes of suspended sediment washed over the screen, and it was over. Nothing moved.

"And we shall know our enemy by the numbers of their dead upon the battlefield," Mitch said.

The two biologists whooped, gripped forearms, and slapped backs. Skip drummed his fists against a wall panel. Mitch pulled Kate into his arms. They were kissing, quite unexpectedly, before she could fully grasp whatever emotion had just overpowered them.

"Guys," Skip said, batting at their shoulders with the back of his hand, until they broke their spontaneous embrace. "Something's up with our camera. Lookie-lookie."

Judging by the scenery that raced past the monitor, the camera appeared to be soaring. Gelatinous trees crumbled and fell, as the lens rocketed up the crater wall, smashing through every obstacle in its path, and rocketed off into the open ocean. In the empty depths of the benthic zone, only the streaks of light emitted by bioluminescent organisms betrayed the camera's movement, reminding Kate of science fiction movies, when spaceships in hyper drive, blasted through the gulfs of rushing stars.

"Think we're caught in a current, or ..."

"The reel," Mitch had barely uttered the words, before he was rushing for the bridge door. His footsteps clanged down the metal stairwell, before he could be seen sprinting out across the main deck. He was headed in the direction of the submarine camera reel, which was spinning at such terrific speed that the force of friction had superheated the bearings. Smoke poured from either end of the spool. Remaining coils of free cable were disappearing one layer at a time, down into the ocean, where the line was so taut that it sliced a pale wake, aimed like a laser into the heart of the ocean, where something was obviously taking the camera for a ride. Mitch put his foot against the railing, and pulled back on the spool brake with everything he had. More smoke spewed from the pad of his screaming lever.

"No way that's a shark," Skip said, as the last loops of shielded cable spun from the reel, and down into the sea.

"How strong is that cable?" Kate whispered.

Chapter Fifteen

Never in its life had it been so enraged. Lights of all colors throbbed wildly across its carapace. All emotion. Unable to think. Only explode. Freight training through the heart of the devastation, it detonated whole columns of manna in its fury, in its single-minded rage to kill the tiny intruder with the spotlight eyes. It wanted to rend, disembowel, tear the creature to bloody shreds, but this thing was too small. Its oversized claws could not grasp the little assassin that had somehow taken so many lives. All of them. All of its children lay dead. Snuffed in seconds by this hapless, yellow thing that emitted a beam of white light. Sanctuary, violated. Life's work, obliterated. A thriving colony of new life, erased from existence by this tiny thing, this little bug with the gall to trespass through its territory. And it could not even grab hold of it.

The monster inflated its layered diaphragms and emitted a wild, sonic blast that missed the little target completely, toppling dozens of manna columns, instead. The forest of trees it had labored so long to build, all came crumbling down upon the ruin that was its nest. For the second time in one day, the monster felt the wrenching pains of a new and agonizing emotion. It was worse than fear. It was helplessness—desperation.

This was not fair. It was designed for war. It was made for clattering battles between armored giants that could endure for months, spectacular fights that could make the pillars of a world tremble and quake, trading blows like tidal waves, blasts of sound that rivaled the greatest volcanic eruptions. It was a god of war, designed to engage the ocean's mightiest denizens, to wrench and rip them apart, to annihilate whole civilizations, to blast flying enemies from the skies, to tear massive holes in flesh that released sanguine clouds of blood and innards that would feed worlds of life for months. However, in all its power and majesty, it was utterly helpless against small threats.

Crazed by the futility of its efforts, it extended its proboscis and sucked the intruder into its mouth. It was hard as a rock. The fouled water tasted of death. Something was burning its gills, its eye, making it feel all disoriented and dizzy. Its nest had been poisoned. Its sanctuary was a death trap. For the first time in its existence, it had been beaten, forced to flee, to desert its lifelong nesting ground.

Pinching down on the venomous little invader with the rubbery lips of its trunk, it began pumping its diaphragms wildly, spewing jettisons of toxic water. If it remained here a few seconds longer, it was going to die, but it was not about to die here. Not without exacting its revenge.

It rocketed up the side of the crater, venting water in plumes that swept storms of filth from the sea floor, typhoons of toxin and debris, as it thundered off toward cleaner water, a quiet place, way out in the benthic wastelands, where it could take its time to concoct some way to make this tiny thing suffer for what it had done. But as it cleared the crater rim, it felt the drag of a taut line in the corner of its mouth. It felt as if there were something else, something heavier, attached. It was true. There was something else connected to the creature, by a long sort of fiber that angled up toward the surface world.

They were behind this attack.

Burning red as the volcanic vents of the benthic trenches, the monster wheeled around, searching the surface of the sea in anticipation of engaging a new and larger threat. It yearned for it to be there. Something massive. An enemy that it could charge with an earth shattering war bellow. One that it could grapple, topple, crush, and rip apart with eager claws. Then, it heard something. It heard a familiar sound. It was the burbling purr of one of those vessels, ridden by the surface dwellers of this age, and instead of growing louder, the sound of this one was becoming more distant. Heading away from the nest. Retreating. Escaping. The thin fiber that was attached to the tiny creature between its lips was beginning to tighten. These two things, the boat and the little assassin, they were actually one.

The monster drew titanic volumes of water into its bladders, and then expelled it through the complex whorls and channels of its vocal funnel, vibrating the fleshy cordage of that strange organ at its core that served as an instrument of music, as well as violence. Low and long, it blew in a moderate timbre that escalated sharply into a trumpeting wail. This was a song that it had not sung in many thousands of years, not since the day that its Life Mate was slaughtered, the day that it had pounded an entire island of surface dwellers beneath the waves. This song was its oath for vengeance.

The monster rose from the sea floor, with a mind inflicted upon the surface dwellers the exact measure of devastation and suffering that they had inflicted upon its own colony. But first, it would have to follow them. It would learn exactly where they lived by tracking this ship of murderers right back to their home. Venting water from its diaphragms, it pushed itself gently, stealthily in the escaping vessel's wake. This boat, it would destroy, but not before it showed them something. It would show them horror and death on a scale to which their miniscule brains could not possibly fathom. There would be not just one colony exterminated, on this night. No, there would be two. And this time, it meant to destroy them all. All of them. Every filthy vermin in their colony. It would show them what it meant to lose everything, and then, it would defecate upon their nest. No column of their precious manna would be left standing. Not a single egg left uncrushed. It was going to follow them back to their surface sanctuary, and it would send every one of them to the After.

Skip brought down the axe in ferocious arches; each swing kinked the cable, chipped and dented the *Savannah's* rail, but the braided-steel casing of the cable refused to sever. The boat listed dangerously to port side. Whatever was on the end of that line was perhaps the greatest fishing story of all time, but they wanted loose of it. As Kate's gaze travelled down the taut line, down into that swirling black water, she felt the loathsome connection to whatever had hold of them, both physically and figuratively. She felt its pull. She felt the boat moving backwards by the sheer power of an unearthly will that could be calculated in kinetic tonnage. Whatever was down there was positively monstrous. The whole ship was threatening to come apart. She clung to the groaning, popping framework of the bridge, unable to do anything but grit her teeth and watch the disaster unfold.

The ship's dual diesels roared, throwing up white pillars of seawater. Mitch throttled the vessel starboard with everything she had. To let up for even an instant would mean their capsize into shark filled waters. Even at full throttle, they were being towed swiftly in reverse. Frothy water slopped up over the stern of their lopsided deck. The sound of shattering glassware and crashing instruments emanated up from the lower laboratories. Tumbling pots and pans clattered through the galley. By now, they were tipped nearly perpendicular to the water. The stern dipped repeatedly beneath the surface. They were going down. Kate closed her eyes and emitted a strangled cry, as Skip kept right on swinging. Even as a surge of oily water sloshed over his ankles, the clang of his axe head resounded repeatedly, against the rail.

At last, we meet, Kate thought. After a lifelong journey along a winding and pointless road, she'd been led irrevocably to this place, this moment in time, this physical connection to that entity of the depths that had haunted her, and had hunted her, for twenty-five years. It had led her here. She was its intended prey. She was the one that it had singled out from the herd, as all great predators do, to pursue her, and only her, with the deadly single-minded deliberation of a shark upon a blood trail. All her life, she'd been nothing but a doomed target. And all along, she'd somehow sensed this awful truth. She wasn't crazy, after all. The intuitive part of her mind, residing somewhere in the lightless depths of her core, had always known with nightmarish conviction, that her body and her soul were owned by that thing, *this thing* that lived on the other side of her false world of wheat and sunshine, through that rip in the flaxen fabric of her reality, forever anchored to her soul by an unbreakable cable. There was nowhere on earth that she could've run. She was married to it. And tonight, her dark groom would at last have its way with her. Although it could have happened anywhere, it was going to happen here on its own terms in the heart of its lair, where she would be utterly helpless against that monstrous will that would never be satisfied until it at last dragged her screaming from her tormented surface world, down into the depths of its own. This was no coincidence. None of this was. This was fate. And anyone unlucky enough to have been close to her, when that final moment of reckoning came knocking, was doomed to share that fate with her.

Suddenly, the boat righted. With the tremendous crash of equipment catapulted port to starboard, the ship wagged back on its keel. Skip and his loosed axe went spinning across the deck to slam gracelessly into the racks of shark tagging lances that were lashed to the starboard rail. Dozens of computer age spears clattered down upon him, like a jumbo game of pick-up sticks. Mitch was launched from his position at the helm, right into Kate's arms. Together, they crashed to the bridge floor. Eye to eye, nose to nose, they shared a few heavy breaths of disbelief beneath the bower of swaying fitments and receivers, all dangling by their cables. The ship was motoring smoothly forward, once more. The great tug-of-war, it appeared, was over.

The sound of Skip's approaching footsteps preceded the bridge door being slung open, with a bang. "You guys alright?" he said, breathlessly, clinging to the steel jamb. Mitch rolled off Kate, and helped her back to her feet. "Dude," Skip said, with his hand upon his forehead, "I hope you got some insurance on this thing."

"You cut the cable?" Mitch asked.

Skip shook his head. "Whatever was down there pulling, just let go, or snapped off, one. We're probably still dragging three hundred yards of line, but we can't bring it in. Winch is totally fried."

Mitch ran his fingers through his hair, exhaling a sigh through his teeth. "Yeah, we can probably rig it over to a secondary spool and bring it—what in God's name do you think that was? There's nothing out there that could—uh-uh. There's nothing down there that strong. No way." Mitch kept shaking his head, pointing accusatively at the sea. "What was that?"

Skip's brow gathered between his gleaming eyes as he moved in close to Mitch, nodding with new certainty, and breathing heavily through his nostrils. "Mosasaur, dude. That's exactly what that frigging was."

"We should probably get down to the lab," Mitch said, "check the galley, everything … see how bad the damage is."

"Shoot, that sub camera alone probably cost a cool million. What's our story going to be for this one, Chief? Shark research gone horribly awry?"

"I have no idea. Look, maybe you ought to go—"

"Check the lab. On it."

"Hey, guys?" Kate asked, from the instrument panel, where she stared down at the monitor associated with the submarine camera. She pointed her fingertip at the screen, where bubbles and motes of debris rushed past the glowing spotlight. "The camera is still live."

Frowning, Mitch slipped over to join her at the bridge panel. He placed his palms on the edge of the board and stared down at the screen. "Sure enough. We've still got the camera. But it's not really behaving like a towed camera."

"What do you mean?"

"Well, I guess I'd expect it so be, y'know, spinning." Mitch made a swirling gesture with his index finger. "Not all level and balanced. Look at that."

"Probably just the design of the sub body. It's made to plane, even-Steven. Relax." Skip hoisted his flattened palm in a high-five gesture. "We still got the million-dollar camera, bro!"

"And a lot of broken laboratory glassware. God knows what else."

"Rogue wave," Skip said, narrowing his eyes. "That's all we tell them it was. Rogue wave."

"Wait a minute," Kate said, tapping her blunt fingernail on the screen. Her eyes grew wider. Her chest began to rise and fall. "Look. At the top and bottom of the screen."

Skip cocked his head.

"What are you seeing?" Mitch said, squinting.

"Here and here. At the very top and bottom," Kate repeated, "there's like a—a border. That wasn't there, before. See?" She pressed her finger against what looked like a pale and bristly header, spanning the top edge of the screen.

"Probably just the frame of the submarine body."

"No, I don't think so. That was not there, before. And, I swear I saw it move. Is there any other view we can get from this thing?"

"There's a rear-view."

A breath caught in Kate's throat. "Switch it on."

Mitch eyed her questioningly, as he leaned over the camera control board. He switched off the forward camera with the flip of a toggle. The screen went black. He then switched on the rear-view camera. There was a flash of electronic static, but the screen remained dark.

"Are there reverse floodlights?" Skip asked.

"I think so. Yeah." Mitch's index finger hovered around the control board until he found what he was looking for. Then, he switched on the lights.

What appeared on the screen was a vacillating hole. Pillowed folds of tissue surrounded a gulping orifice, rimmed with concentric rings of spines. Beyond that, a terrible portal led into a gulf of impenetrable blackness.

"What the heck are we looking at?" Skip whispered.

"We're looking down its throat," Kate replied, her voice cracking. "It's still attached."

"But there's no tension in the line. No drag on the boat."

"Then it has to be—"

All three sets of eyes rose from the monitor, turning slowly astern.

"—following us."

Beyond the main deck, out over the transom, there was a shape. Barely discernible, a quarter-league distant, it was less a definite object than an aura of dim light, emanating up from the depths of the ocean. It was the color of hot coals. Not the vibrant coals bedding a friendly, crackling fire, but those embers of deepest red, the remnants, unfed and untended, that brooded hotly into the darkest hours of the night, when voices are lowered, pacts are made, and acts of treachery are admitted. The glow encompassed a massive acreage of ocean, as though an island of fire burned beneath the sea, but this was no island. Not by the smooth wave that folded over its domed back, or the curling wake that fanned off to either side. This was an object in motion, and without a doubt, it was following them.

"Cut that damned cable," Mitch choked, "get us loose of it."

The order didn't seem to register. Skip's eyes were wide, but unseeing. He stood frozen before the rear window, paralyzed with awe.

"Go!" Mitch shouted into his ear. "Before that thing dives again!"

Skip jolted upright and into senseless motion. He nearly ran right into the wall, before veering toward the door. Kate watched him stumble and fall over the rolling shark tag lances. However, he collected himself, retrieved the axe, and went back to work on the braided steel cable. This time, he swung the blade with a madman's ferocity. The submarine camera was no doubt an expensive and important piece of surveying equipment, and the connecting cable had clearly been designed to prevent its loss, due to entanglement with reefs and rubble. The lines were heavily shielded. The spool and reel, to which the line was attached, were very sturdy, mounted to the deck upon a massive steel plate that was studded every two inches with hex-bolt heads. The whole contraption appeared to be specifically designed to not ever come off, not under any circumstances. Sparks sprayed from the rail with every blow from the axe, until one errant blow overshot the rail, and split the axe handle neatly in two. Skip stood there with his new wooden stake, while the axe head cartwheeled down into the sea.

"It broke," Kate said.

"The cable?" Mitch never looked away from the bow, which slammed like a wedge through the waves. He was clenching the helm with all the intensity of a racecar driver, on the final lap

"No. The axe."

"Go see what you can do. There are some tools down in the forecastle, right across from the lab in a bunch of blue lockers. See if you can find some bolt cutters, a hacksaw, anything."

"Do you—have any idea what that thing behind us might be?" Kate asked, her voice trembling.

Mitch shook his head. He turned slowly, casting her a hopeless glance that stripped away any possibility that his knowledge of the sea would suffice to see them through. Whatever was pursuing them was something outside of his scope of knowledge and experience, and out of his control. Mitch was just as scared as she was.

As she descended the stairs to the main deck, she looked out over the dark water in the direction of the glowing thing. The sight of it reminded her of certain things that she'd seen on television shows that dealt with the mysterious, the unexplained. They weren't normally the types of programs that she watched, but on occasion, she'd flipped through the channels, and settled on something that managed to capture her attention, purely out of its strangeness, like the subject of unidentified submarine objects. Like a UFO, but underwater. Enormous glowing shapes that had baffled sea captains for centuries.

But the thing she saw trailing them, it didn't exactly glow. Glowing implied a soft, even inviting, light source. This seethed. And although it seemed natural to want to understand its motives, maybe even connect with it on some level, there was an unmistakably malevolent quality emanating from this thing.

She was no biologist, like Mitch, but she was aware that throughout nature, across all boundaries between species, there were certain colors, certain displays, that conveyed specific emotions. Threats were universally understood, between all creatures, great and small, designed to broadcast an unmistakable message when something was angry, and should not be trifled with. As Kate gazed out over the taffrail, into the raging lake of fire, what she felt was hatred, hatred on a level that she could not comprehend. It took quite a lot to get her riled, and so far as she could remember, she had never really hated anyone. Not like this. The ocean boiled with the red heat of vengeance. The thing that was following them, and she was certain, meant to kill them.

Her feet half-stepped, half-slid, across the main deck, where Skip was fighting with the terminal connection between the spool and the cable. There was a stainless steel fitting about the size of a coffee mug, which he was trying in vain to loosen. It did not seem to be budging.

"I need a big pipe wrench, or something," he gasped.

"Mitch said there's a tool locker just inside, right across from the lab. Maybe we can find something in there."

Skip followed Kate into the forecastle. She located the light switch, and he rushed for the blue locker doors. While he rummaged, Kate turned in the direction of the lab.

It was a wreck. But at least the collection of instruments scattered all around the floor were things familiar to her, tools with which she was experienced, more so than whatever might be stashed in that locker. It was a biological laboratory, after all, stocked with much of the same surgical equipment as could be found in any hospital emergency room. She crunched through the carpet of shattered glass. Jagged beakers, test tubes and flasks rolled woefully around the floor. An entire shelving unit of biological specimens had tipped over, smashing vials of all shapes and sizes, releasing hundreds of erstwhile captives in a reeking pool of formaldehyde.

Kate picked her way through the rubble, slipping once on a wrinkled eel. Behind her, the clatter of wrenches and sockets on the forecastle floor assured her that Skip had not yet found whatever it was that he was looking for. Then, she saw it, serrated and gleaming, against the far wall. She gasped at the fortuitousness of her find, edging through the field of sharp points toward the cordless bone saw. However, just as her fingertips fluttered over the stainless instrument, the lights went out, and Kate felt herself flying through the air. The <u>Savannah</u> had just been stopped again, as suddenly as if it had slammed into a concrete wall.

When the lights flickered back on, Kate found herself floating in a pond of blood and formaldehyde, amongst a school of pickled fish. The specimens all gawped back at her through sunken and bleary eyes. The pain that she felt was not so much by the innumerable cuts from broken glass, webbing her hands and her forearms, but by the blunt trauma that had been inflicted to her shoulder when she was hurled against the laboratory wall. A dull ache moaned from her shoulder, all the way to her core, but the bone saw was right in front of her nose.

She seized it in her bloody fist, hoping to God that its battery pack still held a charge. As she rose to her feet and crossed the laboratory, beneath flickering tubes of light, she froze at the sound of rushing water. This was not the sound of an influx of water, as might be produced from water spilling through a ship's ruptured hull, but rather, it was the cascading tonnage of millions of gallons of water, roaring down a mountain's slopes.

The problem was there were no mountains at sea.

The lights cut out, blinking on and off intermittently with the serpentine hiss and crackle of electricity. The unmistakable smell of smoldering wiring sizzled in the air. Darkness, then light. Kate called out for Skip, then Mitch, but there came no replies. The ship was silent, but for the lap of waves against its hull, the nervous chatter of broken glassware. Then, all ordinary sounds bowed down to one so alien, so unlike anything of the surface world, rumbling so tremendously low that Kate could feel it inside her chest in the marrow of her bones. The monotone rose in timbre to something of the mournful bellow of a war horn, resounding over some battlefield of antiquity.

Kate clasped her ears and screamed, as the deafening blast permeated every solid object on the ship. It seemed to separate molecules, stretching the space between every cell of her body, until she felt on the verge of vaporizing into a chuff of red mist, if the sonic shockwave did not relent. But it did. It stopped, just as suddenly as it had commenced.

Her body trembled and her ears rang in the unfathomable silence that followed the attack. She made no mistake, it had been an attack, but she feared that the attack was not over. In fact, it had not even begun. That blast was just a taste of the awesome power that could, and most like would, be unleashed at any instant. And if that small sample could in any way be amplified to a greater level, the effects would be unimaginable. Perhaps liquefying.

Kate's steps to the laboratory door were heavy ones, as if she wore a pair of leaden boots. The after-effects of the blast were so weakening that it felt as if every fiber of muscle in her body had somehow been shaken loose in its cordage. Glass crunched underfoot. The lights flickered out, with an electric pop, and they did not come back on. Blackness enveloped the *Savannah.* Something thumped against the hull. Kate listened, as it dragged itself woodenly along the length of the vessel, as if exploring it, with the most horrible caress.

It knew she was here. This was it. Her nightmare had found her.

Chapter Sixteen

Kate lurched for the laboratory door, which was discernible by the light that burned around its seam. Before her, stood Hell's gates. On the other side, she knew, awaited the devil. Her personal demon. It was here to collect her soul. None of this seemed any real surprise. Her personal demon was real. It always had been. It had always been waiting for her, since the moment she first communed with it on the banks of a lonely cow pond. She would burn for what she'd done. This was her penance. It was her deserved punishment for her stupidity, her negligence, her cowardice, for her lifetime of avoidance, for running from her fears, from her family, from her tragedy, from herself. Burning in Hell was what she deserved for failing little Jeffrey, and she accepted her fate.

Kate grasped the handle and she opened the laboratory door. The fire in the sky was blinding. It towered over her like a gushing Vesuvius. Gouts of pulsing lava streamed from its molten core in blazing rivulets, setting the seas all around ablaze in hellish glory. She stepped out onto the deck, awash in the brilliance of the looming fountainhead of hatred. And when it glowered down full upon her, through its volcanic eye, Kate felt the smug satisfaction flowing through the hot veins of this forgotten elder god, this destroyer, this Charybdis, this bane of the ancient seas, this conjuror of whirlpools and swallower of ships, this hellhound of Poseidon. It was real. Somehow, a girl from Kansas had managed to invite its apocalyptic fury.

Kate trudged woodenly across the deck, shielding her eyes in the searing light. If she was enough to satiate its hunger for destruction, then she would be the sacrificial lamb of this era, would her death spare the lives of innocent millions. It was better this way, she thought. It was better to die hoping that her life had made a difference, than to live to bear the loss of another in her stead. That burden was too great, and even if she escaped her demon now, there would come another day, when Hell's gates would spring wide to receive her. There was no escaping your fate. No matter how far or how fast you ran, no matter how well you hid, or how many other innocent people you threw in front of you, your personal demon would always get you in the end.

"Here!" Kate cried, throwing her arms out to her sides. She marched astern and clambered up onto the taffrail. "I'm right here! Take it! Take it all! I'm done!"

The seas between them boiled. Masses of slithering tentacles parted to make way for a larger organ that only beginning to take shape. Membranous folds gradually tightened, slack rose, between expanding bands of cartilage, stretching, tenting, to form something of a bridge of sallow tissue. It rose, streaming water, until the gaping mouthpart was revealed, wavering over Kate like a black duct straight to Hell. The reek of its eager stomach fluids poured from the tapered end of that trunk, lit dimly aglow by the pale spotlights of the submarine camera, still lodged somewhere, within. The frayed length of cable still dangled from the corner of its rubbery lips. As those lips gaped wide, trembling with anticipation. As the gaping mouth descended over her, Kate realized, with an added measure of revulsion, that her death was going to be captured on film.

At the final moment, she was struck by a jolt of recognition. She knew this thing, and she realized that this monster could be no devil. It was no entity from her nightmares. It knew nothing of her, specifically, aside from the fact that she had been involved in the extermination of its offspring. It was one of them. An adult. A parent to the nest of parasites. This was no harbinger of penance imposed upon her for the death of little Jeffrey. This was a sea monster, a threat to all of humanity, a hidden menace whose shadows she'd been chasing, all the way from Kansas City—and she owed this damned thing nothing.

She leapt back, as the trunk dropped, and it clamped its lips upon the steel rail. The monster emitted a lugubrious groan of dissatisfaction, pulsing hotly with every nuance of hate. This was evidently not the soft morsel that it had been anticipating. Kate sprinted across the deck toward the forecastle. The lights in the bridge flickered on, backlighting Mitch's sturdy silhouette as the twin diesel engines suddenly roared. Kate almost laughed out loud with joy at these hopeful sights and sounds. Never in all her life, had she felt so full of conviction, so filled with certainty that she wanted to live!

She seized the grapples on the camera cable spool, and brought the bone saw to life with a flip of her thumb. The instrument whined hungrily as she bore down on the cable with the whirling serrated blade. Sparks sprayed from its teeth as it bit deeply into the braided steel. In a matter of seconds, she'd accomplished what a large man with an axe had failed repeatedly to do. She turned as the severed cable plunged into the sea and watched as the burning candle inside the monster's trunk was snuffed. They were freed, if only it would release its grip on the taffrail.

The diesel engines spewed geysers of foam into the creature's face. Black clouds of exhaust funneled up into its snout. Its enraged coloration cooled to a yellowish hue that conveyed some aspect of surprise at the becalmed vessel's sudden surge of power. But it refused to let go.

Kate turned to look pleadingly up at Mitch. As she did so, she noticed something else, something that filled her heart with the promise of possibility. It was a twinkling string of lights on the horizon, just off the *Savannah's* bow. Destin! It was the skyline of Destin, Fort Walton Beach, Pensacola. They were within reach of civilization.

Turning astern, Kate strode calmly, purposefully, toward the transom. The creature noticed her advance. Its fire returned, boiling up from its core to trickle down over its domed shell like glimmering streams of magma. It narrowed its cyclopean eye, glowering balefully down upon her, as its tentacles backpedalled furiously, whipping the sea into froth.

Kate dropped the bone saw to the deck with a clatter. She traded her tool for a weapon, bending to retrieve something that this ancient monster might remember and appreciate. Hefting the shark-tagging lance into her hand, she made a running start for the taffrail, before lobbing her techno-tipped spear directly at the eye of the beast. The lance wobbled through the air in a lethal arch, before plunging exactly and deeply into the center of its pupil.

Kate slammed into the rail as monster released its grip, the engines roared, and the boat launched forward. The *Savannah* was free. Kate pulled herself up from the deck to relish the sight of a squalling sea monster, writhing in a chaos of foam and slapping tentacles. Its bluish strings of bioluminescent lights flickered on and off in what appeared to be some sort of a physiological meltdown, as the defeated Charybdis sank back down into the sea.

Kate clung to the rail, tears of relief spilling pale streaks down her cheeks. At last, the nightmare was over. Her penance was complete.

"Kate?"

She turned toward the sound of the voice to find Skip teetering in the forecastle doorway, giant pipe wrench in hand. He looked just like a clubbed Neanderthal. It appeared he'd taken a hard concussion to the head. The right side of his face was badly swollen. His eye was nearly closed.

"Found that wrench."

Kate rose to her feet and staggered over to help him. "You need to lie down, Skip. Looks like you've suffered some head trauma. Might even have a fractured orbit, under there."

"Me?" Skip raised his hand to tap his fingertips tenderly around the swollen region. "I think I must've fallen down in there. There's tools everywhere."

"You're still a little loopy, buddy. Let's just get you lying down for right now. We'll be back in Destin in just a few minutes, and then, we'll get you over to the hospital. Okay?"

"Okay."

Kate led him over to a coil of rope, where she eased his bulk down into the makeshift chair that its hollow provided. "I'm going to go see if we've got some blankets in there, maybe an ice pack. You stay right here. Don't try to get up, you hear me?"

Skip hoisted a meaty hand and gave her a thumbs-up.

"Good." She turned in the direction of the forecastle, changed her mind, and hustled instead up the short flight of stairs to the bridge. She wanted to assess the condition of everyone on board, identify all injuries, establish priorities, before starting a treatment plan, and attempting to locate whatever first aid supplies, they might have available. Really, beneath all of that engrained protocol, she just wanted to see Mitch. She wanted to ensure herself that he was alive and well.

He left the helm to meet her in the doorway with a powerful embrace, rocking gently. Beyond, the glittering lights of the boardwalk, Destin's high-rise hotels sparkling on the near horizon like myriad life forms of a thriving reef colony. The briny essence of the sea unfurled from the waves that smashed into foam across the bow. Kate clenched her fingers into the back of his shirt, his hair, as their lips came together. Maybe she'd judged his watery world a little too harshly. What was Kansas, after all, but an aging scrapbook of old memories? This could be her new sanctuary, her nest. All of this. It could be her new place in this world. He could be. At last, she felt as though it was safe to fall in love with another person, to devote herself to a man, and to a place in this world, because she knew, without a doubt, that she possessed the strength to defend all she loved. Love wasn't a gamble, not when loss was inevitable, but life was very much a gamble without it.

"You'd better strap yourself in," Mitch said, pulling away from her embrace to reengage the *Savannah's* helm.

"What?" Kate furrowed her brow, staring at him with her arms dangling limply at her sides. With Destin Bridge in sight, and the harbor just beyond, he was still throttling the ship full-tilt, still manning the controls with the same maniacal desperation. "What's wrong?" she asked, feeling almost hurt by his hasty disengagement from what had been one of the most meaningful moments of her life.

Mitch extended a finger to point at the Shark Tracker screen. There, at the tip of his index finger, was a single orange blip. Based on its position, it was directly behind them. When the realization hit her, it was almost too much to bear.

"No!" she cried, spinning around to plant both palms against the rear window. Directly in their wake rose that seething mountain of red hate, smashing through black waves like an infernal battering ram, still aglow from the fires of some hellish forge that had resurrected her fallen devil from the pits of damnation. The monster was death incarnate. Its mass of glowing tentacles was a roaring crematorium. Sprays of seawater, vaporized into mist, were billowing plumes of smoke. "No!" Kate pummeled the glass with her fists, as the monster thundered down upon them. "Why can't you just leave us alone?"

The points of its claws rose from the sea, slicing white trails through the water. It extended its arms, reaching for them. It spread its shears wide. They were not going to make it. The Destin Bridge loomed just ahead, but they were not going to make it. The monster was going to beat them to the finish line.

"That thing won't make it under the bridge," Mitch shouted. "It won't fit!" He began to swerve the boat to and fro, performing an evasive maneuver that kept their stern out of reach of those snapping claws. The creature seemed to have trouble seeing them through its ruined eye. The tagging lance still dangled from the pupil, tenting the translucent membrane, where viscous fluid wept in a milky trail. Kate shrieked, as one set of shears raked clumsily against the starboard hull. They could not outmaneuver it forever. The *Savannah* was trapped between its claws.

"Hang on!" Mitch straightened the helm as they reached the Destin Bridge, making for a dangerous beeline between the centermost pilings. The monster's claws found purchase. With an earsplitting squeal of rending metal, the chase ended, as the monster slammed headlong into the bridge.

Only half a dozen vehicles were on the bridge when the barnacled mountain of chitin collided with concrete and steel. Three rows of pilings exploded into powder, as the bridge itself parted for the beast. But its terminal velocity was insufficient to send it wholly through. It was trapped at Crab Island. Its carapace wedged between rows of pilings, it could only thrash the water, tentacles glowing like hot wires, trumpeting indignantly in the shy morning light.

Just out of reach of the creature's slashing claws, the *Savannah's* engines gurgled a flood of seawater that rushed into her hull, as she tipped her bowsprit to the lightening sky. The ship had been neatly transected, from transom to mid-deck. Kate was relieved to see Skip swimming for shore. He was going to be fine. Mitch, on the other hand, was questionable.

"Mitch!" Kate shouted into his ear, where a stream of blood flowed from some injury, within. He'd been thrown sideways when the ship was transected, and he'd taken the corner of the radiophone receiver directly to his temple. This type of trauma was survivable, if he was hospitalized immediately. Pressure needed to be relieved from what appeared to be a cranial hematoma, and that was a procedure that could only be accomplished in the emergency room. She had to keep his head elevated, keep his core temperature as low as possible. The sea, it was his best and only hope.

Kate fought his limp arms through the holes in a personal floatation device. She cinched it tightly across his chest. This would suffice to keep him upright in the proper position, and the seawater would cool his core temperature.

The ship was going down. Great belches of air escaped the forecastle hatch, as seawater slithered up through the hold, the laboratories, and the tool lockers. They had to escape the bridge, before it was swallowed.

Kate dragged Mitch across the rear window, which was now situated beneath them. His body left a smear of blood across the glass. She couldn't tell where his injuries were, but there was no time for a treatment plan. Only time to escape. She let him loose. Mitch dropped through the hole to plunge headfirst into a cloud of crimson water. He resurfaced in a matter of seconds, upright and bobbing like a weary castaway. There was no time to locate a second life preserver. The water was almost to the bridge door. Kate sat down on the edge of the glass, took a deep breath, and slid out into the ocean. She was swimming for the first time in twenty-five years.

She swam toward Mitch, hooked him under the chin in the bend of her elbow, and began towing him away from the sinking *Savannah*, lest the two of them be dragged down in her undertow. She swam hard, scissor kicking the water with her legs, and slashing with her free arm, until at last, she felt as though she'd delivered them to a safe distance. The glass box that was the bridge filled in gulps with emerald water. With a hiss of expelled air, it vanished into the waves, followed by the blunt curve of the bow, and finally, the bowsprit's needled point. The ship was gone in a boiling vortex that dissipated into a spiral of foam.

Then, a great claw closed upon their bodies.

Kate turned, but she did not scream, when she looked down to find that she and Mitch were both pinned tightly across their chests between the two massive blades. Their edges were serrated and scarred from ages of misuse. From their evil hooks to the mighty flesh hinge, inscribed with the glyphs of untold battles.

Here was the terrible Charybdis, a troglodytic progenitor in the history of ancient gods, and living proof of a godly path of evolution. For clearly, gods themselves had evolved alongside the ones who worshipped them. Ancient pantheons of wrathful destroyers, from the age of fire and steel, eventually birthed the benevolent fathers of a kinder, more contemporary age. This thing was nothing but a sad relic of bygone beliefs that had somehow outlasted any timeline that the looms of evolution might've spun. It shouldn't be here, but it was. And now, it was going to kill her.

Kate was frightened, but no longer terrified. She felt cheated, but no longer damned. Clutching Mitch tightly to her cheek, she glared hotly into the eye of her destroyer, armed with the new confidence that she'd been brave enough to have loved and lost. Kate pulled Mitch in, and pressed her lips to his injured temple. If there was to be some cosmic record of her last act on earth, she preferred that be it. She closed her eyes, and waited for the inevitable. Kate was done.

Chapter Seventeen

It held them in its grasp, the two assassins. This was not the first time that it had clutched surface dwellers in this manner. What came next was less than satisfying. It would be over too quickly. These two deserved far worse than an effortless and empty gesture that would halve their bodies. They deserved to suffer, as it had suffered, over all that it had ever loved, only to see destroyed by these parasites that depleted the seas of all their resources, which polluted the waters, netting and slaughtering every variety of creature unlucky enough to be birthed into the seas of this planet that they infested. It had never encountered a more loathsome race of beings, too cowardly to avenge the loss of their own, too cruel to be endowed with the capacity to love, as it had loved, all that these vermin had taken.

How times had changed that these surface worms should be allowed to carry on with their wanton destruction of this world, to survive the demise of all the infinitely more powerful and majestic wonders, more deserving than they, to rule the seas. There was a time when it was worshiped as a god by these same creatures. It recalled those bygone years of regular sacrifices, when surface creatures were trussed and delivered by wooden boat to the various places that it once had haunted. It recalled the seaside bonfires, the ceremonial gatherings, officiated by decorated ranks who had taken the time to learn their songs, to craft immense bejeweled instruments that imitated the nuances of their language. They would croon hymns of praise by the first light of a cool, rising moon, summoning their elder god from the deep. Whole islands became temples, where tribes of faithful acolytes once beseeched them to annihilate their enemies. Whole races and religions had been exterminated, false gods driven howling from their sanctums with sonic blasts that melted walls, whole civilizations pounded beneath the waves. Those were the greatest of eras, when it was honored and respected by the lower life forms in its servitude. Now, it was a very different world. A world in which it no longer had a place.

It glowered down upon the two creatures, which clung to one another in its grasp. These two, they would have to represent all surface dwellers, from one side of the ocean to the next, for they were all that it had strength left to punish. It gazed down into the eyes of the one, who held the other, and as the lives of these creatures hung in the balance of seconds, it saw something, something unexpected that gave it pause. The capacity for love.

This one had leapt into the sea to save the life of the other. This one had shown the courage to avenge the deaths of all of its kind, by launching a perfect strike against the nest of their destroyer. This one possessed the warrior's spirit to have confronted an indomitable enemy with naught but a pointed stick, and with that simple weapon, dealt a blow to the all-seeing eye of an elder god. This one, only this one, seemed somewhat deserving of its respect.

Perhaps an act of mercy was a fitting one, granted one warrior to another, when there was only strength left in its claw to perform a single act. Slowly, it released its grip on their bodies. It watched the pair of surface dwellers swim away in the direction of the rising sun.

Tumults of piping seagulls stirred the glittering dawn. They emerged from their roosts to flock the monster's carapace, lighting upon its back, pecking parasites from its barnacled armor. The monster did not mind their gentle attentions, reminiscent of its regular cleanings by the scads of benthic scavengers that had forever trailed it for thousands upon thousands of years. Its body had sustained generations of creatures. Galaxies of life had revolved around its lonely existence in their center.

Its cyclopean eye swiveled skyward, where a squadron of jets roared overhead. Maintaining their perfect formation, they dipped their wings to shift direction, cleaving an arch through the skies in one harmonious movement, just like a school of minnows evading a predator. As it gazed upon the surface world in its final moments, the monster beheld the beauty of one world in the reflection of the other. Their colonies rose from the beach in colorful reefs, where a variety of creatures milled about a common habitat, on wings, on four legs, and on two. It was a thriving colony, much like one it used to know. Nevertheless, the window of time for that colony, and for all of its kind had closed.

The domed back of the rising sun breached the horizon, casting gilded sprays of dazzling light. As its dim eye beheld that glorious hillock of effervescence, it swore that it heard a familiar song. A reverberating trill, ghostly beautiful. So distinct that it could only be produced by one other who'd ever lived. Tapping its last reserve of energy, the monster replied to her with a gentle trill of its own. It reached for the haloed sun, trembling, as the light in its great eye faded. At last, it would feel the embrace of that reunion in death, between two creatures who were mated for life.

The End

www.ingramcontent.com/pod-product-compliance
Lightning Source LLC
Chambersburg PA
CBHW071508170626
46811CB00007B/2770